WITCH 13

Published by Oblivion Publishing
Cover design by Ross Nischler

ISBN: 1-7355251-5-4
ISBN-13: 978-1-7355251-5-0

First Edition Paperback

Printed in the United States of America

To the Chavez family.
Rick (Mr. Chavez). Sally. Vanessa. Jesse. Crystal.
And Ricky.
Since first grade, man. Since first grade.

Witch 13

"13 Witches"

They walked together,
old as time,
they'll take your soul,
but don't take mine.

Skin like milk,
hair like ash,
they'll kill anyone,
who crosses their path.

Hats full of stitches,
make your wishes,
because coming for you,
are the thirteen witches.

— Unknown

PROLOGUE

A WITCH.

That was seven-year-old Madelyn Lamprey's first thought when she saw the woman standing there in front of the tree, still as a statue. In fact, Madelyn thought she *was* a statue initially, like an old Halloween decoration someone left out, maybe to try and scare her. So when she had seen the witch down near the river, she'd froze in her tracks. She began to retrace the events that led to that moment in her head, not believing the thing right before her own two eyes. This had been her routine for the last four months, but Halloween had come and gone, and now it was December.

There shouldn't be any witches in the forest, she thought. *Especially not here.*

There was a soft, cloying wind that evening. The forest was littered with the fossils of dead leaves. After supper she'd rinsed her plate and silverware off and set them to dry in the wire rack, just like she was supposed to. Her parents had already started up the evening news, and that was boring with a capital B. So while they were busy listening to the "exciting new developments" about the accident on Old Ferry Bridge, she'd slipped out of the sliding glass door into the wintry air and closed it so softly it wouldn't make a sound. She was careful to wear her winter coat and gloves: the last time she'd been outside, her fingers had nearly turned blue by the time she'd gotten back home.

They lived on a nine-acre property that held a forty-year-old colonial-style house, a two-story guest house, and trees as far as she could see. She loved the way the gravel sounded when their car climbed the driveway. She loved watching her father repair bicycles down in the shop at the bottom of the hill. But most of all, she loved exploring the beaten rock path in their backyard that led down to the Connecticut River. The stones were smooth and round and they reminded her of a fairy tale, like there might be a big shiny castle waiting for her on the other end. She liked to imagine beautiful white horses with hulking knights riding on top of them. Sometimes she'd start to see a dragon there too, in the forest, but she'd wish the thought away before she ever really got a good look at it.

The trail twisted away from the house, but not too far. Her mother and father had warned her about what could happen if you strayed too far away from the path, warned her about what could happen if you couldn't find your way back before dark.

Which is why she always listened.

She stayed more or less on the trail, and the only times she went anywhere near the wall of black forest surrounding the Painted Mountains was to see if maybe she could spot a deer just beyond the trunks, hidden away in that other magical world.

Madelyn carefully marched along the path, weaving down the hillside, her mouth curled into a dreamy smile, humming to herself. She counted the stones as she descended the path, kicking her feet at the little weeds sticking up from between the rocks. She made a note of the mist creeping along the woodland edge, pretending she was somewhere where magic *did* exist.

As she breathed in the fresh winter air, her sinuses began to burn. The air slowly decayed, peeling away and leaving something else in its place.

Madelyn stopped and curiously lifted her head to see the river lazily carrying past below. She listened to the water slip between the wet, moss-covered stones, and for a moment, she forgot all about the smoke.

She'd smelled burning oil before. Father's car engine leaked oil constantly, and when it burned it smelled worse than a dead possum.

She wrinkled her nose and lifted her eyes away from the safety of the trail to the top of the tree line.

Far in the distance was a plume of black smoke feeding into steely gray clouds. Her eyes widened as the thought crossed her mind that it might be a tornado forming, but she shook her head because she remembered that tornados didn't happen way out here on the East Coast. They happened more in the middle states, like Kansas, where Dorothy and her house had been swept away to Oz. She'd learned that in Mrs. Avery's second grade class.

The beautiful view in front of her slowly began to transform. The "mist" wasn't mist at all; it was smoke. Dirty, filthy smoke that was seeping in from between the trees on the right side of the trail.

Was the forest on fire?

The river was nearly gone now, obscured by the dark smoke rolling across the land. She could feel it sticking to her skin and clothes. It made her eyes itchy and her face tingle. As the last of the river was swallowed up by the burning air, a panic began to crawl over her like bugs. She started to brush her hands against her arms to scrub the burning oil smell off and looked down to remind herself that the trail was still there. She wasn't lost yet; she could still follow it back to the house.

She waved her arms at the air, beating away the smoke.

That was when she heard it.

A giggle, sharp and abrupt. Like there was another little girl out here, too. She halted in place, confused and curious, and turned toward the opposite side of the trail. The side that *wasn't* burning.

She heard it again, faint among the sound of the lazy river.

She threw a glance over her shoulder and watched the smoke seeping out between the tall trunks.

There was another giggle, louder this time, and she drew closer. She wanted to call out, but hesitated. Who could possibly be on their property this late? Mackenzie, the young girl who lived next door? Not a chance. The Millers would never let her go this far away from home.

She began to step toward the sound but stopped, warily regarding the trail. She bit her lip, then shook her head because she knew she needed to be brave. She needed to warn Mackenzie or whoever was playing out there that a fire was coming. There was a dragon in their midst.

Her chin held high, she hopped off the trail, scuttling across the hillside toward the tree line.

"Hello?" Her voice came out stronger than she expected, and hearing herself gave her the courage she needed to move faster.

A shadowy figure passed between the trees, startling her and causing her to stumble back.

There was another snicker ahead, and she almost thought it sounded older than before. Like it wasn't young Mackenzie Miller out here, but a woman instead.

Madelyn arrived at the edge of the forest and stopped. Her hands grew sweaty and her heart was beating so hard she thought it might blow up. She was still, peering into the shadowy veil beyond.

"Hello?" she called. This time her voice didn't sound so brave. It echoed in the dark place beyond where she could see.

Dry twigs cracked and she jerked her head to the right.

It wasn't Mackenzie.

No more than twenty feet away stood a woman.

Madelyn's heart slowed and she stepped away from the forest, partly relieved to know she didn't have to go any further. The woman was facing away from her, standing so close to the tree you'd think she was talking to it.

The woman didn't move; she was still, like one of those Halloween witches people put on their porch to scare away kids like her.

Madelyn approached, and the smoke began to curl away. She could see the woman clearer now.

A witch.

Madelyn recognized the tall, pointed hat.

"Hello?" Madelyn said timidly. "Are you okay?"

The woman didn't answer.

Madelyn slowed as she neared the stranger.

"What are you doing out here?" she asked.

Witches weren't real. She knew that. But even the fake ones weren't supposed to be out when it wasn't Halloween, and it was two weeks until Christmas.

What was a witch doing in her parents' backyard? The thought made her a little uneasy.

Madelyn took a step forward and looked closer at the woman's clothes. She had the straight, pointed hat just like witches do, and a long black dress that hugged her body. She'd never seen anything quite like it.

Madelyn squinted harder at the bizarre outfit.

Her clothes look like they're made of ashes, she thought to herself.

The ash reminded her of the fire, and when Madelyn quickly turned her attention to the other side of the path she was amazed to find that the smoke was gone. She could see the river again at the bottom of the hill, only it looked even better than before. Beautiful even. Clearer than she ever remembered it. She could see fish swimming below, and even the smooth rocks buried in the sand.

Something wasn't right. Where did the smoke go? Why couldn't she smell it anymore? She crinkled her nose and looked back at the strange person standing in front of her.

The witch towered like a giant above Madelyn, her black hat rising into the sky.

Why was the woman facing the tree? Why wouldn't she turn around and talk to her?

The peaceful sounds of the forest had returned and quelled her anxiety a touch, enough so that she was able to work up the courage to take another step closer.

The smoke gone, she stepped right up to the witch, noticing that she smelled like sweets and cinnamon and everything delicious. She breathed in that intoxicating scent, and her eyes felt heavy. She put out a hand to steady herself on the tree but was careful not to touch the witch.

"Excuse me, but...are you okay?" Madelyn repeated. Her head felt weird and light, like she'd just got off that spinning ride at the carnival that went so fast you could climb up the walls without falling.

When the witch still didn't answer, Madelyn turned her head up and finally saw her face.

At first she was scared, because the witch looked more dead than alive. She'd seen them on TV before, but they never looked quite like this.

"Do you need help? Hello?" Madelyn asked, short of breath.

The woman's skin was whiter than white, and her lips looked more blue than pink. Her hair was as inky as a black cat, with eyes much too large for her head.

Madelyn began to feel warm inside, and a euphoric feeling washed over her. Her body continued to heat like a bathtub filling with warm water, and she wiped her damp forehead with the back of her coat sleeve. If you'd asked Madelyn Lamprey how long she gazed at the witch, she would have told you she didn't know. And that was the truth.

What she *did* know was that she was hot. *Too* hot. She felt it building, and her skin began to ooze with sweat. She marveled at the witch a moment longer and smiled, then calmly began back to the trail. Only instead of going back to the house, she started back down the path.

She hummed to herself and wondered if the dragon had started the fire in the woods, or the witch, but she didn't care either way.

She reached the end of the stone path and tilted her head down at the river. The water was peaceful, and she wondered why she'd never tried to swim before. The weather was a lot warmer than she would have thought for winter. She pulled off her shoes and socks and unzipped her coat, letting it fall to the wet dirt, oblivious to the plumes of frigid air coming from her lungs.

Madelyn reached up and tucked the loose strands of hair behind her ear. She took one last look at the river, then stepped forward, letting the water gently lull her in.

And just before her head was fully submerged, she almost thought she heard her parents screaming her name.

Then, she drowned.

CHAPTER 1

SHERIFF STERLING MARSH ran. She ran faster and harder than she'd ever run before. She didn't know where she was running to, only what she was running from, but that was enough.

Her body was dowsed with sweat, muscles burning, chest on fire as she slammed a fist down on the button and disengaged the treadmill. The pain in her knee was back, but it was manageable.

It was precisely 8:45p.m., a mere hour and fifteen minutes before her shift was scheduled to start. Sterling, a thirty-six-year-old woman born to an English mother and an East Indian father, gracefully swung off the treadmill with a thump and toweled off her face. With eyelids etched as dark as an Egyptian pharaoh, her almond-shaped eyes were stark upon first glance. Cracked, plum-colored lips and skin that glistened with an olive sheen left most strangers believing her of Middle-Eastern decent, but she never cared enough to correct them. *She* knew who she was, and that was all that mattered.

While her parents hailed from London, she'd been welcomed into the world kicking and screaming not long after their arrival in the United States during one of the worst storms of the century. They'd revealed this fact on her fifteenth birthday, and she wondered if it meant anything to be born on a night when the world was so angry.

Her father, Ovi, worked odd jobs and long hours, but he'd always come home at the end of the day with a flower in his hand to tuck behind her ear just as the tired red sun was slipping behind the mountains. Perennials. Blue Stars. Daisies. It didn't matter; they were all the same as far as she was concerned. All Sterling cared about was watching him pull up in the driveway in his beat-up Mercedes with the mismatched fender and the missing driver's side mirror. Her mother, Anna, would be waiting on the porch with her arms folded and a frown on her face, forgotten like a ghost. But Ovi...well, Ovi could do no wrong as far as his little girl was concerned. She adored him as much as she adored sun flowers and snow angels and her pink bicycle with the wicker basket on the front. She loved his thick English accent and the neatly-trimmed mustache under his bulbous nose. She loved the old striped tie he'd wear everyday that she'd picked out for him at a thrift store in Maine when he'd went up for business. But most of all, she loved the way he'd laugh music and his eyes would close like he was so happy he couldn't take it.

Ovi, fascinated with their new home, shuffled them about the East Coast while her mother tended to Sterling as the years passed. Aside from her looks, Sterling couldn't have been more different than Ovi and Anna. While her parents loved to eat and indulge in the finer things in life, Sterling instead felt an urgency inside trying to escape. An instinct that told her to get away. To run.

So that's exactly what she did.

A bit of a late bloomer, she'd always been an awkward child, cursed with two left feet and cheeks rounder than tennis balls. But she'd always enjoyed moving, and treasured the feeling of letting her short legs carry her in a whirlwind up and down their property through the swaying Silver Feather Grass while she waited for her father's Mercedes to round the bend putt-putting up the cracked driveway, dodging fallen trees and bushes like spot fires. And as the years rolled by and she entered high school, she took her love for running to new places, embracing her competitiveness and desire to push herself by joining her school's Track and Field team. Before long, Ovi and Anna had watched as Sterling's puffy cheeks chiseled away into stone, revealing the face she knew really belonged to her.

But that was a long time ago.

Ovi was gone now.

And she was a shadow of the woman she once was.

Sterling took a few swallows from a Hydro Flask before easing onto a yoga mat on the side of her bed. Her stomach had gone soft, and her jawline wasn't quite as sharp as it had once been, but she still felt that side of her hidden away inside, dormant. She spent the next ten minutes stretching every aching tendon and limb, controlling her breathing like her life depended on it.

She hadn't slept. She never did. Even back when she *could* sleep regularly, she didn't. But now that the choice had been ripped out of her control, she wished that she could. She craved the control and desperately wanted to be back behind the wheel. She loathed the powerlessness she felt at not having that choice anymore.

So instead, she punished herself by running in the hopes that by pushing herself beyond her physical limits, she would *finally* be able to rest. This had become her routine. Some might have even called it a ritual. After exhausting herself working twelve-hour days under the grateful service of the town of Drybell, she'd come home and run no less than five or sometimes six miles, imagining herself in the forest on the other side of the wall-sized plate glass window. She watched the quiet trees and the endless horizon, and not once had she ever regretted leaving the city. Her mother, Anna, thought it was stupid that Sterling ran on a treadmill when there were miles of sprawling open forest trails at her doorstep, but Sterling didn't agree. The Painted Mountains, the gloomy mountain range surrounding Drybell, was the furthest thing from safe. Everyone in town knew as much. Besides, using the trails would have been irresponsible with her erratic schedule. How would the station contact her if she went out of range? What if they needed her?

Her cellphone rested on the corner of the dresser, a crackling voice coming from the speaker.

"Hey Ling, it's Mum again. I'm sorry I missed you on your birthday, but I suppose maybe you were working again. Hopefully you got my voicemail. I, uh…" There was a pause and the woman sighed. "I have something for you here that I wanted to give you—for your birthday, I mean. I know I haven't gotten you anything for a few years, and I thought it might make up for it. Heavens, I hate leaving messages. My voice sounds like a hundred-year-old man. Anyway, I wanted to surprise you, but I don't have your address and I don't know how else to get this to you. I love you, Little Star. I hope you're not eating those awful microwave dinners every night."

The voicemail clicked dead. She picked up her mother's tarnished gold ring from the desk and slipped it on. She felt the cool metal around her finger and grimaced, then twisted it off, setting it back on the desk.

The ring was beautiful, even after all these years. But no matter the luster, something just didn't feel right when she put it on. Like it could never truly be hers. A relic from the First World War, the ring was a family heirloom handed down from Sterling's great-grandmother to her grandmother, to Anna. And now to her.

Sterling and her mother used to speak once a week on Friday evenings ever since the move all those years ago, but not anymore. Those days had come to an end.

Sterling avoided calls altogether now with the exception of work, but still listened to Anna's endless voicemails. Hearing her mother's voice made her feel closer to family, even if she could

never bring herself to speak to the woman again.

After a scalding shower, she put on her uniform and walked to the living room, powering on the television with a remote before retreating to the attached kitchen.

She pulled open the refrigerator door and winced, the light nearly blinding her glassy red eyes. There was a perpetual darkness clouding around them, and Chase hadn't let her forget that fact.

After she rummaged through cartons of leftover Chinese takeout and triple shot energy drinks, she decided to break routine, grabbing the milk instead. A habit that carried over from her old life reared its head and before she knew what was happening, all the ingredients were laid out on the granite countertop.

Sterling was pleasantly surprised with herself as she prepared the smoothie, the first relatively healthy thing she'd eaten that week, if at all. She listened as jumbled voices poured from the television, erupting in a string of static. She heard words like STORM and ROAD, but couldn't make out the rest.

This wasn't new information. She'd heard about the incoming storm earlier that morning from Georgia, the receptionist down at the station.

Sterling flipped off the television, the static replaced with wind. It howled and whistled, and where some people would be unnerved, Sterling found it comforting. Branches playfully tapped the outside of the living room window, and she scolded herself for not cutting them last weekend like she had planned. The wooden fingers reaching for the house would need to be dealt with if she was going to hang the Christmas lights in time. She added the lights to the mental checklist of "Chores she may never get to" and chugged the strawberry banana smoothie like it was the first truly good thing she'd drank in years. The smoothies were a pre-meet ritual in college. The sugar overload gave her a head rush and the strawberry banana smell unburied hazy memories of intimate midnight conversations in her dorm room with then-girlfriend/long jump up-and-comer Heidi Harris, but she reminded herself that that was her old life, and it wouldn't do her any good to think about it now.

"Fuck..." she muttered.

She licked her dry lips, savoring the taste. She relied on the sugar then, and she still does now. She chased the smoothie with a tall glass of water and returned to her bedroom, switching off the living room light on her way out.

Sterling grabbed her leather duty belt off the back of the chair at her desk and swung it around her hips. The weight somehow managed to surprise her despite the countless years she's worn it. She fastened it, then inspected and chambered her Glock 22, sliding it into the holster.

Standing in front of the easel mirror in the corner of the bedroom, the belt and its numerous pouches looked bigger on her than she thought they rightfully should. Sterling frowned, straightening her posture, then pinned her badge to her dress shirt.

As she fastened the polished metal star on her chest, an unsung power exploded throughout her body like a succession of fireworks. The uniform changed her every time, transforming her into the person she always aspired to be, had become. All the control she felt was so close to slipping away rushed back, flooding into her like a drug.

And it felt *good*.

The shine on her badge had dulled, like a metal locket that'd sat at the bottom of the ocean for the last century. Only in Sterling's case it hadn't taken a century to tarnish her luster, just a month. She imagined herself there, lying at the bottom of the ocean in the cold, surrounded by darkness watching the light break as it faded away on the surface. She wondered if she'd prefer it there, away from the rest of the world, where it's quiet. Where she could be alone. The answer scared her, because with that revelation came the unavoidable truth that she'd become even more disconnected than she ever wanted to believe possible.

Sterling took one last look at herself in the mirror and noticed a shard of light dancing on the collection of tarnished trophies buried in the closet. They sparkled under the layers of dust and years of neglect and she forced herself to avoid looking at them.

She collected the resignation letter resting neatly on the desk, all the more certain she was making the right decision. She read it two more times, then another three, until she was absolutely convinced that it was perfect. Part of her held to the hope of finding a typo.

Judgment Day would come tomorrow. The Chief was scheduled to return from vacation in Miami, but if the weather was any indication, that wasn't going to happen.

Sterling stared down at the letter as if she literally held her future in her own two hands. And maybe she did. But she clung to a shred of hope that there would be other opportunities. Other paths. Other roads to run.

Yet despite this, all she saw were the words that would end everything she knew and everything she would have known.

As she read the first line again—*I, Sterling Marsh, tender my resignation*—the static returned from the TV, shrill and abrupt. Caught off guard, she snapped her head toward the dingy living room. She went to draw her firearm, but stopped before the gun was all the way out of the holster, cognizant of how badly it ended the last time she drew her weapon.

The sound hissed from the living room; it reminded her of the snow from the television sets in the nineties, but she knew hers was too modern to experience any such phenomenon.

She stepped beyond the lighted threshold of her bedroom.

The static cut off.

The living room was a maze of shadows, lit only by a cold bluish moonlight. Sterling stepped into the room and flipped the light switch, but there was only darkness. She watched for any sign of movement.

Dread wormed its way up her spine, and as her sweaty palm tightened on the gun at her hip, the television screen sprang to life in a bright flash.

Sterling was too baffled to move, and the longer she stood waiting, ready to draw her firearm, the more she noticed that the wind had gone silent.

At first, she wasn't sure what she was hearing. The sound was barely discernable. She thought it might be the remnants of the static from seconds before still ricocheting in her ears, but after a minute she took a step toward the television and realized that she wasn't imagining it.

There was something there.

Sterling carefully bypassed the loveseat and moved slowly past the coffee table until she was right in front of the modest LED flat screen.

The hairs on her arms stood on end, and against all intuition and better judgment she leaned down, pressed her ear to the glass, and listened.

She couldn't fathom what she heard at first, but as the sound carried on, it became louder, clearer.

Her eyes blossomed in terror.

She slowly backed away from the television, nearly tripping over the coffee table.

Because what she heard were children, and she couldn't tell if they were singing, or screaming.

CHAPTER 2

STERLING STEPPED INTO the diner, shaken, and spotted Chase waiting in the corner booth. The overhead fluorescent lights beat against her strained eyes, and the warmth was so overbearing her weary body was racked with a shudder.

She waited in the entrance and watched Chase as he gazed out the wall of glass. He was lost in thought, his golden-blond hair neatly combed to one side, framing a pair of lake-blue eyes and a sharp nose. Sterling figured he was doing what he always did: digging up problems that didn't need digging up just for the sake of keeping his hands busy. Because men like Chase always needed to be reminded that they were needed. The ones she'd dated, anyway. The "Messiah-Complex" she'd heard it called. He meant well, she knew, and while he was a far cry from the boy scout he'd started as, she reckoned he still thought of himself as much, even when the line wasn't so clear.

Sterling considered turning around, maybe walking back out, but before she could his head turned and their eyes met like magnets. Chase smiled his All-American smile and, after hesitating, Sterling couldn't help but reciprocate with one of her own.

He waved her over and she quickly scanned the diner to find they were alone.

"I was getting a little worried," Chase said. "Don't think you've been late once since we started working together."

Sterling sat without a word, scooting in across from him. Her face rife with trepidation, she contemplated confiding in Chase what she'd heard on her television. She went to speak, but before she could get the words out he interrupted.

"Hey—Sterling," Chase repeated with a wave of his hand. "What happened? Where were you?"

The sound of his voice rescued her from her own head, and she shook off the gloom clouding around her.

"I, uh…"

Chase stared across the table at her peculiarly, detecting something was off.

"What is it?" he asked.

Sterling licked her lips and said, "Haven't been feeling well. Think I'm coming down with something."

Chase exhaled, relieved, then fell back against the bench seat. "Fuck," he said. "The flu?"

Sterling shook her head. "I don't think so."

Chase propped open a menu and began scanning the specials. "You know what they say: Soup, fluids, water, yada yada. Although for me, a greasy burger always does the trick."

Sterling was silent. She listened as a buzz serenaded the diner, whereupon her eyes fell on a blue neon clock. The hum it produced was dreadful, reminding her of the television. Children's screams floated up from the depths of her mind, and she couldn't decide if she really heard what she thought she heard, or if she was so exhausted that she imagined it.

Chase tipped his menu to the side and glanced at her, arching his eyebrows. "Eat," he said.

"You talk to Georgia? What do we got tonight?" she asked, attempting to evade him.

"For God's sake, eat something, Sterling."

"I'm not hun—"

"*Eat.*"

Eating was the last thing she felt like doing, but that was what Chase did. He knew she had to be reminded to eat, funnily enough, like a child, the same way Anna would nudge her plate closer while Sterling glared at her. She didn't feel like eating then and she sure as hell didn't now.

The waitress, Judy, a Drybell local with a checkered apron and a nest of frizzy red hair and raspberry lipstick, made her way to their table.

Chase ordered a black coffee and a tuna melt.

"And for Sterling?" Judy asked.

Sterling hesitated, only to find Chase staring daggers at her from across the table. She tapped the menu on the palm of her hand. Chase's expression was pleading, causing Sterling to crumble like a house of cards. "A slice of cherry pie, no whipped cream." It wasn't Apple Rhubarb Crumble, but she supposed it would do. There was a pause, then: "Thanks, Judy."

Judy smiled and tucked the two menus under her arm before disappearing through two batwing doors.

Chase said, "You know, pumpkin is the official state pie here. What would our forefathers think?"

"They wouldn't think much, Chase: they're dead."

Chase rolled his eyes, shaking his head. "C'mon, Marsh, I'm trying here. Help me out, will ya?"

Sterling looked at Chase while demented screams and hollow echoes carried on inside her skull like a carousel. She honed in on them, willing them to a hush, the buzzing transforming into a sharp ring.

"I'm sorry, buddy, this thing is kicking my ass," she said, rubbing her eyes. "Took some ibuprofen in the car. Hopefully it kicks in soon."

Chase eyed her suspiciously, as if he didn't quite believe her, then nodded. "Yeah, okay."

A silence settled over the table and Chase said, "Look, I'm sorry. I don't know how to make this 'not awkward', so I'm just going to say it."

"Chase—"

"I think you're making a mistake." There was a finality to his voice that she didn't like. She knew this was coming, and knew that by coming to the diner to meet him she'd have to suffer through "the speech," but she came anyway. Was it an obligation she felt to her deputy? Did she do this out of duty? Or was it because part of her hoped that he might *actually* be able to talk her out of it?

"I just don't get it."

"You don't get what, Chase?"

"I mean, come on. You were made for this, Sterling," he began. "This job. This life. How can you not see that?"

"You really still believe that after what happened?" she questioned, taken aback.

"*Especially* after what happened," he argued.

"He's dead because of me. That man is dead because of what I did. *Me.* He had kids, you know."

"I *do* know, yes. All the better," Chase said.

Sterling sat there dumbfounded.

Chase shook his head and looked around. He leaned forward, voice low. "People like that—people who do the kinds of things he did? For these kids, his family? Where I'm from that's a mercy. They would have grown up without him either way, the only difference is that now they're not gonna have to worry about visiting him behind bars. It's better this way."

"Better how?" Sterling asked.

"Because now they don't have to make that choice. They get to go on with their happy lives none the wiser. And while it might hurt now, he'll slowly fade from their memory and their lives will be all the better for it."

Her father came to her then. She saw him there in her mind's eye that last Christmas they'd spent together as a family. She saw him smiling at her as he walked in the door, his hair graying at the temples, shoulders hunched like the weight of the world was hanging on them as he unraveled a knitted scarf from his neck.

Goodbye, Little Star, he'd said. *Don't let your light go out.*

She shook her head. "You don't forget people just like that, Chase," she said with a snap of her fingers. "And despite what you may have heard, time does not heal all wounds, and we sure as hell *aren't* our memories. What we *are* is what's left after the crash," she said, tapping a finger on the table. "Just this mangled mess of nothingness and broken promises and lies and deceits and everything we can't ever see or hold again. *That's* what those kids are. And no, I do not for a second believe they're better off."

"You know what I mean, Sterling. You *are* this job."

Sterling scoffed. "So why the investigation? Why the administrative leave? The tests? All of it."

"You *know* why, Sterling. It's procedure. Not just our department—every department."

Sterling shook her head. "And what if I said that's not the problem? Then what?"

"*Not the problem*?" Chase repeated. "What do you mean? What other problem would there be?"

"I mean, what if the problem isn't that I killed him?"

Chase regarded her oddly, like he didn't understand what she was hinting at.

"What if the problem is that I'm glad I did?"

"I think you'd have to be crazy not to be," Chase lamented.

Sterling found comfort in his words. Comfort in the thought that she acted just as any other human being would have if put in the same situation.

"You were just protecting yourself. That's all. My only regret was that I wasn't there to protect you."

"I don't *need* protection, Chase."

Chase nodded. "I know, I know. It's just...I don't know. I guess I feel like I should have been there with you that night. Maybe this whole thing could have been prevented?"

Sterling leaned forward. "No," she said. "Don't do that."

"Do what?"

"What happened between us does not mean that you owe me anything. It was one night, and it has zero to do with why I'm leaving."

"Are you sure that's all it was to you? One night?"

The table began to vibrate, interrupting their conversation. Chase picked up his phone and glanced at the screen before immediately sending the call to voicemail.

"Jennifer?" Sterling asked.

Chase nodded.

"Why don't you answer it?"

"Because I don't want to do something stupid, like get into a fight with my wife right before an eight-hour shift."

"Or maybe it's the fact that she doesn't know you're sitting here with me right now," Sterling added.

Chase didn't reply, only watched flickers of white light beyond the serrated black mountain peaks.

Sterling paused as Judy arrived at the table with their orders, setting their plates down in front of them and sauntering away.

Sterling picked up the fork, watching dark cherry syrup trickle down the tines. Her mouth was bone-dry, and she regretted not ordering a glass of water. She held the fork in her hand, watching the red seep down, then held it up to her mouth, running her tongue along the cool metal.

Chase watched, mesmerized, as it streaked across her tongue in a long red vein. She savored the tart flavor, then swallowed before carefully slicing into the crust. Crimson filling oozed out so dark it looked like blood. Oblivious to Chase's gaze, Sterling finally took a bite, then wiped her mouth with the back of her hand.

She looked up, surprised to find Chase's intense blue eyes burning into her. He stared at her, and she remembered seeing that familiar gleam in them once before.

And where it led.

They finished their meal, and Sterling picked up the tab. They made their way to the front doors where they were greeted by their reflections. Sterling stole a glimpse at them standing side by side, fantasizing about them strolling through town, arms linked, while they laughed and shared candy apples and stole kisses before the sun sank behind the mountains. She mused whether their child would inherit her dark features and skin or Chase's fairer complexion, and she realized she'd stopped breathing.

Chase saw the longing on her face, gently shaking her back to reality. "Sterling?"

Sterling turned to him, shaken by her reverie, and was painfully confronted with the truth that this imagined life would never be, no matter how much she wanted it.

"We've gotta go, Boss," he said with a sad smile.

She nodded her head, starting forward. The more steps she took, and the closer they got, the more the glass doors turned to smoke and mirrors, transforming them into two ghosts rather than people.

As her fingers slipped around the door handle, Sterling took one last look at herself in the mirror, wondering how she had arrived at that point. That exact moment in time. She thought about how many different events must have gone wrong for her to be there, in the diner with Chase at that precise moment, and the bleak thought was so overpowering she almost burst into tears.

Don't let your light go out.

Before she could pull the bar, the door swung toward her.

She stepped back to avoid being hit and found Chase's wife, Jennifer, standing motionless in the entrance, her face frozen in disgust. Sterling beheld the hate boiling in the woman's eyes.

Jennifer's gaze shifted past her, and Sterling watched all the unspoken rage melt into sadness as Jennifer discovered Chase waiting behind her.

The trio stood frozen in time: Jennifer with one hand on the door, Sterling caught in awkward shock, and Chase with a Styrofoam box of leftovers in one hand, his wallet in the other.

Sterling frowned, the sadness on Jennifer's face nearly unbearable, and she wished she were anywhere but there in that moment. Even back home sitting next to Anna on the couch with the cracked leather cushions.

Sterling went to speak, but before the words could come out, fire exploded in the left side of her face. The buzzing and dead children's voices came screaming back in her head as the force snapped her face to the right, nearly sending her stumbling into the row of booths.

Through her ringing ear, she heard three muffled words.

"You fucking bitch!"

CHAPTER 3

STERLING STOOD IN front of the diner in the wintry night air, breathing in the cold. She watched as Chase unsuccessfully attempted to calm Jennifer while she stormed to her car.

The left side of Sterling's face burned, but she ignored the pain. When she ran, she felt that same fire in her legs, arms, and chest, and while she consciously knew it wasn't the same, the physical sensation didn't feel much different. She'd actually grown kind of fond of it, in a way. She thought of her abandoned trophies collecting dust; remembered crossing the finish line so many times before, and the rush of adrenaline she'd felt every time as people had screamed and cheered her on.

And now there was nothing left but regret.

She listened as they squabbled, watching Chase wave his arms as he tried to justify their rendezvous at the diner. She heard Jennifer scream her name and jab an incriminating finger in her direction. She could only stare on in a daze as the girl unleashed every foul obscenity on her mind, feeling the sting in her face and her bruised ego.

Chase turned and frowned.

She wasn't stupid. She knew what he was saying.

He was telling Jennifer she meant nothing.

That Sterling wasn't the one for him.

That it had all been a mistake.

That Jennifer was his whole life.

Sterling's face flushed with heat. She watched them scream and yell at each other and make a spectacle. She lifted a hand, touching her face. The pain was worse.

Jennifer threw her arms into the air and stomped away, getting into her car and peeling out of the parking lot in a whirl of leaves, disappearing into the breath of the night.

"Jennifer!" Chase shouted halfheartedly. He began to give pursuit, but then turned back, cursing under his breath.

They locked eyes and he frowned. Sterling's heart pulled tight.

A second later, his gaze wandered past her, his expression changing.

Sterling turned and peered the opposite way, finding a teenage girl standing at the edge of the curb, still as a sculpture.

She recognized the girl: it was Kayla Grayson, the nineteen-year-old daughter of Danny Grayson, who owned Grayson's Market, the one and only grocery supply store in all of Drybell.

Captivated, she watched Kayla waiting at the curb, staring off into the night. She could see the girl's breath slowly pluming out in front of her and noticed she wasn't wearing any shoes.

"Hey," Sterling called. "Kayla, right? Kayla Grayson?" She took another step forward, the strong wind drowning out her voice. "You okay?"

There was a swell of electricity and Grayson's neon sign dimmed like an eclipse. The lampposts dotting the street groaned, powering down one at a time. Before she knew what was happening, the entire street sunk into darkness.

"What the hell…" she uttered.

The dark didn't seem to bother the girl. Kayla stared off into space, still as could be on the edge of the walkway.

Sterling glanced over her shoulder at Chase, who was making his way over. "What's going on? She all right?" he called to her.

Sterling shrugged.

Thunder growled. The ground began to vibrate.

Sterling listened closely, watching tiny specks of rock dance across the pavement. The hum grew louder, droning on and overtaking the night air.

An engine.

She snapped her head up to find a large semi-truck speeding down Main Street no more than a hundred yards away.

Shit!

There wasn't much time.

She sprang to life, hurdling over the hedges onto a wooden bench. "Kayla, move!" she shouted, waving her hands. "Get out of the way!"

Kayla didn't react, standing there on the edge of the curb with a blank expression on her face.

The gigantic truck roared forward, nearly as wide as the street itself, kicking up leaves and debris like a moving storm.

Sterling leaped off the bench and hit the ground running. She flew down the sidewalk, dodging parking meters and sidestepping trash bins. "Get out of the way!" she screamed, but her voice was lost beneath the sound of the engine.

She watched in horror as Kayla stepped off the curb, as if sleepwalking through a dream. Her bare feet padded over the concrete, coming to a stop in the middle of the road.

The truck barreled on, dangerously close, the engine like rolling thunder.

She heard Chase yelling her name somewhere behind her. Her heart was on fire and her legs were wobbly from the run earlier that night. She dove over the hood of an old Toyota Corolla and lunged through the air.

The engine was on top of her, blasting in her ears with a rumble that could very well shake the earth to pieces.

She slammed into Kayla, tackling the girl out of the way in time to feel a powerful whoosh of air right behind her. She squeezed her eyes shut as they flew through the air, hitting the ground like they'd fallen out of a moving vehicle. Their bodies viciously tumbled over the cracked asphalt and rolled to a stop. The engine rose to a crescendo, a blatant reminder of the death waiting on every corner, and whooshed past just as abruptly.

Body aching, throat burning like she'd swallowed acid, she rolled herself upright and leaned down to get a look at the girl.

Kayla Grayson looked like she was sleeping. Like she hadn't just narrowly avoided getting splattered all over the front of a big rig.

Panting, Sterling pressed a hand to the side of Kayla's neck and felt for a pulse.

She swallowed, chest rising and falling as Chase ran up and dropped to one knee.

"What the hell happened?! Is she all right?" he asked hurriedly.

Sterling looked up at him in wonder and said, "She's asleep."

She turned away from the window as Chase approached the car. He cursed, opened the door, and climbed into the cruiser.

Beyond the windows, Kayla Grayson was being loaded into the back of an ambulance. Two fire trucks were parked in front of the market, and the firemen were conversing with onlookers who had witnessed the incident. The power had returned, restoring the obnoxious holiday cheer tracking up and down the street.

"Who the hell walks into moving traffic and decides to take a nap afterward?" he said, shaking his head. "What a fucking disaster. First Jennifer and now this."

Sterling stayed quiet, watching the emergency staff scurry like ants.

The town's going to have a lot to talk about come tomorrow...

"Dwight says they're gonna keep her overnight down at Hatton Memorial, make sure nothing's wrong."

When Sterling didn't respond, Chase said, "I'm sorry, Boss. I've never, and I mean *never,* seen her hit anything in my life. I've never even seen the woman kill a spider for fuck's sake."

Sterling looked at him, confused. "What?"

"Jennifer," he explained. "I don't know what came over her."

Sterling did. Although his comment was meant to make her feel better, it actually made her feel worse. Sterling reached up, feeling the side of her face, almost in a state of shock. Not from the pain, but more from the sheer surprise of the act. She looked in the rearview mirror, noticing her skin had reddened. "Shit," she muttered, aware of the questions the mark would bring from the others at the station.

"I am so, so sorry," Chase said. He began to reach for her face, but she brushed his hand away.

"It's fine," Sterling added, twisting the rearview mirror back into place and starting the car. "Didn't know she had it in her."

Chase nodded soberly. "Yeah. Who would've thought?"

The receptionist at the station had her back to Sterling when she walked in. The aroma of butter choked the air, suffocating the small lobby. The robust frontend clerk sat hunched forward in her chair, staring down at a dated cellphone with oversized text that was propped up on the desk with a little stand. Her plump fingers dug around in her lap and Sterling heard crunching.

"I knew it, I knew it, I knew it..." the woman repeated.

A native of Houston, Texas, Georgia Cook was the face of the Drybell Sheriff's Department. The first person anyone saw when they came in, and the last person they spoke to on the phone, Georgia handled everything from parking tickets to impounded vehicles.

Sterling waited a moment, taking in the normalcy of what had been her life. She wondered how many times she'd been in this room before now; wondered if she'd miss it the way she missed home when she left and moved on to college.

Eventually, she peeked over Georgia's shoulder at the screen, where a young woman gave a live interview on the events purported to have occurred in Winterview City, about a hundred miles east. The receptionist was clearly fascinated by the interview, and Sterling wondered whether Georgia really believed in the supernatural, or was merely longing to escape the menial tasks of the grind.

"Aren't you a little old for haunted houses, Georgia?" Sterling asked. Her voice shattered the receptionist's concentration like a sheet of glass. Georgia gasped and the bowl of popcorn flew into the air.

"Whoa, easy old girl," Sterling said, suppressing a laugh.

Georgia turned around, placing a hand on her thundering heart. "Sweet bejesus, woman, don't you know it's bad manners sneaking up on an old lady like that?" she said with a thick, Southern drawl.

Georgia caught her breath, then did a double take as she collected the spilled popcorn and returned it to the tub, noticeably gawking at Sterling's face. She rolled forward in the chair, squinting.

Sterling had hoped her skin was dark enough to hide the red pooling on her cheek, but apparently, she was wrong.

"What in the Sam Hill happened to your face?" Georgia asked. Georgia's candor spoke volumes of her genuine nature, and Sterling couldn't help but be grateful that she had someone in her life that would give it to her straight, so to speak. Georgia rolled forward, slowly putting together who might have been responsible.

"Is that...from...?"

Sterling flashed Georgia a look that told her everything she needed to know, and Georgia returned one of sympathy.

Sterling gently pushed back a few strands of hair from her weary face and Georgia frowned, as if she could feel Sterling's pain. "That bitch is lucky you didn't shoot her."

"I think I had it coming."

Georgia rolled back to her desk and rummaged through the small cooler she kept her lunch in, taking out an icepack and handing it to Sterling. "Here. Won't get that stink of sin off ya, but it'll help with the redness all the same."

Sterling smiled, taking the icepack and pressing it to the side of her face. "Thanks, lady."

The two women shared a tender moment before Sterling eased back on the desk.

"So, what do we got tonight?"

Georgia shrugged, leaning back in her chair. "Tell ya the truth, it's been kinda quiet so far. Not a single call, I reckon. In fact, it's actually quieter than usual if you don't count the squall outside."

Sterling removed the icepack from her face and flipped it over, skeptical. "Really? *Nothing*?"

Georgia shook her head, putting her hand over her heart. "That is the official party line from Our Lady of Mercy in dispatch. God as my witness, not so much as a deer sighting on Iron Mountain Road from what I've been hearin'. Although…"

"What?" Sterling asked.

Georgia sucked in a deep breath, exhaling. "It's nothin' really. Just…well, the storm's been wreaking havoc on the phone lines. Tried calling my son earlier, but there's so much static on the goddamn line I couldn't even get a word in. Luckily, he don't have much to worry about way over there in Texas."

"You try your cell?" Sterling asked, slipping her phone out of her pocket.

"Even worse," Georgia said flatly. "No ma'am, I think we are just gonna have to wait this one out."

"Well, hopefully the storm blows over by morning," Sterling said. "I'm sure we could all use a little break from the world right now, don't you?"

"Uh-huh. Maybe some of us more than others."

"I thought that was you," a voice said.

Rosa Garcia, a short Hispanic woman in her early-forties, leaned against the doorframe leading into the hall. Her giant brown eyes blinked behind half inch-thick prescription lenses. A bulky headset strapped down a head of frizzy black hair and, with the exception of a small gold cross around her neck, she was without flare of any kind.

"Hey, Rosa," Sterling greeted.

Rosa's attention snagged on a brilliant starburst beyond the window, chased by the deep lull of thunder. Mesmerized, she unfolded her arms and approached the window, taking in the ominous flashes carrying on in the night.

"I've got a bad feeling about this night," Rosa said.

Sterling and Georgia exchanged a look.

"You also had a bad feeling about last night, but we're still here, ain't we?" Georgia replied.

Attempting to ease the tension that had washed over the room, Sterling said, "How's my town looking tonight, Rosa?"

Without lifting her eyes from the window, Rosa said, "Quiet. I guess you picked the right day to get out, eh Sterling?"

"It's always quiet this time of year, Rosa," Georgia countered. "At least 'round Christmas. C'mon, girl."

Rosa said, "Let's hope it stays that way."

Georgia and her locked eyes a moment, then Rosa said, "The Christmas party still on? I wasn't sure if you still wanted to."

Sterling nodded. "Yeah. Midnight Secret Santa. Be there or be square."

A Christmas party at the office actually felt like the last thing she wanted to do, but she reasoned it might help get her mind off everything else, including the ache in her face.

Rosa half-smiled, then disappeared into the hallway.

"I swear that woman was born with a scowl on her face," Georgia said, shaking her head. "Would it kill her to crack a smile from time to time?"

"You know she doesn't like this time of year, Georgia," Sterling replied. "Not all of us like being reminded we don't have family anymore."

"And that's another thing. Why you sticking up for that one? She likes you about as much as cats like water."

Sterling shrugged, then reached for a stack of letters in her mail cubby and began sorting through them, dropping them in the trash one by one. As she got comfortable with the idea of a quiet Christmas celebration with her friends at the station, Georgia's mouth spread into a grin.

"I suppose, course, you might be interested to know about the crash that happened this afternoon."

Sterling's eyes shifted up from the mail in her hands, unimpressed. "Ah. There it is." She smirked at Georgia, exhaling as she dropped the mail on the desk. "All right, lady, spill it."

"It was over on Old Ferry Bridge. You know the one, runs right over the river about a quarter mile? Well, Spencer said a big rig turned on its side. Said there was another vehicle involved and the sun was nearly down by the time he got there. Fire, smoke, the works. Took Dwight and his boys more than an hour to put the dang thing out. Leo the Coroner took the driver down to the morgue; body was all burned to hell, the poor bastard. Didn't say much else, other than he found a man down at the crash site."

"A man? Who?"

"Yes ma'am, Spencer brought him in himself about five o'clock this afternoon on the button. He's sitting in lockup as we speak. Hasn't said a word to nobody." Georgia hooked a thumb toward the other side of the building where the prisoner waited in a cold cell.

"So?" Sterling said.

Georgia tilted her head down and gave Sterling an unimpressed look over the top of her glasses.

"Who is he?" Sterling asked.

"Well, it's the damnedest thing," Georgia said, "because, darlin', we don't have the slightest fucking idea. But apparently *someone* does, because we got a phone call within thirty minutes of Spencer bringing him into the station from the *Department of Homeland Security*. And guess what? They have decided to pay us a visit."

CHAPTER 4

STERLING AND CHASE made their way through the corridor toward the two holding cells. Their boots clacked across the tile, and the sky gave them glimpses of the dark world beyond the windows.

"What do you mean you can't get ahold of him?" Sterling questioned. She carried a file folder in her hands, navigating a mess of paperwork as she marched through the corridor.

"I mean we *can't* get a hold of him. He's not answering his phone, and with the reception I can barely get a call out." Chase replied. "I've texted him four times already."

Sterling found this unusual. Spencer King, a fifty-seven-year-old man with a bulging belly and a short fuse, served as her second deputy. The cantankerous old timer was almost as attached to the job as herself, and she couldn't see him ignoring their calls under any circumstances barring death or some sort of life-threatening accident. He'd despised her after she'd swooped in and taken what the self-proclaimed "Protector of Town" called his birthright. It wasn't just that she was a woman, it was that she was an *unmarried* woman, and a driven one at that. God forbid he ever find out about her dating roster.

King was an asshole, but she'd miss him all the same, and it wasn't like him to vanish. *Especially* on a night like tonight.

The pair slowed their pace as they arrived at a steel door more fit for a submarine than a jail. Chase unlocked it and stepped aside to allow Sterling to pass.

"Did you have Rosa try him?"

"Already did it. Nothing."

Unease stirred in her chest and a tingle scuttled in her hands. She ran her tongue along the bottom of her teeth. "Well, I guess there could be a million reasons why he's not answering. But my first guess? He's *asleep*." She said this last word more sarcastically than she intended and wondered if Jennifer's slap was still simmering her blood.

"In this storm?"

"Come on, Chase. You know Spencer; you get a few beers in the guy and he's liable to sleep through a goddamn tornado tearing through his living room."

Chase looked at her apprehensively and said, "Let's hope so, because it looks like it's going to get bad out there."

Together, they arrived at the cells. The station hadn't been updated since its original construction at the beginning of the nineteenth century and still boasted iron bars just like towns from the Old West. Two dank cells with cement floors and walls, a stainless-steel toilet and sink, and a bed that was no more than a slab of concrete. The only light the room got was from the sconce on the wall between two narrow windows.

Sterling and Chase found a man sitting upright inside the nearest of the two cells, his face obscured in shadows.

"Good evening," Sterling said cordially. "I'm Sheriff Sterling Marsh and this is Deputy Chase Adkins. We'd like you to tell us about what happened out on Old Ferry Bridge."

The man silently looked up, considering her. His face passed into the light, and Sterling observed that he was in his early fifties, with short dark hair and the most haunted eyes she'd ever seen. A scar cut through his left brow and his face bore the five o'clock shadow of a man who was running out of time.

"Old Ferry Bridge…" the man mused.

Sterling took a step toward the bars. "That's right. We'd like you to tell us what happened there this afternoon."

"That makes you the one in charge around here then, yeah?"

"I am," Sterling offered with a tip of her head.

The man studied her before taking a deep breath. "Where is he?"

"Who?" Sterling asked.

"The man that brought me in. King."

Sterling cast a look at Chase.

"He's missing, isn't he?" the man asked.

Not wanting to give the suspect an inch, she said, "He's fine. Out on patrol."

"You're a bad liar."

"Hey," Chase warned, stepping forward. "Watch your mouth."

Sterling put a hand on his shoulder, and the unexpected contact birthed an awkward moment.

The suspect took notice.

"Fine," Sterling said, flashing a guilty smile. "You're right. We haven't heard from him." Then: "Why do you ask?"

It was clear the suspect didn't take any pleasure in his prediction being validated. Instead, his brow pinched together and worry clouded his eyes.

"And you probably won't," the suspect said.

Sterling asked, "What's your name, sir?"

The man looked at her and shook his head.

Sterling began to feel her patience slipping, and exhaled with irritation. She took another step toward the bars, flipping up the top page of the report and reading off the paperwork.

"According to this report, at approximately four oh seven this afternoon, Deputy Spencer King reports a big rig crash on Old Ferry Bridge. Emergency services are called and arrive within twenty minutes to extinguish the fire. During his investigation, Deputy King reports finding a 'suspicious person' wandering near the crash site. They are...disoriented. Confused. It is also worth noting that the wreckage of the collision is so substantial that access to the bridge is now impossible. No one goes in, no one goes out.

"Shortly after the suspect is taken into custody, the station is contacted by an individual claiming to be with the Department of Homeland Security. The identity of said suspect is withheld in the database, which is a first for me, but is deemed in the NCIC to be a 'wanted person.' Funny thing is, all known information in the database has been redacted. Imagine that."

Sterling closed the folder. "Now, I'm no genius, but I know that the DHS wouldn't roll out the red carpet for just anyone. So my question to you is: Who are you, and what exactly is it that the DHS wants with you?"

The man remained silent.

Sterling crouched down outside the bars to reach his eyelevel. "Listen to me very carefully. I do not want to keep you in here one second longer than I have to. But I *will* leave you in here for as long as is necessary until you give me some answers. The whole world doesn't fall apart overnight, stranger. It just doesn't happen," she said. "Not here."

Sterling and Chase began to walk away, and just as she was about to step through the door, she heard the man call to her.

"Wait."

She turned to find the man standing at the front of the cell, his fingers wrapped around the bars.

"Sheriff Marsh," he said. "*Sterling.* Be careful."

A chill cut through her bones as the tomb of a jail exploded in a flash of white light from beyond the windows. The concrete walls sang from the rolling thunder, and the wind howled louder than the animals of the mountains.

She glanced at Chase, taken aback, and then at the man, who appeared to be speaking sincerely despite the circumstances.

She nodded at the stranger, confused by his warning, and continued into the corridor.

Chase and the man locked stares before he turned around, slamming the door closed.

CHAPTER 5

"SURPRISE!" THE VOICES bellowed.

"For she's a jolly good fellow, for she's a jolly good fellow…"

The entire staff sung in unison, horribly off-key but the embodiment of holiday spirit. They chanted farewell to her with cheerful faces, bright with happiness and hope, each dressed in a party cone hat and their favorite ugly Christmas sweaters. The lunchroom was alight with Christmas magic. Lengthy vines of spangled bulbs. Sparkling tinsel. Red and green balloons. Two foldout tables at the far end of the room were lined with plastic reindeer goblets complete with antlers like she'd seen in that one movie. A generous bowl of spiked eggnog and all variety of cookies, cakes, and muffins dotted a plethora of silver trays.

Chase. Georgia. Rosa.

They were all there.

For her.

Except Spencer and the Chief, of course.

She checked her cellphone for any calls from King but saw nothing. He'd turn up sooner or later.

"Surprise," Chase said unenthusiastically. He smiled guiltily out of the side of his mouth. "Sorry, Boss. Tried to tell them you don't like surprises, but they wouldn't take no for an answer, and neither would you."

A small boy peeked out from behind Chase's leg. His golden hair was parted to the side just like his daddy, and he was fitted with a sweater vest over a baby blue dress shirt held together with a bright red bowtie. Slung over his shoulder was a leather bag two sizes too big. The boy dressed about fifty years older than he actually was and, while Georgia and Rosa found it endearing, Sterling just found it annoying.

She looked down at him, blinking.

"Hey, there he is," Chase said merrily. "Come say hi." He ushered Max out into plain view with a good-natured kick to the behind.

Sterling smiled sheepishly and tipped her head.

The boy was weary with exhaustion, but he held upright well enough for a seven-year-old who was up way past his bedtime. She was surprised the weight of the satchel hadn't tipped him over yet.

"What do you say, Ace?" Chase asked, egging him on.

"Merry Christmas, Miss Sterling," Max said timidly. His chest deflated and a party horn sprung out from his lips with a papery *crunch!*

"Thanks," Sterling said artificially, and it tasted like ashes on her tongue.

"Well don't just stand there, give your Aunt Sterling a hug," Chase said, scooping him up in his arms and thrusting him awkwardly toward Sterling.

"Oh, no, really, it's fine—" Chase lobbed the boy into her waiting arms and she caught him uncomfortably, holding him up in the air. She clumsily took hold of him like she was holding a dead animal.

They stayed there suspended, blinking at each other in awkward silence.

"Isn't it a little late for you to be up?" she asked, making a face like she had a sour taste in her mouth.

Max shook his head. "It's only nine o'clock in California."

"Are you *in* California?" she asked.

Max got a confused look, like he was trying to add numbers, then shook his head.

"Exactly."

Sterling exhaled like she didn't know what else to do. "You're getting heavy, kid. You must be getting old."

"Yeah, I guess so," he agreed. His voice lowered to a whisper. "I didn't want to miss your party, so Daddy said I could come down and visit, but that it's a secret. Cool, huh? Me and Georgia are gonna hangout until Daddy can drop me off at home later. Georgia says Santa Claus is coming soon, and if I've been real good this year he's going to bring me something special."

"Santa Claus?" Sterling cocked her head. "You don't say?"

She looked up and saw Georgia and Chase glaring at her, their faces tense.

"It's true!" Max exclaimed. "Cross my heart."

"I see…" Sterling smirked. "Well, you're in luck, because I have a feeling your Dad knows him pretty well. And, uh, I think I even met him once down at the Silver Dollar—"

Rosa elbowed her in the side and she winced.

Max's eyes lit up like a slot machine. "You did?!"

Sterling nodded. "It's true," she growled, eyeing Rosa. "And I'll tell you what, he was putting away eggnog like you wouldn't believe. *Almost* had to give him a ticket, but I let him off with a warning on account of all the kids needing presents. I guess it's a good thing I did, huh?"

"Yes ma'am." Max bobbed his head. "He made it to our house, didn't he, Daddy?"

Chase folded his arms and nodded. "It's true, I saw him

myself. Left Max lots of gifts under the tree."

"I bet he did," Sterling said, laughing sarcastically.

Chase swiped a few frosted snowman cookies off the table and popped them into his mouth, crunching. "Jennifer had to go down to the office to grab some papers for the hearing tomorrow about the river."

"The river?" Rosa asked, perking up.

"She says something's wrong with the water levels. I guess the state's getting involved. I try and stay out of it."

Rosa's face darkened. "Probably nothing…"

"Figured I'd let Max here join the party and just drop him off at home once things settle down. Last day of school, right, Ace? Why not celebrate?" he said, playfully slapping Max on the shoulder.

Max flinched, but nobody else seemed to notice.

Sterling smiled pensively at Max, like she was trying to figure him out. What was there to figure out? He was a kid. Messy. Smelly. Expensive. What more did she need to know? She commended Ovi and Anna for raising her for those eighteen years because God knew she wouldn't have been able to. She gave Max a phony squeeze, then set him back on the floor.

Georgia—who was wearing a grin longer than the Mississippi—stepped forward and threw her arms around Sterling, patting her on the back the way a caring grandmother would. "We're sure as shit gonna miss having you around here, Sterling. I'd try and talk you out of it, but I reckon by now you've about made up your mind." She grabbed a platter of frosted cupcakes off the table, offering her one.

Sterling waved them away, attempting to politely refuse. "Oh, thanks, I just ate about an hour ago—"

Georgia looked at her straight-faced, then thrust them at her. Sterling guessed she should probably get used to that sort of thing for the night. "I spent *all weekend* baking these damned things, and I just about burned the first two batches," said Georgia. "Now I know you wouldn't have an old woman slaving away over a hot stove for nothing, now would you?"

"I want one!" Max interrupted from below, tugging on the tray.

Georgia bumped him out of the way with her leg and said, "Where's your manners, Maxy? You wait your turn. This is Sterling's special day."

"Special how?" Max asked. "Is it her birthday?"

"Because," Georgia explained, shaking her head, "she's been good to us, and we want to show her that we're grateful, because we are. Because Drybell takes care of its own."

Sterling nodded a reverent thank you, then took a cupcake off the platter. "Thanks, old girl." She peeled off the cupcake liner, then took a bite of the rich chocolate, her melancholy face thawing to something warmer. "Mmm…" she said, chewing rich cake. "You haven't lost your touch."

"It ain't Yorkshire pudding, but I figured best not compete with your mama," Georgia replied with a wink.

"I want one," Max begged.

"For heaven's sake, here," Georgia snipped, rolling her eyes.

Max swiped the dessert out of her hand and scampered away, cozying up alongside a mountain of gifts at the base of the Christmas tree.

"Manners, Ace," Chase scolded.

"You're really giving it up, ay Sterling?" Rosa said. The side of her face was trapped in the warm, quaint glow from the Christmas tree.

Sterling nodded. "Guilty as charged. But I think you'll make do just fine without me."

"Probably," Rosa agreed, walking forward, "but that doesn't mean we want to."

"Oh," she said, caught off guard. There was an awkward silence. She'd never heard Rosa say a single nice thing to her in all her ten years in Drybell. "Thanks."

Rosa forced a smile that didn't suit her.

Chase cut in. "Come on guys, let's cut her some slack, huh? What else is she gonna do, spend the rest of her life sitting around Drybell arresting Jimmy Hayworth every other weekend for running stop signs on his bicycle? Pluck the occasional cat out of the tree? Let's face it, the gal's moving on to better things."

There he goes again, Sterling thought. *Always trying to be the hero. Always trying to rescue me.*

There had been a dream before. A beautiful one where she lived out her days growing old in the rocking chair on her front porch, watching the sun rise behind the mountains.

But it was just a fantasy.

It wasn't real, and it never would be. Because life isn't a fairy tale.

"In fact," Chase added charismatically, collecting four goblets from the table and filling them with eggnog, "I would like to propose a toast." He distributed a glass to each of them, then raised his own. "Sterling Marsh," he said, exhaling. "That first night together, you saved me from that rabid pit bull and somehow managed to tase me in the process."

She laughed the first true laugh she had in a while.

Chase continued, "You remember, the one that got loose from Old Lady Gomes's place? Anyway, I knew since that first night that I had met someone special, and we're losing someone just as special, if not more. It breaks our hearts, but your legacy will live on here in Drybell."

Chase attempted to hide his true feelings beneath his tales, but his eyes were filled with sadness and it gutted her inside something fierce. He continued on, "You are one of the finest people I have ever had the pleasure of working with. You're hardworking, driven, and we love you for it. May you find whatever it is you're looking for out there."

The two stared at each other intimately, the group's glasses hanging in the air.

"To Sterling," Chase declared.

The group said, "To Sterling!"

They toasted, and Sterling finished the eggnog in three swallows while the others followed suit.

Chase licked his lips, setting the glass on the table and clapping his hands together. "Now, is this a funeral, or a party? Music, Georgia?"

"Right," Georgia said, snapping her fingers. She ambled over to the table and dug through a cardboard box on the ground, sliding out a record.

Sterling arched her eyebrows. "A record player? Where in the hell did you guys dig up that thing?"

"On loan from the Drybell Antique Mall until next week." Chase grinned at her like a schoolboy. "Spared no expense."

A couple quick scratches cut the hum of twinkling bulbs as "Rockin' Around the Christmas Tree" hissed to life.

Sterling filled up the eggnog goblet a second time, then wandered over to the Christmas tree, where Max was fiddling with something in his hands.

"What's that?" she asked.

Max looked up at her, then held up his hand to reveal a small cube covered with multicolored squares resting in his palm.

"Rubik's Cube," she said.

Max nodded.

"You like puzzles?"

"Yeah. I guess," he said with a shrug. A beat, then, "Do you?"

Sterling shook her head. "Nah. I was never any good at them. Couldn't concentrate long enough to see it through, you know? I was more of an outdoors kind of kid."

Max kept on, working the thing in his hands.

"What about 'em?" she asked. "Do you like, I mean."

He twisted and rearranged the squares, spinning the plastic sides and realigning sections at a time.

"It's fun," he replied.

She didn't know why she expected a more profound response. He was seven, after all. For all she knew he'd probably just learned how to ride a bike, or tie his shoes. All the stuff kids did at his age.

"I don't have to listen," he added.

Sterling raised her eyebrows. "Listen?"

He nodded.

"To what?"

"Anything," he mumbled. He turned and glanced at Chase, who was on the dance floor with Rosa and Georgia working up a sweat, and Sterling understood: he was talking about Chase and Jennifer. She'd seen their house once before, and with that square footage there wasn't much chance Max wouldn't hear their voices from any room in the house, even *with* the doors closed.

She thought about telling him that it would pass. That things would get better when he was older. She heard her mother and father's voices, clashing at each other like guns going off. She remembered sprinting out the front door and over the porch steps, racing through the fields surrounding their house. She'd find that old tree with the knot for a heart and climb into the hollow there, her heart pattering like a hummingbird.

She considered offering a few encouraging words, thought about telling him that things would get better once he was away on his own.

But she didn't.

Why should she lie to him?

"What happened to your arm?" she asked.

Max froze, twisting his head up at her.

"No point lying. It's my job to know when people are telling the truth."

Max sighed. "A boy at school."

Sterling shook her head and got down on one knee so that she was eye level with him.

"He hit you?" she asked, voice low.

Max hesitated saying anything else, but could see she wasn't going to let up. He nodded, ashamed.

Sterling grit her teeth and felt her fist clench.

"Max?"

Max kept on with the puzzle.

"Look at me."

When he didn't, Sterling reached down and took the cube from his hands. She gently nudged his face toward her and looked him straight in the eye. "You're a lot smarter than people treat you. And since I know that, I'm going to tell you something I wouldn't normally say to a kid. Just call it free advice."

There was an eruption of laughter and she glanced over her shoulder to find Georgia attempting to teach Chase and Rosa how to line dance. Georgia was in the groove, but Chase had two left feet and Rosa was stiff as a wooden plank in a breeze.

"There are a lot of bad people in this world, Max. People that will want to hurt you. Make you feel bad about yourself. Belittle you. Bully you." She paused, watching a small train pass by under the tree. "I don't care what anyone else says, if a boy hits you—*hurts* you? Well, then you just hurt him right back. Don't ever let anyone treat you like that, because once they start thinking it's okay, it's only gonna get worse."

She smiled sad-like, then said, "I promise you. You don't stop it now; it'll only get worse. You might not understand right now, but when you get older, you will."

"Everything all right over here?" Chase asked, boogying over. "What're you two talking about?"

Sterling looked at Max and she could tell he'd understood.

"Ace?" Chase repeated.

"He was showing me his puzzle," Sterling answered, handing the cube back to the boy. "Weren't you, Max?"

Max nodded, turning his attention back on the puzzle.

"We've been missing you out there. How about a dance?" Chase asked, out of breath.

Sterling gaped at him. "Are you kidding?"

Chase stared at her stone-faced.

"Dance? Me?" she asked.

Chase chuckled. "Yes, dance. You know, cut a rug, tear it up? Get 'jiggy' with it, all that bullshit."

Max stopped what he was doing and looked up at his daddy like he'd lost his mind, then shook his head and went back to his puzzle.

"Who *are* you?" Sterling sneered.

"Come on, Marsh," he argued. "This is it! Your swan song. Last night on Earth." His eyes twinkled and there was a familiar electricity. "It's your last night. I mean…why the hell not, right?"

Sterling considered him, admiring his boyish charm. God, she was going to miss him. She relented with a groan, her mouth pulling into a smile as she raised her goblet. "I'll tell you one thing right now: I'm going to need something a hell of a lot stronger than whatever's in this."

His mouth hooked into a crooked smile. He extended an arm and she took it. He put a chivalrous hand on the small of her back, ushering her out to Georgia and Rosa, who were twisting away with a drink in hand, laughing and singing along with the music. They saw her coming and began whooping and cheering like her own personal cheerleaders.

The music went on as they danced and ate sweets and talked, and before long the menace of the impending storm had faded into the background, granting them one last quiet moment of Christmas reprieve.

CHAPTER 6

BILLY CAPSHAW RACED down the aisle, past a blur of cereal boxes, Pop Tarts, oatmeal, and cake mix. He buttonhooked as he emerged on the other side, swinging past the tortilla end cap and down the bread aisle, recklessly knocking items off the shelves as he went.

His mother, Elaine Capshaw, didn't notice. She never seemed to notice the things he did, too busy scheming how to get her next fix. In this case, she was actively engaged with the male cashier ringing up her groceries, philandering like a schoolgirl in church while she doctored up a bad check.

Billy had the whole store to himself. He hadn't seen a soul in here besides that policeman in the brown uniform.

Cops, Billy thought. That was what his mother called them. Sometimes she called them pigs, too, but he didn't know why. She said they were bad, that they wanted to take him away from her and bring him to live with his grandma in Idaho. They were always coming by the trailer at night: the woman who vaguely reminded him of Princess Jasmine but older (his sister watched *Aladdin* on repeat) and the man with the yellow hair and the blue eyes. Sometimes even the fat old man, who looked like the buttons might shoot off his shirt like bullets. The very same one who happened to be here in the store right now. Billy hated him worst. He smelled like alcohol and stunk like one of his uncle's pigs, and Billy had to pinch his nose anytime he came by their house.

Yuck! Of all the luck, he thought. *Where is he, anyway?*

He had to be careful not to be seen, otherwise the cop might take him away like they did with the bad people.

To jail.

He shivered.

He listened to the shrill beeps from the scanner bounce off the walls from the front of the store like sonar.

His shoes screeched as he skidded to a stop.

Candy! There was an entire wall of it, going up so high he couldn't even tell what was at the top.

He blinked rapidly, overwhelmed by all the colors.

It all smelled sooooo good. Chocolate and taffy and coconut.

His mom would never buy him any. She'd rather he starved to death eating cold broccoli and cans of spaghetti sludge than buy him a Snickers bar or, God forbid, some M&M's.

His eyes slid over to the periphery, where he could make out the man scanning the food. He had on a red apron, a skinny black tie, and a mop of hair that looked like it was barely attached to his head. Billy saw a hint of green pass through his hands and recognized it immediately.

Broccoli. Barf!

He grimaced like he'd eaten something rancid.

His eyes narrowed as he spotted a pack of Jelly Bellies. His favorite! He anxiously glanced both ways to make sure no one was watching. His hand shot out and snatched them off the metal rod, stuffing them into his pocket a little too quickly and raking his fingers across that hard piece of metal on his pocket. He jerked his hand out just as quickly and felt pain flare across his hand.

Ouch!

He looked down at his skin but only saw red.

He thought back to earlier that day when he'd seen that stupid boy Max touching his crayons and his body tensed. He'd showed him what happens when you touched Billy Capshaw's things. They were *his*, no one else's.

The Jelly Bellies were in his pocket. Suddenly he was teetering on a dangerous ledge, thrilled at his newfound skill. He waited for someone to come. To scream and yell at him, tell him he was under arrest, going to jail and then to Idaho where it smelled like potatoes everywhere you went!

But nothing happened.

No one came.

His eyes inched wider, ravenous for sweets, and he reached out, stealing a bag of peanut M&M's and a Baby Ruth bar and shoving them as far down in his pockets as he could (but mindful of that stupid button this time).

Chocolate wafted into his nose. His head went light and the world began to tip.

He smelled…cinnamon?

He wrinkled his nose and rotated his head toward the back of the store, where long white counters followed along the wall. Normally there was tons of foam trays laid out on the shelves. Red meat. Slimy fish. Raw chicken. Some things he didn't even know what they were. But the shelves were empty now, and the dim glow tracking along them was turned down like his old nightlight.

He rolled his tongue inside his cheek, squinting.

A giggle.

It came from around the corner, toward the far end of the store.

He turned, looking back, and heard his mother and the man at the counter talking.

The titter came again, drawing his attention back the other way.

A girl? She sounded his own age, maybe a smidge older.

What is that? he thought curiously.

He carelessly reached out and ripped a hole in a plastic bag stuffed with suckers, peeling the wrapper off a lollipop and popping it into his mouth.

Cherry.

There was a long creak and something wet plopped on his face.

He recoiled in disgust, stepping back. He reached up and wiped at his face, inspecting his fingers.

Water?

He slowly craned his head up at the ceiling, where long metal beams crisscrossed overhead. They were painted so that they'd blend in with the ceiling, but they still stood out like a sore thumb, infested by rust and mold. He traced the dangling lights from the front of the store to the back, noticing they dimmed the further back they went.

There was another giggle, like it was right in his ears.

He about jumped out of his skin, biting down on his cheek as the sucker shifted in his mouth.

Ow!

He winced, yanking the sucker out like an infected tooth. He scowled at the thing, then chucked it over the cereal boxes. He reached up and probed the inside of his mouth, retracting his fingers to find bright spots of blood.

Another fat drop of rain sliced down his cheek. He looked up and glared at the ceiling like it was aiming for him. He shuffled back and watched another drop plunk right on the floor by his feet in a wet splat.

This stupid place is falling apart!

Another snicker whispered in his ear, so soft he barely heard it.

He spun toward the sound and saw the darkness at the other end of the store. The floor under his feet vibrated like an earthquake was beginning. His eyes spread open and he put a hand on the shelf just in case the earth started to rattle.

When nothing happened, he slowly padded down the aisle, finding the long white shelves of the meat department glowing in the dark. His heart was beating faster, but he didn't know why.

Billy turned around, nervously looking for his mother.

He could barely see them now, way down at the opposite end of the store. He looked around but didn't see anyone else, and for a brief second, he almost hoped he'd see the policeman.

He turned back and was faced with two black doors that were taller than any he'd ever laid eyes on before. There were thin plastic windows in both of them all scratched to hell, and they didn't have any handles like the ones at home or school.

He heard the storm outside the store, could hear the rain washing against the front windows overlooking the street. Thunder rumbled and he felt it in his chest. In his teeth. His hands.

His mouth hung open as he gaped at those ginormous black doors. He swallowed, taking a step back.

He heard his older brother, Benny, in his head, scolding him like he was no better than his little sister. He'd dared him to go down to the basement, into the room with that big metal thing with all the pipes. He'd said no, and Benny had let him know with a slap to the face that that sort of behavior was unacceptable in the Capshaw family. No brother of his was gonna be a wimp! It was already bad enough that he had a sister to deal with, but according to Benny, having a brother who was a wimp was much worse.

Come on, don't be a baby! What are you, scared? That's it, isn't it? Billy's scared of the dark! Aren't you, Billy?

In the end, he'd relented to the goading, let himself get sucked right into Benny's dumb game. He'd gone down those creepy wooden steps into a darkness that smelled like something was rotting down here.

Didn't you ever wonder where Dad was buried, dummy? he'd

said. *Mom wouldn't tell you because you're too small, but he's down there. She couldn't afford to bury him in the cemetery like she wanted, so she just put him down there instead. Don't believe me? Go on, see for yourself.*

Billy had stayed down there with his eyes squeezed shut and his hands over his ears and, to his relief, he never saw or heard a thing.

When he came back up the steps ten minutes later, practically shaking to pieces, Benny was gone. Billy had walked all around the house, thinking maybe his brother was playing a trick on him, but he never could find him. His baby sister was in her bedroom, humming "A Whole New World" to herself while she poured tea for an entourage of stuffed animals. Billy had gone outside with his baby sister and called for his brother, but he never could find him.

No one ever did. He was just…gone.

That was over a year ago now.

He'd gone into that basement a boy and come out a man.

Billy sucked in a breath of confidence, puffing up his chest and lifting his chin high. His fingers reached through the air, passing through the mist rolling out from the meat section toward the black doors. He heard a wet sucking sound as his fingers met the doors.

He halted, rolling his eyes to his feet.

His shoes were immersed in a pool of red syrup like flies in a flytrap. He began to pull his foot out and heard a sticky squelch. Disgusted, he tugged the other foot free with another suck, clearing himself.

The red ooze was leaking from under the doors.

Maybe this isn't such a good idea… he decided.

Buzzing wound up in the air like a hundred flies. He listened to it, cocking his ear toward the sound. A groan traveled through the walls, and the tubes of light sputtered like they were coughing.

He spun around to find someone standing there.

The figure was a shadow in front of the empty white shelves.

She hadn't been there a minute ago. Couldn't have been. The air buzzed, wrought with bleach and blood, and Billy wondered where all the meat had gone.

The stranger didn't move. It was a lady, but he couldn't see much else. She was wearing some sort of coat and a long black dress, and she had really white skin, like those twins he had in his class at school. His teacher said that they had something in their bodies that made their skin extra white, but he couldn't remember the word. Come to think of it, though, this lady looked even more white than the twins were!

Billy studied her, raking his eyes up and down her strange clothes, and snickered again that someone would be so dumb to dress up like a witch when Halloween was months ago. The white lights tracking the walls fluttered, spilling open hollows of darkness.

Suddenly the woman didn't seem so funny anymore.

He stood there watching the woman who was dressed like a witch and a fist began to tighten in his chest, like this woman wasn't anyone he should be talking to.

The lights crackled, flickering again and leaving him engulfed in the dark with the unnerving figure.

He spun on his heels and began to walk away when his foot kicked something soft.

Down at the base of his feet, a weird hat was lying on the tile. It was big and tall, and it reminded him of something he'd seen in Halloween shops and old books. He picked it up and it was much heavier in his hands than he guessed it would be. Fascinated, he ran his fingertips over the surface, rubbing over wrinkly patches that felt like his own skin. He noticed something swaying in the air and grabbed at it, stretching it taut in his fingertips.

A fat gray hair; it was stuck between the stitches in the hat. He turned the thing over in his hands, noticing several others sprouting out as well. He wrinkled his nose, plucking one from the hat with a sharp *plink!*

He smirked, pleased with himself, then lifted the thing up and wrenched it over his unruly brown curls.

"Oh, look at me, I'm a dumb scary witch," he mocked under his breath, sticking his tongue out at the woman.

There was a shudder in the walls, and the fluorescent tubes behind him dimmed again.

He turned around and gasped, noticing the woman was only a few feet away now.

She moved!

His skin crawled like bugs. His mouth was dry, and there was a mist of cold sweat on his back. His smirk fell away as he watched the creepy old woman stare at the empty meat wall.

The lights flickered and the tubes hummed with the flow of electricity.

He wasn't having fun anymore, he decided. He looked to the front of the store and saw his mother loading the bags into the cart.

Time to go.

His eyes slid over to the woman, making sure she was still there.

He grabbed the wide brim of the hat and pulled. There was a pinch and he felt his skin wrench up with it.

"Ouch!" he growled, wincing.

That's weird...

His eyes widened as he felt the thing move on his head like it was alive, like a giant spider was on his head, squirming. Almost like...it was *breathing*.

He panicked, jerking again, harder this time, stumbling forward a few steps. A pressure began to build around his head, like it was caught in a giant vacuum tube. He began to whimper, sucking in short, empty breaths. He spun around, desperate for help, for anyone, but only the woman was there.

He took handfuls of the hat in his hands, and just as he went to yank it off, the hat bit down on his head like a shark's mouth lined with serrated teeth.

There was a white-hot flash of pain all around his skull and something warm trickled down his face.

Blindly, he reached his hands up and brushed them over his face. He held them up in a daze, like he was about to teeter over, and a cold bolt of terror shot through him. His blurry vision pulled into focus and he saw that his hands were wet with blood.

His eyes shot to his mother, who heaved the last of the bags into the shopping cart, politely taking the receipt from the checkout man with a cheeky grin and casually jotting something on it before handing it back to the man.

Billy's eyes began to sting and he realized it was from the blood; it was hot and spilling down his face. He tasted copper in his mouth and spit it out. He let out a whimper and realized he was crying now.

He opened his mouth to scream and there was a flutter of air. His vision went black as the hat sprang to life, plunging down his face with a blinding pain, slurping down over his head like the mouth of a snake. A horrible buzzing exploded in his ears like a million flies. He frantically clutched at the hat as he shrieked for help, attempting to pry it off. He held on for his life as the horror slithered down further, cresting the edge of his chin and completely engulfing his head.

He gasped, trying to pull in air and only getting a mouthful of flies. He tore at the thing with his chewed fingernails, falling to his knees. The hat bit into him again, swallowing him whole, and unexpectedly he was transported back to the basement, smelling that horrible smell with his eyes closed and his hands over his ears. A frightening thought occurred to him then: that maybe Benny had found the same hat somewhere in the forest that day, that it had eaten him alive, too, and that was why nobody had ever found him.

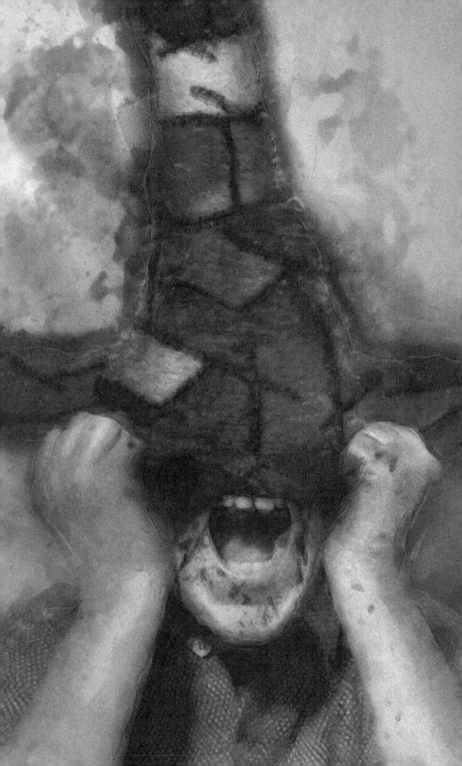

He gasped, straining for air and choking on blood and flies and his own tongue instead. The hat twisted tighter, muffling his horrified screams as his head went dizzy and he felt like he was falling.

Then, there was only darkness.

Less than five minutes later, Elaine Capshaw rolled down the cereal aisle calling Billy's name, finding nothing but a witch's hat and a pool of blood.

She listened as the speaker clicked on and announced, "Cleanup on aisle five."

CHAPTER 7

ROSA SAT ALONE in dispatch: a small, perpetually dark room with no windows. The carb coma was right on schedule, but her body was fighting it. The two monitors in front of her cast an emerald glow on her face, and she wondered how long she'd been staring at the idle interface. She sat upright in the chair, stiff as a board, her headset dangerously quiet. She waited there, drumming her fingers on the desk with unease, as if expecting a call that would never come.

Normally the silence didn't bother her. In fact, it was one of the things she loved about the job. Ordinarily, it was peaceful. Serene even. Where most would run through a checklist of every single rotten thing about their job, instead, Rosa counted her blessings. She didn't have to sit around and force herself to pretend to be interested in the trivial day-to-day details of her coworkers' lives. Didn't have anyone looming over her shoulder, checking her work and telling her what she was doing wrong, or doing right, for that matter. There was almost a point in her life where she'd given up hope, resigned herself to corporate slavery and condescending managers and even worse customers. After years of working retail at dead-end jobs, she just couldn't take it anymore. Processing refunds at Walmart in the customer service department. Cleaning up filthy, disgusting hotel rooms with soiled sheets and used condoms. Taking fast-food orders from snobby rich teenagers who had the munchies. Dealing with sleazy managers with a laundry list of potential lawsuits and others who sometimes never showed up at all. But she'd done it all with a smile, because she had a sister who needed her and that was that. By that time in her life, she'd lost track of all the places she'd worked, and part of her was glad for that. Not because she thought any of those jobs were beneath her, but because she had been nearly thirty-seven years old and still hadn't a damned clue what she was doing in life.

Maria, her sole sibling and only family in the states with the exception of their mother, Guadalupe, had been at her side through thick and thin. Together they'd braved the world and gotten their hands dirty with grit and sweat to do what needed to be done. To make a home for themselves in a world that was as vicious as a rabid dog. And when Rosa had come home late one evening after a particularly taxing night, she'd realized the hope for a decent life that she prayed so hard for was diminishing.

Then things had changed.

The sky was pregnant with rain. Maria had been assaulted, had a knife pulled on her after she'd walked down the wrong alley. The man had punched her poor sister in the face and knocked the vision right out of her left eye, making off with her purse and half of their rent money. Horrified, Rosa had learned the news about an hour before her shift, but without their rent money, the demand for her to work was even greater. So she'd tearfully said goodbye to Maria at the hospital while her sister was laid up in bed with a bandage over one side of her face, catching a taxi to work.

Ten minutes before the longest shift of her life ended, she was handing out her last Happy Meal of the night to a nice African American man and his son via the drive-thru. The man's hair was close-cropped and graying at the temples. She remembered his eyes were dark brown, like A&W Root Beer, and he squinted when he smiled at her. He'd pulled up to the window in the rain and seen the miserable, defeated look on her face. His expression had softened and they'd shared a look of acknowledgment, commiserating over what life does year after year in a world without hope. She knew that he saw the same sad, middle-aged woman in front of him that everyone else did. She was ashamed. Ashamed she couldn't be there with her sister. Ashamed of who she'd become, that she couldn't take care of her baby sister and her mother. Ashamed maybe more than she had ever been her whole life. She felt humiliated and tired, like the will to live had left her before she ever really got started. She ruminated how long it had been since she'd felt joy, or even a modicum of happiness, and a bleak image of the world running her over like a subway was devastating and terrifying all at once.

But then something unexpected and wonderful had happened.

While they'd waited there, eyes locked, the boy had leaned forward from the passenger seat and smiled a big, toothy smile. The man's son was maybe nine years old, with a chip in his front tooth. He smiled at her and said, "I see you," with a giggle.

Rosa's eyes pooled with tears hearing those three profound yet simple words because she realized that the world hadn't forgotten her like she thought. Her heart swelled and she burst into tears, quietly laughed as the boy looked up at her.

Had *seen* her.

She still mattered. No matter how hopeless things had become, she hadn't been forgotten, left alone in the dark.

She beamed at him and wiped her eyes, mouthing, "Thank you."

The boy hung there in the window looking up at her in the storm and the man chuckled warmly, nudging him back in his seat.

Where had all of her joy gone?

She'd handed the man the bags after sneaking an extra toy in the Happy Meal.

As it turned out, that kind man had worked for the San Francisco Sheriff's Department for thirty-nine years. Apparently, he'd been enjoying his retirement, roaming the United States and all of its grand attractions in a pilgrimage to show his boy everything he'd missed out on himself as a child. The Grand Canyon. Mount Rushmore. The Empire State Building. The Statue of Liberty. The Seattle Space Needle. Lagrave's Lasher Cube and the Great Suttershade Anomaly. Everything a young boy could hope to see in his childhood.

Impressed with her ability to multitask and perceptive of Rosa's longing for more, he suggested she apply herself as a dispatcher. "Give it a try. It might change your life," he'd said.

And thanks to one seemingly trivial act of kindness, and with her hope restored, apply she did. She couldn't remember being so excited about doing something, least of all anything pertaining to work, that one dark cloud always reminding her she could never escape the gloom.

Six months to the day, she was at the academy, training on everything from communication codes to emergency procedures while Maria recovered from the attack in an apartment Rosa couldn't stand. The sheer amount of information was overwhelming at first, trying to take it all in, but before long she had graduated from training, transferred, and taken up the reins as the sole dispatcher at the station, filling in for the late Dan Underwood, who'd given in to a long, painful bout with colon cancer.

Rosa never forgot that nice man and his son, and found herself thinking of them often. She wondered what might have happened if they'd never come to her window that horrible night, and she was grateful to them for saving her life.

The haze of green light from the monitor pulled her back to her spot at the drive-thru window. She saw herself standing there at the window in her uniform, needles of rain blowing in from the dark night. She remembered the routine. The repetition. The dread she felt while Maria was confined to a hospital bed, unsettled thinking about how bad the city had gotten. She thought of her boss, Stanley, with his bulging belly and the oily wisps of hair pasted across his bald head, the way he'd waddle over with his clipboard and look at her like she was less than nothing.

"Your productivity is starting to worry me, Rosa. What's the disconnect?" he'd ask her, and she'd shake her head because she didn't know what he wanted her to say.

She shuddered thinking back about how he made her feel as he tapped the pen on the clipboard and gave her the stink eye. He'd stood there and slowly looked her up and down, ran his tongue over his flaky, disgusting lips like his skin was falling off.

"I'm at my wit's end. You're just not getting this, girl," he'd scolded. "Don't know what else we can do. But maybe what you need is for me to give you a little more training *personally*."

She'd nearly thrown up in her mouth, excusing herself to the bathroom and exiting out the back door into the rain. She didn't even bother telling anyone she was leaving because she didn't know where she was going herself, only that she wanted to be anywhere but there.

A spell of nausea came over her, all too aware how badly she was marred by old memories, tortured by the knowledge of all the years she'd wasted before they'd found sanctuary in Drybell.

She had friends now. A family. Georgia. Chase. Even Sterling.

Her eyes fell. She exhaled, troubled, and realized that she was more by bothered by Sterling's resignation than she thought she rightfully would be. It was no secret that she wasn't Sterling's biggest fan by any stretch of the imagination. Sterling was like her sister in some ways, those moments where you could never actually agree on anything and you fought like an old married couple. The two had butted heads on more than one occasion, rarely going out of their way to talk to each other unless it was absolutely necessary. Rosa couldn't quite put her finger on what it was she didn't like about the girl. Maybe it was the way Sterling saw the world as a half-empty glass, like people only really existed to help themselves. Or maybe it was that contemptuous tone Sterling had when she spoke to her, like anyone that didn't carry a gun and a badge didn't have the right to know what was going on around here. Like they weren't as essential to the happenings in Drybell.

But she *was* essential. Just as essential to the town as the others.

Drybell needed her, and she needed it.

But what did it matter now? Sterling was leaving.

Her chest deflated with guilt. She shook her head, chiding herself for being so petty these last few years. She should have tried harder, made some part of a reasonable attempt at a friendship with the woman. A civil rapport at the very least. Maybe if she had then none of this mess would have happened in the first place. It was agonizing, the thought of not knowing what type of changes were in store once Sterling was gone, and she cringed picturing what might happen to her life.

She popped a bite-sized snowman cookie into her mouth and chewed.

She'd put on a happy face for the Christmas party, just like she'd told Chase and Georgia she would. She'd even had a glass of eggnog and made polite conversation with them, something she'd tried to distance herself from as much as possible until now. Hell, she'd be remiss to admit she hadn't had fun! She'd even danced a bit like she used to when she was younger, before she'd grown up and forgotten what it was like to know joy. She'd forgotten how much she'd liked dancing, how alive it made her feel. The funny eggnog glasses. The desserts. The campy Christmas lights she'd found at the Market on a two-for-one special. Even the Secret Santa had gone off without a hitch. She couldn't help but snicker when Sterling had opened the wrapping and found a small bobble head of herself; a perfect caricature of the Sheriff down to the tiniest detail, including her dark eyes and lips, her trademark raven ponytail, and even the glittering gold star on her chest. Rosa quickly realized that her pathetic idea of fun lately had been hunting down a new pot for her Marigolds and baking homemade enchiladas and tamales for the neighbors' block parties (according to Georgia, she was the only one in Drybell who could cook authentic Mexican cuisine) she never bothered to attend. One time, Rosa had cooked them all breakfast at the station, and Georgia had quipped that a tortilla and beans never went with scrambled eggs no matter what anyone else said. Rosa rolled her eyes because Georgia was Georgia and nobody was going to change her mind. Sterling on the other hand, welcomed the new. Rosa knew Sterling's dark features came from her father's side, a man Sterling rarely ever mentioned, even to the others. She remembered that Sterling's mother was white and that her father was Indian, and she remembered being a little jealous that Sterling had probably been privy to both English and Indian cuisine growing up. She'd seen a photo of the family sitting on the corner of Sterling's desk and noted Sterling's odd expression, her mouth pressed into a flat line even as a toddler.

Rosa heard laughter echo through her head, and moments from the party replayed in her mind like home movies. She saw herself walk up to Sterling as the woman tossed her plate into the trash and refilled her coffee.

Sterling looked tired. More tired than she ever had before. She smiled at Rosa halfheartedly, like she'd done all she could in this life and was ready to throw in the towel. Rosa knew that feeling all too well, having experienced it most her life. She finally understood: Sterling wasn't her enemy. And it finally hit her, what she hadn't liked about the woman all these years.

The truth, as much as she didn't want to believe it, was that Sterling was just like her. Or at least, who she had been before she'd found Drybell and invited peace into her life at Our Lady of

Mercy's Sunday service. Sterling was like a wolf caught in a trap, bleeding herself dry and gnawing at her own wounds.

She'd blinked at Sterling in wonder, appalled with herself, and thrown her arms around the girl, squeezing her tight. Sterling had stood there awkwardly, finally patting Rosa on the back with a relieved smile, like she'd finally put to rest the last thing that needed to be said before she said goodbye.

And as Rosa had embraced her, pouring all the hope and prayers she had into the woman, she remembered what the man had said to her at the drive-thru and how it had changed her life. She gazed at Sterling, feeling something like empathy and love, and said, "I see you."

Sterling had looked at her strangely and smiled, not knowing what to make of her words, and then said, "Look after the place for me, Rosa."

And that was it. She'd taken a few cookies on a napkin patterned with reindeer and snowmen and made her way back to dispatch to sit in the dark terminal, alone with her thoughts.

Rosa straightened her back, twisting her head.

The wind howled beyond the walls. Tree limbs snapped distantly like bones, dropping to the floor of foliage. She concluded that they must be close since she could hear them through the concrete walls of the station.

She heard a ring that sounded far away, unlike the sounds of their ringtones.

Something from an older time.

The payphone on the edge of town.

Rosa shuddered.

She'd been at work that night. It was three hours into her shift when she'd gotten the call. At first, she didn't recognize the voice while the woman murmured strange words.

But after a moment, the woman had muttered something in Spanish and it whipped her like a leather belt.

Maria.

Her sister's voice was dreamy and soft, and Rosa feared she'd been drugged. The woman murmured strange things into the phone like she didn't know what was happening while Rosa suffered a complete breakdown in a matter of minutes.

Then, quite miraculously, she knew.

The phone booth.

She'd grabbed her keys and ran out of the building like it was on fire. Within minutes she was on the outskirts of town, her car skidding through a lake of red mud to a stop. She spilled out of her car onto the wet earth. She could see the phone booth up ahead. The thing was on the verge of being swallowed by the black forest. She saw the ghastly bluish light inside and the sheen from the chrome and something shifted in her stomach like snakes coiling.

She heard Maria's subdued voice in her head, sobbing as she listened to those last words before the line went dead.

"No tengas miedo, hermana."

Rosa fought her way through the mud and rain, wading on her hands and knees to the phone booth like a beggar. Panting, scared beyond belief, she'd opened her eyes and beheld the inside of the booth.

Maria's dark eyes were pried open, her head angled toward the ceiling. Her face was warped in a way that was unnatural, and Rosa burst out sobbing hysterically, clutching at her cross. Maria's hair and clothes were soaked, and her body was contorted up against the inside of the phone booth, her knees pulled tight to her chest. Rosa remembered the way her sister looked, the way her mouth was in an *O* like she'd been screaming when she'd died. Sometimes, in her nightmares, Rosa imagined what Maria might have seen just before she passed, but nothing she ever came up with would ever be as awful as not knowing itself.

Branches splintered in the darkness. The ringing carried on, on the other side of the glass, growing louder, closer, but she knew it wasn't possible.

The heavy sounds of falling branches rose to a crescendo as the ringing crept into her ears, caressing her mind like a dying hand. She pictured Maria's body twisted up inside the phone booth and thought back to that horrifying grimace and her skin, like all the blood had been drained out of her.

Eyes glued open, Rosa braced her palms on the sides of her chair to stand just as a call came in.

The ringing choked off, leaving only the steady breath of the wind and the faint melody of a Christmas record spinning down the hall.

"911, what's your emergency?" she asked, shaking it off.

On the other line, she was greeted by silence.

Rosa listened as the wind rustled the forest. She imagined the autumn leaves drifting down the highway, drawn to the phone on the edge of town, and suddenly it was three years ago. Everything was...familiar.

"Hello?" A pause. "Is anyone there?"

She listened for a minute more, her heart pounding with blood.

"If anyone's there, make some sort of noise—"

"*Ducks. The ducks. They're on the water,*" a voice whispered. "*There's ducks, so many ducks. I see them.*"

Rosa jerked forward in her chair.

A woman.

The voice was hushed, speaking in whispers. It was familiar.

No. It can't be, she screamed inside her head. *She's dead.*

Rosa said, "Hello? Ma'am? Are you all right?"

"*The ducks—they're swimming; I see them on the water. They're beautiful and white and...*"

Something was wrong. The rambling, nonsensical nature of the call chilled her blood, and it was like she was reliving that night all over again. A cyclone of alarm was building in the pit of her stomach.

"Maria?" she said, and she hardly recognized the accent that came out of her mouth. "Maria, is that you?"

"*Ducks. Ducks. Swimming.*"

She felt her body melt into a puddle. Thank God. It wasn't Maria's voice. The disorientation was the same, though. The whispering. The nonsensical sentences.

Focus, Rosa. Focus.

Her instincts kicked in, and she began trying to gather all the information she could. "Listen to me, Ma'am, I need you to listen to my voice. Tell me what's going on. Where are you? Are you hurt?"

She noticed Sterling watching her from the doorway out of the corner of her eye.

Rosa continued pressing for details, her professionalism unshakeable. "Ma'am? Are you there? Talk to me."

There was an audible break in the woman's entranced tone; her voice crackling into the headset, familiar and panicked. "*Rosa?*"

Rosa's heart dropped.

"Jennifer?"

Sterling stirred in the doorway, eyes narrowing.

Jennifer's voice was choked with sobs as she tried to speak, hysterical, frightened. "*Rosa...you have to get Chase—someone's here; in the building. Something's happening.*" Jennifer's voice rose as she spoke, and Rosa deduced that the only thing preventing her from screaming was the threat that whoever was there would find her if she did.

"*Where*, Jennifer? Tell me where you are." Rosa remained cool and professional as she talked, as if it were any other person calling. She had trained herself to be as detached as possible, aware that if she lost her composure, it could cost someone their life.

"Jennifer?" Rosa repeated.

Sterling stood at her desk, leaning forward to glean what she could while Rosa typed.

Sterling mouthed, "Where is she?"

Rosa held up her hand, listening. "Jennifer? I need you to tell me where you are, sweetie."

From the other end of the line, Jennifer whispered, "*She's out there. I can see her—I can* feel *her. Oh, God. She's in my head, Rosa. I can feel her in my head.*"

Rosa heard muffled sounds, like furniture moving and a body dragging across carpet.

"Who?" Rosa asked. "*Who* is out there, Jennifer?"

"*I don't know. I don't want to look at her, Rosa. I don't want to look. I can't look.*"

"It's okay, Jennifer. I just need you to tell me where you are. Where are you?" There was pause. "I need you to tell me where you are."

Rosa was holding her breath now. Her first impulse said the payphone, but then she realized that was impossible; she'd have heard the storm and the rain. She looked at Sterling, and Sterling looked at her, and then finally, after an agonizing full minute of silence, Jennifer said two last words before the line went dead.

"City Hall."

CHAPTER 8

LEAVES WHISKED PAST the windshield as Sterling rocketed to the other side of town. The call had come in less than ten minutes ago, and Sterling knew she should be able to make it to the other end of town in five.

To City Hall.

After the phone call she'd instructed Rosa not to utter a word to anyone. She knew Chase; he'd panic, plain and simple. She couldn't have him spiraling, compromising her investigation or possibly escalating the situation.

So what did she do?

She'd made the call. A unilateral decision to go it alone and find out what was going on. It was a risk, of course. But more of a risk to bring Chase, who might do something rash. She hadn't caught the entire exchange between Rosa and Jennifer, but she'd heard enough.

Rosa had said Jennifer sounded strange. Confused. Disoriented. She'd said she didn't sound like herself, which gave her more cause to leave Chase out of it. She could handle it on her own.

And if she couldn't? Then maybe, just maybe, she'd see about calling him.

If only King would answer his goddamn phone...

She liked that option better.

The prospect of a quiet night was slowly becoming less of a possibility.

Sterling wheeled the cruiser sharply to the right, cutting through a grove of tattered trees that arched over the road. The wind had picked up substantially, and she felt it fighting against the bulk of the car. She thumbed through her phone as she drove, playing another voicemail.

Anna's voice spoke to her through a blanket of static.

"Hey Ling, it's Mum again. I just arrived back in the States this afternoon. The funeral was lovely...the flight, I'm afraid, left something to be desired. Quite dreadful, in fact. Your Aunt Mae said you sent some money down. Thank you for the help with the expenses. Not sure we'd been able to bury him properly without your help.

"I thought maybe you'd make it to London, but I guess you had to work..." There was a moment of silence on the other line and Anna exhaled, clearly upset. "You know, you don't want to see me, fine, I get that. I can't make you want to see me. But your father, Ling? That man loved you more than anything on God's green earth. He doesn't have a thing to do with what's going on between you and I, and you should have been there today. It would have meant a lot to him.

"I wanted to tell you that Jimmy and I are moving in together. I know it's not what you want to hear but it's my life and, well, I have a right to decide what's best for me, don't I?" There was a pause and Sterling could hear cars rush by like Anna was driving. "Look, Ling. I know you don't fancy the idea of anyone replacing your father. Hell, I don't either. But he's gone now and Jimmy is here and that's the reality. That's my life now, and Lord knows you haven't made this easy on me. So please, Ling…you are just going to have to accept that he's a part of my life now and he's not going anywhere. I love you, Little Star."

The line went dead and Sterling's hands tightened around the wheel hard enough to put dents in the plastic. Anna didn't know what she was talking about. She never did. No matter what Sterling told her she just didn't want to listen to a word of it. Because it was easier to pretend. To live in an illusion than reality.

The parking lot was virtually abandoned aside from five or six cars, and a hundred yards across the parking lot sat City Hall.

As the car reached her destination, a knot the size of a fist formed in her chest. Her left eye twitched just as the silhouette of Drybell's single opulent building rolled into focus.

The structure was obscured in layers of dense fog, and the tall light posts in the parking lot flickered nervously as the cruiser passed by below. Sterling sensed that the atmosphere surrounding City Hall possessed a threatening quality, and she wondered if it was all in her head, or if there really was something sinister at work.

She slammed down the brake pedal, skidding the car across the asphalt. She turned and peered out the passenger window, where at the top of the stairs were two glass entrance doors. Instead of the bright white light she'd been accustomed to seeing inside, there was only darkness.

Sterling exhaled, then threw open the driver's side door and stepped out of the car. She reached back inside and pulled out a Maglite.

The emergency lights cycled on the roof of the car, casting the world in a harsh blue and red tint. She'd grown used to them over her time in law enforcement, but seeing it now was slightly more unsettling. She threw a glance over her shoulder at the parking lot, where nothing moved but the surrounding trees swaying busily in the wind. This corner of Drybell was desolate, and it made her feel more alone than she already did.

She pressed down on her radio. "Dispatch, Unit Two is ten

twenty-three," she announced. The storm raged, and she wondered if Rosa heard her over the intensifying wind. She tried again, "Repeat, Unit Two is ten twenty-three, come on back."

She waited a moment, doing a quick scan of her surroundings. "Dispatch, you there? Rosa?" Sterling shook her head, and for a split-second she regretted not bringing Chase along.

Don't be an idiot. Everything is fine.

As the tempest bellowed around her, she turned on the flashlight, drawing her firearm. She carefully marched up the concrete steps to the entrance. The flashlight beam struck the glass doors, snuffed out by the darkness within.

Sterling stepped closer. She tugged on the handle, expecting it to be locked, but it opened. Surprised, she lost her grip and the heavy door swung closed like a slab of granite. She looked up, expecting to find someone watching her from the other side, but found empty panes instead.

She secured a better grip and jerked the handle, shouldering it the rest of the way open.

A draft of hot, dry air rushed out of the building like she'd opened a portal to Death Valley, leaving a buzzing sound lingering in a tunnel of darkness.

As she passed through the barrier of the entrance, the air became noticeably thicker. Cloying and hungry, it draped over her face like a veil of death. Her breath was two white plumes, and she thought this strange as she didn't remember seeing it outside. After the initial surprise wore off, she found the air almost tolerable. Pleasant, even. The building smelled like sweets and candy; milk chocolate and blueberry muffins. Years of baking desserts at Christmas with her grandparents in London fluttered through her like moths, and the cold encasing her heart slowly began to thaw.

She caught herself being lulled into coziness and shook her head, brushing off the nostalgia. She continued on her investigation, the flashlight and pistol held out in front of her. The beam of light sliced through dust motes dawdling in the shadows, giving her fragments of the deserted lobby, which possessed newly renovated tiled walls and floors.

She paced toward the check-in desk, and her light scaled the wall behind it, gradually finding a giant metal insignia of the town seal. She admired it a moment, then shifted the light higher, where a second-floor balcony followed along the room's perimeter.

"Hello?" Her voice echoed off the vaulted ceiling, consumed by the darkness. She swung her light back down and traced the floor up the nearest wall, discovering a light switch panel. She toggled the switches, but nothing happened.

The distant sound of buzzing grew louder in her ears, but she couldn't quite trace where it was coming from.

"Hello?" she called again. "This is the Drybell Sheriff's Department, is anyone there?"

Only the steady song of the wind spoke to her.

Anxiety pumped through her blood, charging her with pure adrenaline.

"Jennifer?" The name rang out over and over, vanishing into the building like the throat of a sprawling cavern.

She decided on the first right, ascending the stairs to the second floor. The funnel of muddy light gradually revealed a path to a long balcony. She waved the light below, finding patches of the abandoned lobby.

"Where the hell is everyone?" she muttered to herself. "Jennifer?" she shouted again.

A sob cracked the silence, the spine-chilling sound unnerving in the dark. A shudder passed through her.

She rocked the light to the opposite end of the balcony, where two mahogany doors waited.

"Hello?"

The sobbing continued, faint and distant, buried somewhere in the building.

"Is anyone there? This is Sterling Marsh with the Drybell

Sheriff's Department. If someone's there, please say something!"

The sobbing swelled higher, but there was still no answer.

Alarm rising, Sterling's hand tightened around the gun.

She moved swiftly to the doors, throwing them open and then stopping in her tracks.

A sickly sweet odor lingered in the air, so overpowering it was on the verge of disorienting. The flashlight slipped from her hand, somersaulting through the air, the beam skittering across the wall and clanging on the floor. She held at the mouth of the darkness, taking slow, deliberate breaths. She felt something there, but the guise of blackness shared no secrets.

The gun trained in front of her, she dipped down and scooped up the flashlight. The shaft drug up the wall, slowly unveiling erratic, red smears.

Sterling's mouth fell open in gruesome wonder.

She took a step closer, raising the light to find the wall's mint paint slathered with a primitive four-foot drawing. An insect whizzed past her ear, landing on her face.

A fly.

She reflexively swiped at it, and it buzzed away.

Her heartbeat caught in her throat, her pulse jackhammering. As she studied the macabre art, she drew in a deep breath, slowly exhaling the cloying air.

Blood. There was no question. And any chance she had for a final quiet night went up in flames. She couldn't help but feel resentful. She knew it was selfish and illogical, and that there was something terribly wrong, but she felt cheated, like the whole universe was using this final act to kick her when she was down.

She swung the light to the opposite wall, which was covered with dozens more of the demented icons. She studied them, taking in every line and curve. The work of a cult most likely, but she also didn't rule out the possibility that they were simply just jumbled letters and symbols sketched by a severely disturbed individual. She raised the light up and something cracked inside her, like part of her mind had literally broken off.

Above her, the ceiling was decorated with more grotesqueries. She tried to fathom how someone might have accomplished this feat, but the logistics boggled her mind.

The wails resumed at the other end of the hall, snagging her attention. They resonated through the darkness and she recognized them as child-like, driving the urgency higher.

She shook off the unease of the room, marching to the door at the end of the hall.

As she went to reach for the knob, the sobs abruptly ceased. Her hand lingered in the air, a quizzical expression on her face.

She waited for it to resume, but it didn't, and just as the silence had all but smothered the hall of blood, a sharp cry broke out back at the balcony overlooking the lobby.

Sterling spun around, patrolling ahead.

The cries continued.

It was an adult female now.

Sterling retraced her path, stepping through the moonlight back to the balcony. She froze, the flashlight beam trained across from her.

She brought the light up and her heart sank.

Jennifer stood on the railing. A noose made up of various wires was fastened around her throat. Her face was twisted in a horrible grimace, and Sterling could make out the faint gleam of tears streaked across her filthy cheeks.

"Jennifer?" Sterling's voice snapped Jennifer out of the trance. She lifted her head as though it had a hundred-pound weight hanging from it.

Her dazed eyes found Sterling's and she began sobbing again. "Help me...Sterling."

Sterling cautiously took a step forward. She scanned the balcony, but they were alone. No one else was here.

"What are you doing, Jennifer?" The apprehension in her voice was evident, but she still clung to the professionalism that she'd taken so much pride in up to this point in her career.

A caressing whisper in the back of her mind told her this was a pivotal moment in her life, that whatever she said next was going to tell her everything she needed or wanted to know about herself.

"I don't want to do it, Sterling," Jennifer whimpered, eyeing the steep drop to the cold tile below. "But I can't stop—she's inside my head. I can feel her."

Sterling took another step forward, peering over the railing at the lobby, which looked like nothing more than a pit to the abyss. They were at least fifty feet from the ground, but it was so dark she couldn't see it.

"She wants me to jump, Sterling," Jennifer cried.

"Who, Jennifer?"

Jennifer didn't respond, only kept weeping softly.

"Who?" Sterling demanded. Her stern voice boomed in the cavern, and the resonance momentarily shook Jennifer from her hysteria.

She brought her tortured face up, glowering at Sterling.

"*Who's* here?" Sterling repeated, softer this time.

Jennifer's fear molted into anger. "This is your fault, Sterling!" The crazed woman attempted to step down off the railing, but couldn't will herself to move. She stayed there, her feet on the edge of the railing, the makeshift noose hanging limp around her neck.

"Why couldn't you just leave us alone, Sterling?" Jennifer wept. "Of all the people in the world, why did it have to be Chase?" The words were as sharp as a blade and cut just as deep. Sterling's eyes closed, heavy with shame.

"I—" Sterling began.

"He was the only good thing left in my life, and you took him away. You ruined it!" she screamed. "And now I'm going to die."

CHAPTER 9

MAX LOOKED ON, entertained as Georgia dug through a tall cabinet in the lunchroom.

The smell of mashed potatoes and gravy lingered in the air. Ham and hot chocolate and all of the fixings he'd need to put together his sandwich later. The "Moist Maker." A sandwich he'd learned about from *Friends*, one of his favorite shows. Most of the food had been wrapped in aluminum foil and carefully packed into the fridge by Rosa, along with about half a dozen Tupperware containers. The nonperishables had been left out on two long folding tables at the edge of the room.

A scratchy record twirled over on the bookcase, belting out "Holly Jolly Christmas." Max liked Christmas music. Maybe even more than the eighties songs Mommy liked to play on her iPod while she exercised. There was just something so comforting about Christmas songs, like all the people singing them were smiling and laughing and having so much fun. Or maybe he liked them because Christmas was the only time he didn't have to listen to his parents fight and say things he'd get his mouth washed out with soap for saying himself. He reckoned people just acted nicer in general when Christmas was near, and guessed it was because they wanted to stay on Santa's good side. But he was thankful for that, because even the grumpy people he knew gave him presents sometimes near Christmas. Besides, everyone knew boys and girls on the naughty list didn't get presents. And he wanted as many as he could get.

He smiled, listening to the cheery music. The sound warmed the room with the steady crackle of static and a melody from days gone by. He'd watched the record spin around and around, and he was baffled how that pancake of shiny black plastic somehow made such wonderful sounds.

Can they fit those inside of cellphones now? he pondered.

"Chess. Checkers. Connect Four," Georgia uttered. She stopped, peeking her head around the door. "Any of these sounding like your cup of tea?"

"I don't drink tea, Georgia. I'm a kid, remember?"

Georgia sighed. "It's an expression, sonny. It's a way of saying you like something."

"Oh," Max replied. "No. Not my cup of tea, Georgia. Sorry," he said with a shrug, softly singing along to the music. "Have a holly, jolly Christmas…"

"My you are a fussy one. All right, all right. I'll keep at it," she said, disappearing behind the door. "I don't suspect we're gon' hear a peep out of the phones tonight. Guess it only makes sense we try and entertain ourselves for a while until your daddy can bring you home."

Bored, Max adjusted his bowtie for maximum bowtie visibility, then hopped onto the counter as Georgia kept a running conversation with herself. He reached into his leather satchel (a thrift store find from Mommy after he'd become obsessed with Indiana Jones) and dug out his Rubik's Cube, carefully beginning to manipulate the sides. He remembered Daddy working up a sweat in the garage, going through and cleaning out the rafters so they could sort through all the boxes up there.

Mommy had been after him for weeks about it and she hadn't let up. She was tired of doing all the work around the house. She didn't think it was fair that she had to go to work and come home and work some more. She said she had two jobs and it wasn't right that she had to fix everything around the house too.

Daddy did not like that.

She was right, though. Most the stuff they'd found in those dusty old boxes *was* junk. Even by kids' standards. Aged black and white photographs. Some old film reels. A mismatched shoe and a jacket filled with moths. And dust bunnies the size of tumbleweeds. Daddy had cursed up a storm while he'd sat there patiently, and at one point he'd cut his hand wide open on a rusty nail. While he'd went to the kitchen to wash up, Max had stumbled upon maybe the only thing of significance in the whole garage: the colorful little cube he now held in the palm of his hand. He'd taken the curious thing in his small hands and forever solidified his love for games and puzzles.

"Sweet lord, where in the world did we get all this junk?" Georgia grumbled, grabbing a misplaced booklet and fanning herself. He saw her wipe the sweat from her forehead through the crack in the door and her makeup smeared a little.

Max chuckled, giving the cube's face one final twist.

The red side: it was complete. *Only five left,* he thought.

He kept working the puzzle as Georgia continued sorting through the cupboard. He heard a jangle as she shuffled games around the inside of the cabinet like a puzzle itself, the little pieces rattling inside the boxes as she worked through them all.

The noise stopped and a box stuck out from behind the door. "Hungry Hungry Hippos?" Georgia asked.

Max sighed and said, "That one's for kids."

"Oh, well, for kids? Good riddance, where is my mind tonight?" she said sarcastically. "I didn't realize you was looking for something dangerous. Let me see what else Grandma Georgia

can dig up in this old graveyard."

"Max?" a voice said.

He looked up to find Rosa standing in front of him.

"Oh. Hi, Rosa," he said politely.

He liked Rosa. She was all right, as far as grownups went. She didn't smile really, and he didn't know if it was because of him, or because she just plain didn't like smiling. She didn't have any kids or a husband, and Daddy said she was the "Queen of Uptight," although he had no idea where that was. All he knew was she didn't say a whole lot, and when she did, she wasn't funny like Georgia. She looked mad all the time, like someone had eaten her lunch without asking. He certainly didn't like her as much as he liked Georgia, but she was nice enough when he was around, so she was okay in his book.

"Who's that now?" Georgia piped up, riffling in the cabinet.

Rosa said, "What're you two up to in here?"

"Rosa?"

There was a crunch as Georgia stuffed a couple of the games back in place. She stepped out from behind the doors to the cabinet. "Ah, our own Lady of Mercy," she said with a grin. "Didn't think you'd step foot from that room once you were settled in. To what do we owe the honor?"

Rosa ignored her, coldly motioning to the cabinet. "I hope you're not making a mess. I just sorted that cabinet on Monday." She leaned over to peek inside and Georgia scoffed innocently, blocking her view.

"Well, it just so happens we was looking for a game, weren't we, Maxy?"

Rosa looked down at Max doubtfully, and he bobbed his head in agreement.

"What about you?" Georgia asked. "What're you doing here? You come back for seconds?"

Rosa cocked her head, as if she didn't understand the question.

Georgia said, "Why are *you* here? I don't suspect you're looking for a game yourself?"

"Oh. Yeah. I just wanted to stretch my legs. The phones have been quiet tonight."

"Ah," Georgia said, nodding. "I was just telling Maxy as much. Have you seen Sterling? I need her to sign off on a few last-minute details before tomorrow."

Rosa shook her head. "I haven't seen her, no."

"All right...?" Georgia said, arching an eyebrow.

"What?"

"Nothing," Georgia shrugged. "Just as well, I'll track down that woman yet before the night is through, hear you me."

Rosa sure was acting funny. Max couldn't put his finger on it, but it was almost like she seemed nervous about something, and he remembered when Daddy had asked him if he'd opened that special box of chocolates Mommy kept on the dresser. He guessed his face probably looked about how Rosa's did now.

"Say..." Georgia said. "You feeling all right, Rosa? You look like you've seen a ghost."

Rosa smiled uneasily. "My head is killing me. Too much sugar, I think." Then, "I don't think I've ever had a night this quiet since I started here. I don't like it."

Georgia laughed. "You're telling me, girl. Between the sugar cookies and the carrot cake I've got enough sugar to send me into diabetic shock."

There was definitely something wrong. Max listened to the storm and decided that nobody should have to be alone on a night like tonight. "Do you want to play with us, Rosa?" he asked.

Rosa shrugged. "Thanks, but I have to get back to work now. You two have fun, though. Maybe you can help Georgia put those games back where they're supposed to be when you're done," she sneered.

Rosa looked at Georgia and Georgia flashed her a funny smile.

After she'd gone, Max said, "How come she didn't want to play with us, Georgia?"

"Ah," she said, shrugging it off. "Don't you worry about Rosa. She's just being a sourpuss because she doesn't like lightning." She hobbled back to the cabinet and began rifling through the games. "Don't mean we can't still have fun, though."

Max smiled.

"Ah, here we go!" Georgia exclaimed as she slid out a long box.

The game looked *old*. Like something Daddy and him would have found in the attic. The box was falling apart; the surface was yellow and crispy, and the corners were held together with tape, tape, and more tape. On the cover, there was a group of kids and three witches.

"Which…Witch?" Max muttered.

"Goodness, child, ain't you never heard of Which Witch?"

Max shook his head.

"Oh, well, you are in for a real treat, my friend." Georgia closed the doors to the cabinet and set the game on the table. Leaning down, she blew the dust off the top and pried off the lid. "My three older sisters and I used to play this game all the time, although if you asked me now, I'd say *they* were the real witches."

As Georgia unfolded the board and began setting up the walls, Max reached down and took a blue piece of plastic from the box. There were three more like it. Red. Green. Yellow.

"What's this?" he asked, holding it up.

"That…is *you*," she said, bopping him playfully on the tip of his nose.

"I don't get it?"

"Look closely now."

He held the thing up and squinted.

"It's a boy!" He quickly took another from the table, closely inspecting it. "And this one's a girl."

"I'll tell ya, child, you are sharp as a tack tonight."

"What are these?" he asked, scooping up a handful of smaller matching tokens in his hand.

Georgia plucked one from his palm and impishly brought it up to his face like a spider. "Eek, eek!"

He looked at her unimpressed, eyeing the thing pinched between her fingers. It was a tiny critter with a wiry plastic tail.

"A mouse?"

"Heavens no. A rat," she corrected. She carefully placed them on the board, straightening the warped cardboard walls. "*That* is what happens if the witch gets hold of you: She turns you into a rat."

"Oh," he said, gnawing the ends of his fingernails.

"Child, do not make me get the hot sauce," she said, brushing his hand away from his mouth.

He wasn't sure if he liked this game. Rats. Witches. Spell Cells, whatever that was. But he thought of Billy Capshaw and knew he wouldn't have chickened out if it were him, so he played along.

"And this," she said, holding up a polished ball bearing no larger than a quarter, "is what you gotta watch out for."

Max gently took the thing from her fingers and held it up, finding his own reflection staring back at him.

"It's so shiny," he said, captivated.

Georgia chuckled.

"What is it?" He turned it over in his fingers, but everywhere he looked his reflection was there staring back at him. It flickered with white as lightning lit up the world beyond the windows.

Rolling thunder shook down the mountains through the forest. Georgia leaned down close and whispered in his ear.

"That, is the storm."

CHAPTER 10

JENNIFER WAS FACEDOWN on the tile. Blood slowly seeped from her mouth and ears, her limbs set in awkward, broken angles around her as if she'd been run over. The wire noose had snapped; her weight had driven her straight into the ground.

Sterling stared down at Jennifer's body, her face wrought with sadness and guilt.

Jennifer was dead. Sterling knew, but she kneeled down anyway, feeling for a pulse. Jennifer's skin was warm, glazed over with sweat. Her hollow green eyes were frozen open, staring into the nothingness that was her new life.

Tears slipped across Sterling's cheeks as she held her fingers against Jennifer's throat. The back of her hand went to her mouth, and it was all she could do to keep from suffering a complete and total breakdown.

She gazed miserably at the lifeless body. Jennifer's pale skin was smooth, perfect even in death, and Sterling bitterly realized that she would never be as perfect as Jennifer, even when her time came.

Sterling reached down, softly closing Jennifer's eyes with the reverence of a caring mother the way she hoped someone would treat her when she was gone, even though she knew it wasn't what she deserved.

For the first time since she could remember, something stirred deep within her. A finality sank in the moment Jennifer's eyes were closed, and the gravity of what had happened hit Sterling like a brutal kick to the stomach. A whimper escaped her throat; the loss and anger and sorrow bleeding in, and before she knew what was happening, she fell back on her butt, sobbing, scrambling away from the corpse that was Jennifer.

Her back slammed into the front of the counter as the heavy flashlight rolled across the tile. She heard the metal grind as it bowled over the floor while her chest heaved. In an act of self-castigation, she forced herself to experience every emotion she'd been fighting to lock away, finding herself nearly as hysterical as Jennifer by the time the memories were etched into her mind. She shuddered, thankful she was alone, where no one could see how badly she'd lost herself, turned to a shell of her once glorious identity.

She leaned her head back, thudding it against the counter over and over. "Stupid, stupid, stupid."

She listened as the flashlight continued to roll across the tile. The funnel of dusty light wheeled along the wall to her right, stopping on an adjacent doorway.

She needed to call emergency services.

She sniffled, wiping her face with her jacket sleeve, composing herself the best she could before trying her radio.

"Dispatch, this is Unit Two, code thirty-three at City Hall." She waited, taking in the silence and the darkness. "This is Unit Two requesting immediate assistance."

Silence.

"Rosa, are you there? Chase?"

But there was only static.

She pulled her phone out of her pocket, but the screen was dark.

"Shit! Shit! Shit!"

A child-like giggle stirred from beyond the doors.

Sterling startled, seizing her firearm and awkwardly standing up.

"Hello?" she shouted, her voice nasally and congested. "Is someone there?"

Silence.

She turned and gave Jennifer's body one last look, knowing she could do nothing more to help the girl.

She trained her Glock in front of her and swung down, grabbing the flashlight from the floor. She took a deep breath, then proceeded through the doors.

The beam from the flashlight was fire in the darkness. She saw bits of dust floating in the air and remembered her mother telling her that dust was primarily composed of human skin. The same dust she now breathed in.

She scaled the wall with the light, slowly unveiling more grotesque symbols decorating the paint. At the end of the hall were two additional glass doors, both smeared with dried blood.

"Sterling."

The whisper was as clear as day. The hairs on her arms stiffened and her glassy eyes widened. She stopped there, surrounded by countless crimson markings, and called out again, "Is anyone there?" She hated the way her voice sounded in the building; the oppressive silence amplified it like a megaphone.

She was met only with further silence.

A bloodcurdling scream tore through the building.

Sterling spun around, eyes darting about the hall. She imagined she was inside a tomb, trapped within a living nightmare.

There was an electrical hiss, like a power line shrieking, and a flash of light exploded on the other side of the glass doors where she spied multiple dark shapes.

Her pulse was climbing again, and the only thing she could do to keep from screaming was continue on.

A weak, child-like moan skittered from beyond the doors.

Mustering up what little courage she had left, she used her shoulder to shove the doors open.

The air temperature ratcheted up again. The flashlight sputtered, snapping off as she stepped into the room and took another step forward, crunching over glass. She stopped in her tracks; the sounds of her shallow breaths absorbed by the darkness. She smacked the flashlight with her palm, the device flickering back to life.

Sterling gasped.

Dozens of ghastly figures stood motionless along the walls, their eyes vacant, faces turned to the wall as if being punished for some unspeakable crime.

Sterling recognized some of them, the majority being city workers and clerical staff. She'd conversed with several of them on occasion, but under the circumstances they were barely recognizable, more like ghostly husks of themselves.

"This is Sheriff Sterling Mar—" Her speech puttered out like a dying car as she beheld countless more bodies high on the walls, pinned there like dolls. Her eyes blossomed in terror as she witnessed the impossible.

Her anxiety screamed and she had to force herself to breathe, unable to rationalize what was right in front of her, even though she knew it to be true. Although she had learned to trust her instincts fairly early on in life, after the events of last month, she thought maybe she shouldn't.

She whipped the beam across the room, attempting to make sense of the levitating bodies. She tried to speak but nothing came out, the prospect of what was unfolding before her too frightening to understand.

There was a hum and the faint heat from the flashlight went cold, leaving her in the darkness. "No, no, no," she said frantically, batting the flashlight against her palm. She began hyperventilating in the blackness, attempting to get her breathing under control.

In and out, Sterling, she told herself.

In and out.

A droning started to climb; carrying through the air, rising like a tea kettle on the verge of boiling.

She fought with the flashlight, cursing it, and just as the thought of running screaming out of the building started to become appealing, the structure groaned, rattling the foundation.

There was an electrical hiss, followed by a surge of power. A rolling clack chimed throughout the building as if it were a giant clock, the room flooding with sections of weak, gritty light.

The emergency lights, Sterling thought. *Thank God.*

A wave of relief poured into her body, smothering the panic like water on fire.

She smiled at the dead flashlight and tossed it away, thankful for small victories, then looked up in wonder to find the bodies gone.

And a mere few feet from her, a witch.

CHAPTER 11

A WITCH.

That was Sterling's first thought when she laid eyes on the figure. Wearing an intricate black dress and a tall, pointed hat, the figure reminded her of a witch torn straight from the storybooks, only not nearly as comical. No, there was nothing funny about this witch. There was an edge to her like a blade; everything sharp with purpose.

She held there cautiously, studying the stranger. She considered the possibility that the shadows were playing tricks on her, but the longer she waited, the more certain she was that this wasn't in her head at all. There was in fact a witch standing in front of her.

Or at least someone dressed like a witch.

Which meant that there was someone here, just like Jennifer had said there was.

Sterling's hand tightened around the pistol.

The figure faced the wall. She remained motionless, and the only way Sterling knew she wasn't just a leftover Halloween decoration was because she hadn't been there a moment ago. She wasn't sure if she was more unnerved that the horrible floating people were gone, or that there was a now a witch here instead.

"This is the Drybell Sheriff's Department," Sterling announced. "Turn around *slowly*, and put your hands on your head."

When the woman didn't move, Sterling realized silence had reclaimed the building.

"Hey! I'm talking to you," Sterling barked. "Turn around and keep your arms where I can see them."

The witch was still.

"I'm not going to ask you again."

When the woman still didn't yield, Sterling exhaled a frustrated breath and began forward. She threw glances to the sides of the room to ensure no one was lying in wait to ambush her.

A warm tingle began to thaw her chilled muscle and bone. She felt her blood slow and with it, her reflexes. The cool, wintry air in her cells evaporated, and her body flushed with a heat she hadn't felt in a long time.

The woman wore some sort of scented perfume—Sterling was sure of it. The closer she got, the more she found herself breathing freshly baked spiced cakes and rich, hearty cocoa. There was also chocolate chip cookies and Figgy Pudding and another scent she couldn't place. The sugary fragrance was so overpowering that Sterling had to fight against letting her mind retreat to her grandmother's kitchen in London in that cozy two-story apartment with the blue door. A place so much more pleasant than here.

She snapped to, and the reality of Sterling's predicament caused her mood to sour. She decided to abandon all attempts at pleasantries. "Turn the fuck around, *now*," she growled.

The woman didn't move.

Sterling raised her gun and stepped forward, the barrel inches from the back of the woman's head. She considered how easy it would be to give in and pull the trigger, just one more nail in her coffin, but she couldn't.

The wind whistled beyond the towering glass panes overlooking the parking lot, playfully vying for her attention. The faint outline of the moon shone buried beneath the veil of clouds.

Focus, Sterling.

She honed her attention back on the witch.

The woman sported an intricate black dress and some sort of coat, with a tall, leathery hat. Sterling swung the flashlight up to find that the hat contained dozens of sprawling lines fastened with crude stitches. She took note, then gently pressed the barrel of the gun to the back of the woman's head. As she shakily placed her other hand on the woman's shoulder, she felt a charge of pins and needles jettison through her hand, like touching static-charged laundry that had just come fresh from the dryer.

"I don't know who you are, but you so much as *twitch*, and that wall is gonna be the last thing you ever see."

The witch was still. Sterling slowly rotated the woman, whose hands were slack at her sides, until they were face-to-face.

Sterling blinked rapidly, caught off guard by the witch's brilliantly unsettling eyes, the irises and pupils pools of silver-gray like twin moons. Sterling gazed at the contours of the witch's face, which were lean and pale, her high cheeks framed with wispy black strands. The woman's purple-tinged lips reminded Sterling of a dead body; parted just enough so that she could discern a gap between her two front teeth. There was something beautiful about the witch the same way there was something beautiful about death, and Sterling was both terrified and exhilarated.

This night might be getting interesting yet.

CHAPTER 12

MADNESS WAS TAKING over, and the night was still young. The cruiser idled in the parking lot of City Hall. The emergency lights pulsed, and tendrils of fog crawled from the jagged edges of the forest.

Sterling found herself embroiled in a mounting horror, the likes of which she'd never experienced. The culmination of so many uniquely bizarre sights in one evening rattled the very foundation on which she'd established her keen logic. Ghosts, monsters, witches. These weren't quantifiable things; they were just fairy tales, bedtime stories at best. Besides, criminals weren't so different. Weren't human beings just as capable as any monster? Could they not aspire to enact just as much harm, if not more? Murderers and rapists may have even posed more of a threat, as far as she was concerned.

Contemplative and unsettled, she shook her head, doing everything she could not to think about the stranger sitting in the backseat.

Inevitable as a dead-end, her gaze warily lifted to the rearview mirror, where she glimpsed the silhouette of the witch against the moonlight behind a grid of steel.

She looked away just as quickly, as if she'd caught a glimpse of the sun, but the silhouette remained there in her mind's eye, malevolent and ominous.

Her communications problems served only to further unravel the threads that held together what had become an exceptionally delicate situation. How could she even have begun to explain what she'd seen here? What had happened? She saw no possible outcome in which she wasn't crucified for her actions or determined by the department to be unfit to serve.

Despite all this, she tried her radio again.

"Dispatch, come in." There was a pause. "Dispatch, this is Unit Two, come in, over." While she waited for a response, she pulled her cellphone out again to find a black screen. Hadn't she charged it?

The witch's tall hat rested on the passenger seat beside her, a ghastly patchwork of stitches and mismatched fabrics. Sterling picked it up, carefully examining the odd object. She ran her fingertips along the rusted metal sutures, coming to the conclusion that this was no mere mass-produced accessory; clearly it was fashioned by hand and was incredibly worn. Ancient, even. As she turned it over in her hands, a feeling she could only describe as hopelessness came on like the beginnings of a cancer. She'd experienced something similar when she'd learned of her father's diagnosis all those years ago, and somehow it seemed just as vicious, this drowning inside. She grimaced at the hat in disgust, tossing it back on the passenger seat.

In the rearview mirror, the witch blankly stared forward, oblivious to the world. Sterling considered that the witch was blind, as she hadn't reacted to anything around her, but didn't rule out the possibility that it could all be an elaborate ruse.

After handcuffing the suspect and reading her the Miranda Warning, Sterling had escorted her outside and into the patrol car without incident. Despite the vacant human being she appeared to be, the witch had allowed Sterling to guide her out of the building easily enough.

Almost as if the witch *wanted* to be taken.

A chill colder than liquid ice broke through her spine, flooding the warmth. Sterling's hands shivered uncontrollably, fumbling the knobs on the radio as she attempted to contact dispatch again. Her muscles began to freeze from the inside out, and the wind-chill blasting through town clawed at every vulnerable bit of her skin. Despite all this, the lingering heat remained, whether from her own beating heart or something else she wasn't sure. A lapping tide of dread and fear perpetually washed over her, drowning her one minute at a time. The image of Jennifer's battered body lying in a pool of her own blood was seared into her brain, and she didn't think she could ever unsee it.

Sterling jolted as an ear-piercing static exploded from the radio. The pitch screamed and depressed in a horrible surge of rising and falling pulsates.

"Shit!" she shouted.

Ears on fire, she twisted the knobs, cutting the noise off. She hit the radio with her fist in frustration, sinking back against her seat. She pressed her eyes closed, shutting out the cold biting at them.

When she opened them again, she took a long, deep breath, then exhaled. She ran her tongue over her chapped lips and glanced at the rearview mirror again.

The witch was still, as if she hadn't heard that horrible sound explode from the radio seconds ago.

"What's your name? You from around here?" Sterling asked. "I'm talking to you." When the witch didn't answer, Sterling sighed. "You're not making this easy on me, you know?"

Sterling chewed her lip, on the verge of falling apart in tears again. Her eyelids felt like they were made of lead, and she wished she were back home in bed, buried under the covers where it was warm. She turned and peered over her shoulder at the witch. The silhouette was threatening in an oddly passive way, and the woman's silence only served to make it worse. "No, you're sure as hell not from around here…" she reaffirmed, adjusting her rearview mirror.

When the witch still didn't answer, Sterling decided to try a different approach. She started the car, slowly pulling away from City Hall before eyeing the woman's intricate black clothing in the mirror. "Never cared much for Christmas," she began. "I thought it was just an excuse for relatives to meet up once a year, pretend like they give a shit about each other. Food was the best part, I think. From what I remember, anyway. You talk. Eat ham. Drink eggnog. Hell, I'd be lying if I said I wasn't partial to a little dessert every now and again." She paused as the car sailed across the black ocean of asphalt, her gaze finding the witch's dead eyes in the mirror. "But I always thought there was something…disingenuous about it. Like they never really wanted to be there in the first place." A beat, then: "That's my take, anyway."

Sterling wheeled the patrol car to the left, back to the main highway. The car lurched onto the pavement, the witch swaying in the backseat. "But Halloween," she said with an ironic smile, "now that was always more my thing."

The darkness engulfing the car gradually began to fade the farther from City Hall she got. The cruiser drew closer to the center of town, a dazzling display of lights breaking up the gloom with the warm glow of holiday cheer. The facades of the buildings lining Main were traced with thousands of colorful bulbs, the result of the annual Drybell Christmas Light Contest, of which Sterling participated only once, her first year in town.

Sterling flipped off the emergency lights; she didn't want people to panic.

"You know why I like Halloween?" Sterling asked the witch. She looked up at the mirror as if expecting the woman to answer, and when she didn't, Sterling said, "Because you can be anything you want. And people will look at you and accept you, because that's what they're supposed to do. Nobody questions you. Nobody tries to tell you to act this way, or that. You can just...*be*. Ain't that some kinda nice fantasy?"

She was ten years old, back in her old bedroom. Ovi and Anna had been arguing all month about what costume she was going to wear that Halloween. Her mother had her mind made up that Sterling was going to go as a cat this year. She'd even bought the little plastic ears and outfit in the vacuum sealed bag and purchased the makeup for the whiskers. The problem was, Sterling didn't want to *be* a cat. She'd had her eyes on a witch costume at the corner drugstore. You see, on a trip to Blockbuster one particularly dull night, she'd stumbled upon a VHS tape called *The Wizard of Oz* and decided shortly after that it was her new favorite movie. She remembered the silly, whimsical songs and the vibrant colors. But most of all, she remembered the witch. Not the one with the fluffy pink dress and the crown. The other one, with the black hat and green skin and the broomstick and flying monkeys. Sterling remembered thinking there was just something so fascinating about the witch, the way she lived in that ginormous castle with all her monkeys, her crystal ball, and those men with the spears. She connected with something there, thinking back. Maybe because the Wicked Witch saw the world the same way Sterling did now. Halfway through the movie she'd decided that *that* was what she wanted to be. She wanted the green skin. The broomstick. The black hat. She wanted it all.

Sterling frowned as the car passed down Main, thinking back to that night. Anna had led her into the living room, so excited she was practically shaking. Her mother had slipped the cat costume out of the paper bag like it was something so precious (designated by the Jean Juliet Costume company as "Scary Cat") and Sterling remembered audibly gasping.

She'd looked up and seen Anna's excitement deflate like a car tire. She felt a pang of sadness remembering the way Anna's elation had withered like a dying plant, and with it any chance of them bonding the way a mother and daughter truly should. She wondered if that was the moment her mother was finally forced to accept the truth that she'd never compare to Ovi in Sterling's eyes, and she felt a physical pain in her heart that she'd wounded her mother that way, like she'd done something terribly wrong by trying to be who she really was. Like fuel to a fire, Sterling had vetoed the cat costume, along with her mother's plan to win her affection, and in the process sabotaged her parents' marriage further.

Two weeks later, Sterling and Ovi were in the living room. Ovi was carefully running a makeup brush over her face when her mother walked in the door from the market, her arms full of paper bags crammed with candy for trick-or-treaters. Anna had looked at them like they were strangers, studying her daughter all dressed in black with her tall hat and green skin, and she could have sworn she'd seen tears glisten on her mother's cheeks in the light. Anna had set the bags down, thrown the cat costume in the trash, and retreated to the bedroom, where she remained the rest of the night. Ovi, upon seeing the sadness in his daughter's eyes from disappointing her mother, said something Sterling would never forget.

"Stay true to yourself, love."

The cruiser rolled down Main, past sparkling facades and dying lights. After a moment of quiet, Sterling pumped the brakes, bringing the car to a stop.

While the familiar Christmas lights ordinarily brought her a glimmer of hope, instead she felt a vice crushing the life out of her, an iron maiden formed of hard, sharp emotions.

What the hell was she going to tell them? How was she going to explain Jennifer's death to Chase? The people at City Hall? Any of the fucked up things she'd seen tonight.

Without warning, she heard Anna's voice erupt into the car.

"Hey Ling," she began, and the shock of her voice after the

horror of the last hour nearly brought Sterling to tears. She scrambled for the phone, wrestling it off, but the touchscreen wasn't responding. "It's Mum again. Just went for a walk this evening and it was so lovely out and I couldn't stop myself from thinking about you. Remember those walks we used to take around the lake during summer after your meets? I'd take you to that ice cream place you fancied. What was it called... Dairy Queen, and you'd get a banana split with extra cherries and the bloody thing would melt before you could finish it?

"God...you were incredible, Ling. I don't think I'd ever been so proud of you. There wasn't a thing you couldn't do. Still isn't. You could fly...

"I wish you'd talk to me. I could really use your voice about now."

Anna sobbed quietly on the phone and a knife twisted in Sterling's heart that she'd forgotten was there. "I had to go in for X-rays this morning. Don't worry—it's nothing serious. Doctors say it's just a sprain. I think I'll be able to get back to work in a couple of days." She laughed, and Sterling missed that laugh terribly. "Don't know what to do with all this extra time on my hands. I tried buying some plants but...well, you know how that turned out. I don't believe a cactus would help me at this point. Anyway, I don't want to keep you. Just take care of yourself, Ling. I love you."

Tears beaded in her eyes as she listened to the line cut off, and silence overtook the car.

She looked in the rearview mirror at the witch just as frenzied screams broke out of the radio in jarring static. Sterling lurched in her seat, seconds away from ruptured eardrums. The noise was so overwhelming she couldn't form a single coherent thought. Her hands sprung for the radio knobs only to find they were already switched off.

The reverberation painfully rose in her ears. Her eyes pulsed with pain, on the verge of exploding from her head. The voices pouring from the radio were the most horrible thing she'd ever heard, the sounds of people being burned alive, or perhaps mutilated by unseen hands. A collection of the worst things she could possibly imagine. She wondered if she were trapped in a room, alone with that sound, if she'd have gone insane.

Unable to take the screams anymore, she threw the door open, drunkenly spilling out of the car onto the pavement.

She clapped her hands to the sides of her head, her body shrinking into the fetal position. As the howls rose in a crescendo of horror, she threw her leg out, kicking the door closed.

The sound abruptly cut off. The fire inside her head sluggishly died down. The searing pain began to wash away like layers of sand on an alien beach, the screams trailing off into the abyss.

Her face slowly relaxed, her eyes warily peeling open to find a twelve-foot snowman perched on top of Grayson's Market staring down at her. A decoration they'd put up every year in December, the snowman wore a shabby top hat and striped scarf. One of its wiry arms was fixed in a demented wave.

Her frozen breath expelled in front of her like a dying animal. All the fight she had was gone, abandoning her like a bastard child. For a moment, she allowed herself to fall into self-pity, a concept of which she had never really tolerated before now. She contemplated just lying there and never getting up, maybe just waiting to freeze to death, or letting some unsuspecting car run her over.

She saw Ovi and Anna staring down at her, wondering what had become of their little girl, how she'd fallen so far from grace.

But no matter how hard Sterling tried to resign herself to fate, she knew fate wasn't done with her yet. She rolled onto her stomach, bracing herself against the car and pushing herself to her feet. She glanced inside to find the witch patiently sitting in the back seat, same as before. As she rubbed her bloodshot eyes, a long creak came from the top of Grayson's Market.

She lifted her gaze from the cruiser to the rooftop and found the snowman leering at her, stark against the night. Under ordinary circumstances, the snowman was a welcomed sight in town—something of a landmark and a pleasant reminder of the small-town life she'd chosen. But now, she noticed something unsettling about the snowman.

The warm smile he normally flaunted was far more sinister in this light, twisted into a sadistic grin, and Sterling wondered if maybe he knew something she didn't. Before she could dwell on the thought, a clap of thunder cracked open the sky, unleashing a torrent of needle-like rain.

Within seconds her clothes were drenched, and she was left staring into the rear driver's window where the witch waited.

Or was it merely her own reflection?

CHAPTER 13

"WHAT THE HELL is wrong with you?"

Chase's words were nearly drowned out by the chaotic whirlwind in the air. Her deputy was furious, just like she knew he'd be. Sterling had made it back to the station, arguably no worse for the wear. The roar of the rain sounded like the world was tearing itself open, so fierce and heavy that she was surprised the town wasn't already underwater. While sections of gray clouds had lingered before amongst the night, the moon had retreated into space, leaving behind a blanket composed purely of cosmic darkness.

Chase fought the wind, prying apart the side entrance door enough to prop it open. He shouted, "Middle of the biggest goddamn storm in this town's history and you decide to go out there *alone*?!"

Sterling groggily climbed out of the running Interceptor and pushed past him through the entrance, anxiously glancing down the corridor to see if they were alone.

Chase watched her as if she'd lost her mind, but she didn't

care. The clock was ticking. Counting down. But to what, she did not know.

"We don't have time for this," Sterling said hurriedly, "I need you to get the State Police on the phone *now*."

"How the hell am I supposed to do that? The lines are dead," Chase said matter-of-factly. "The storm is worse than we thought. Georgia hasn't been able to raise shit. Rosa neither. Spencer is fucking AWOL and I'm sure you've noticed the radios are useless too, which makes it all the more *stupid* that you left without telling me where you were going."

Sterling ran her finger over her lip, nervously glancing at the rear window. "All the lines are down?"

Chase nodded grimly.

So it isn't just the radio…

"Where. The hell. Were you?" he pressed.

He doesn't know about Jennifer, she thinks. *Rosa didn't tell him.*

"I know you like to think of yourself as a one-woman-army, Sterling, but there are other officers here, and that means—"

"City Hall," Sterling interjected. "Okay? About an hour ago, Rosa got a call."

"City Hall?" Chase repeated, his face tensing. "From who?"

What felt like an eternity passed while Sterling reflected on her options. She knew that if she told Chase the truth, things would go from bad to worse, so it was a no-brainer to wait for the storm to clear before she dumped life-changing news on him.

"Jennifer," Sterling finally said with a sigh.

Chase's clenched jaw fell open. "*Jennifer*? And you didn't tell me—"

"She's fine." The lie was out of her mouth before she could even think.

"She's okay; it's nothing," she said, resting a hand on his shoulder. The weight of her secret nearly crushed her on the spot. "There was an intruder. This late at night, she got a little scare, but she's fine now. Everything's fine. Jennifer went home." A potent mixture of guilt, rage, and shame roiled like poison in her blood. Lying to him was the last thing she ever thought she'd do.

Chase's posture relaxed a smidge as he digested the information. The deluge grew louder as ragged wind breathed through the trees. Finally, he said, "Who was it?"

Sterling met his eyes, then motioned over her shoulder at the Interceptor.

Chase cocked his head, peering at the window. He squinted, a tiny crease forming between his eyebrows. "Who the hell is that?"

"I found her at City Hall. Hasn't said a word since I picked her up," Sterling said.

"What was she doing there?" Chase asked, moving closer to the car.

"I don't know. She was just standing there in the dark, looking at the wall."

Chase looked at the witch incredulously. "Come again?"

"You heard me right."

"The wall?"

"Something's not right, Chase."

"What do you mean?"

"There's something…off with her. I can't explain it."

He looked at her curiously, waiting for more.

"Look, Chase, I don't know what's going on right now. I don't know who she is, or where she came from. All I know is that I need to get her processed and into a cell because I am telling you that there is something *wrong* with that woman. I don't know what, and to be honest I don't give a damn. I just know I'm not going to feel better until we get her behind bars."

He regarded her for a moment and she wondered if it was obvious how close she was to breaking. After considering her carefully, Chase finally nodded, "All right. Continental suite it is."

Sterling smiled, thankful to circumvent anymore arguments for the moment.

Chase moved around to the rear passenger side and opened

the door. "Out," he ordered.

"I think she's deaf. Or blind. Or both. There's something wrong with her eyes," she called, trailing behind him. She followed him to the side of the car, then leaned in toward the witch and froze as if she'd been locked in suspended animation.

Back inside City Hall the lighting had been poor. She'd caught glimpses of the woman's face, but parts were always obscured in shadows. Now, under the floodlights outside the station, she beheld the stranger that was the witch.

The woman's dead eyes were like two gleaming mirrored coins. Her skin reminded Sterling of her mother's dolls, unnaturally pallid and smooth. There was a symmetry to the witch's face like a priceless work of art, but her oversized eyes gave her an unnerving, alien appearance, like the people in those Big Eyes Paintings.

"Sterling?"

Chase's voice snapped her out of the impromptu inspection. She tossed a look over her shoulder, finding him waiting impatiently behind her.

"C'mon, Boss, I'm freezing my ass off out here."

"Sorry," she replied, wiping the rain from her face. She reached in and took the woman's arm, feeling that familiar electricity web through her hand and up her forearm. Deep in her chest her heart fluttered, her head filled with static. She couldn't tell if she loved it or hated it.

She sucked in a deep breath, then cautiously directed the witch out of the car.

The woman's long black limbs unfolded as she emerged, a type of surreal nightmare come to life. The floodlights anchored to the side of the building flickered and the car's engine sputtered, the lights on the dash hiccupping. Chase's pupils dilated with intrigue, drinking up the bizarre stranger in front of him.

Sterling witnessed the familiar desire in his eyes, the same eyes he'd looked at her with so many times before. Her face flushed crimson, her skin prickling with pins of jealousy.

"Chase," Sterling said with a stern voice. "Get your shit together; we've got a job to do."

Chase shook off the craving, acknowledging her command, and took the witch's arm.

Sterling wondered if he felt that same electricity she felt, or if it was something special just between her and the witch.

Chase looked down, noticing the witch's bare feet were visible as the wind tossed her clothing. Her skin was filthy and Sterling imagined her feet would be on the verge of frostbite by now.

"Where's her shoes?" he asked.

"She wasn't wearing any," Sterling replied.

While Chase escorted the witch through the side entrance, Sterling popped open the passenger door and snatched the witch's hat off the seat, kicking the door closed.

Inside, the corridor was cold, but marginally warmer than outside. They continued down the hallway toward processing, where Sterling felt her skin thaw like defrosting meat.

She stepped through the open doorway to find Georgia in the corner swearing at the copy machine. She held there a moment, listening to the woman's tirade.

"Georgia?"

Georgia turned around, surprised to find them standing across from her.

"Sterling, you're back!" she beamed, putting a hand on her chest. "You scared the goose shit out of young blood there, he was worried sick." She tipped her head at Chase, who was rounding the corner.

Chase scoffed. "Yeah, well, someone has to," he said bitterly.

Georgia playfully kicked the edge of the copy machine. "Piece of junk that one is. Puts out less than a nun on the eve of the apocalypse."

"Georgia, we have a little bit of a situation here," Sterling said.

"Honey, I don't think anything gonna be worse than the

storm about to plow through here and level this town. I don't have my chains on me; I might have to spend the night here."

Sterling grinned uneasily, then stepped back into the corridor.

"Oh, what's this; where's she going now?" Georgia asked.

Chase smiled halfheartedly, raising his eyebrows and massaging the back of his neck.

A wave of heat clouded into the room. The temperature climbed what felt like twenty degrees as the overhead lights broke into a nervous flicker. The radios on Sterling and Chase's uniforms flared with hisses of static. The copy machine unexpectedly sprung to life, and Georgia whirled around in time to see the green glow skim beneath the cover.

The witch stood in the doorway against the light.

The sudden failing lights combined with the appearance of the unsettling figure caught Georgia off guard, finally at a loss for words.

"Move," Sterling ordered. The witch seemed to float forward, and Georgia couldn't help but ogle the bizarre traveler before her. The entire scene was so surreal and fantastic Sterling wondered if anyone would believe it.

A buzzing sound zipped past Sterling's head. She looked around the room for a fly but saw nothing. Only this time she knew she wasn't imagining it because Georgia and Chase heard it too. The group stood alert while the erratic bulbs sputtered and crackled.

Sterling took a step forward, and a hiss of electricity shrieked just before the room was engulfed in darkness. Her heart pounded, her back drenched in sweat. She listened to Georgia and Chase's frazzled voices and movements in the pitch-blackness.

There was a whirl and a charge of electricity. The overhead lights exploded on again, bathing the space in a ghostly white light.

Sterling's tense face melted into a grateful smile; it fell away as she noticed the witch was no longer standing in front of her.

"Where's..." she muttered, spinning to Chase. Their eyes met and they looked at Georgia, who's attention was glued behind them.

Sterling and Chase exchanged a grim look, then turned around to find the witch in the corner of the room next to the Christmas tree, facing the wall.

"Somebody better tell me what is going on *right now*," Georgia said.

CHAPTER 14

GEORGIA WAS IN the bathroom again. She'd been in and out of there all night since the party. Max thought maybe she'd drank too much eggnog. He'd seen her filling up her glass every few minutes, guzzling the stuff like water, and he gathered she might be in there for a long time yet with the amount she'd drank. Daddy told him he couldn't have any himself, and he hadn't understood why. He was glad he didn't though, because Georgia seemed to be feeling pretty lousy about now. At one point he heard her retch the same way Daddy did sometimes when he'd get home from the Silver Dollar late at night, the small place on the corner of Main Street with the bright neon sign in the window of a funny glass with an olive. Max had asked him before if he could go with him sometime, and Daddy had simply laughed and said, "Sure Ace, maybe someday."

Another heave, louder this time, and he heard water splash.

He cringed.

"Georgia? Are you okay?" he asked hesitantly.

She grunted and he shrugged, pacing impatiently in front of

the door.

He heard a different door open and saw Daddy walk out of his office down the hall, marching toward the side entrance. He noticed car lights pass through the window overlooking the front of the station.

Daddy didn't see him. Good. He didn't like to be bothered when he was doing things in his office, so Georgia usually kept him company in the meantime.

The door opened at the far end of the hall and the sound of the rain roared into the station. The wind was howling like a ghost, and he could smell the forest and the water from the wet pavement.

Miss Sterling was back.

He'd seen her slip away earlier, and no one really seemed to have any idea where she'd went. Daddy had got upset and asked Georgia and Rosa, but they didn't know, just like he didn't know and he'd said a bad word under his breath and walked outside to get some air.

Max swiftly paced over and slid into the doorway to Spencer King's office, peeking out from around the corner and curiously watching as Miss Sterling and Daddy talked.

Daddy did not look happy. He looked the way he did when him and Mommy were fighting, and Sterling looked just about as happy as Mommy had.

He heard Mommy's name and his ears perked up. He listened hard to what they were saying, but it was no use; he couldn't hear anything over the stupid rain.

I wonder what they're talking about?

They walked into the rain and he spied Sterling's car under the awning. That was where they usually parked when they had to bring in the bad guys. He'd seen his daddy do it on multiple occasions, and each and every time Georgia had been there to keep him far away during the process. But not this time, no siree. This time he was finally going to see some action, the nitty-gritty behind-the-scenes stuff that kids never were allowed to watch.

He peeked around the corner, more brazen this time, and squinted his eyes.

The car's headlights were on, and he could see the green glow from the little computer inside. They used computers at school sometimes, but the one in Daddy's car was different. *Boring* was a better word. They didn't have any fun pictures or games, and when he'd asked once if he could play with it on a ride along, Daddy said they were "for work only."

He listened as their voices came closer.

They were arguing, and Max saw someone tall step out of the back of the car.

There he is!

He retreated back inside the office, pressing himself into the wall and holding his breath like he was underwater.

Daddy talked to Miss Sterling for a moment out in the wind and the rain. He listened briefly, then slid around the doorframe, peering out.

I can't see anything!

He exhaled, frustrated. He was tired of hiding. He took another step, right out in the open.

It was a woman.

His eyes widened, mouth gaping and dry. He couldn't believe his eyes.

A witch.

He saw Sterling holding something, and sure enough there was a tall dingy hat in her hand. The witch's skin was white as bone, and Max could have sworn he saw her eyes glow in the night. She just stood there while Sterling and Daddy talked about things he couldn't hear and argued like his parents did.

A door slammed closed and he about leaped out of his skin.

"What're you doing, Maxy? Lord as my witness, I will never drink eggnog again as long as I live," Georgia said tiredly, wiping her mouth. Her eyes snagged on the spectacle outside. "Oh, looks like they're bringing someone in." She exhaled. "All right, come on, youngster, you know the rules."

"But Georgia!" he protested.

Georgia silenced him with a wave of her hand. "Huh-uh, no way. Your daddy left me in charge of you while he's working, and part of that job is keeping you away from questionable types. Now come on," she said, directing him back to the lunch room.

She held open the door and ushered him inside with a playful kick to the rump. "I'll be back in two shakes of a lamb's tail—I need to help Sterling and your daddy for a minute. We got lots of paperwork that needs tending to before sunrise. Now be a darling and stay put until I get back, otherwise all games will be suspended for the rest the night."

Max gawked at her. "But—but, that's not fair!"

"Whoever said I played fair?" she said with a smirk. She winked at him and closed the door behind her.

A few minutes later, he heard the heavy side door slam closed from the wind, practically shaking the whole building.

He took a step back and peered through the frosted pane of glass in the door. Their voices carried closer and closer, making their way down the hall.

Then he saw her.

A real-life God's honest witch.

She passed in front of the door, and he could have sworn it fogged up the way it does when someone breathes on it. He stepped back fearfully, listening to Daddy and Sterling, their voices low as they escorted the woman down the hall. His chest was thumping and his hands were all tingly and warm.

He did not like the witch.

No, he did not like the witch at all.

CHAPTER 15

THE WITCH WAITED in front of the counter, still as ever, with Sterling on one side and Chase on the other. Georgia stood opposite them at the terminal on the counter, the keys clicking away, initiating Live Scan to obtain images of the stranger's fingerprints.

Chase was caught somewhere between pensive and bitter, his face screwed up in a strange look of pure fascination.

"This is one for the books, ay, Sterling?"

Sterling responded with a weak smile, keeping her attention fixed on the witch.

"We're online," Georgia announced, giving a thumbs up. "Ready when you are."

Sterling took the witch's hand, and it was like touching a piece of glass that had been left out in the sun all day. "Jesus," she muttered.

"What?" Chase asked.

"She's burning up."

"Fever?"

Sterling shrugged.

"What's the hold up?" Georgia called out.

"Sorry," Sterling said. "All right, ma'am. Right thumb first, nice and easy." The witch didn't respond. Sterling carefully centered her thumb on the colored glass pad, hearing an electronic chirp from Georgia's terminal.

Chase exhaled in frustration as they waited for the scan to populate.

"That one didn't take," Georgia called out to them. "Try and reposition it."

Sterling nodded, shifting the witch's thumb.

The witch's hand unexpectedly jerked.

Sterling gasped, losing her grip.

"Hey!" Chase shouted, snaring the witch's arm and throwing his body weight. His fingers sunk into the rigid flesh of her neck, ready to wrestle her to the floor if need be.

"Wait! It's okay," Sterling protested, breathing hard.

"What the fuck was that?" Chase asked.

"It's okay, Chase. It's fine," she said, holding a hand up. Sterling calmly retook the witch's hand, watching her like a hawk. She carefully repositioned the witch's thumb on the pad. "All right, Georgia, try that."

Chase stirred like a pent-up dog with nowhere to run. Sterling could see the apprehension in his eyes, see how the worry was digging its claws into him. As the scanner processed, he pulled his cellphone out and began dialing.

"What are you doing?" Sterling asked irritably.

Without lifting his eyes from his phone, Chase said, "She isn't responding to my texts." He finished dialing the number and put the phone to his ear.

"Something's wrong, Sterling," said Georgia. "I'm just getting a black blob on this end. Looks like a damned inkblot."

"Inkblot?" Sterling repeated, raising her eyebrows. "What're you talking about? What's the problem?"

Georgia shrugged, "Don't know. Ain't never seen this before."

"Sonofabitch," Chase muttered under his breath, oblivious. "I can't get through. Goddamn storm is ripping us a new one." He snapped the phone closed.

"*She's fine*," Sterling lied. She watched Chase stretch his neck with a hearty crack. "Chase," she repeated, softer this time, "she's fine."

But Sterling knew that was the furthest thing from the truth. Jennifer was dead and Chase's marriage along with her. But how could she possibly tell him that, especially now?

"What's the problem?" he asked, stepping around to the scanner.

Sterling looked down at the pad, then lifted the witch's hand. The breath was sucked from her lungs, leaving her slack-jawed at the bizarre sight.

"Well, I'll be damned..." she muttered. She reached for the witch's other hand and held it up to the light.

"What is it?" Chase asked curiously, moving closer.

Together, they examined the witch's palms and fingers, which were slicked with sweat and eerily absent of any fingerprints or creases of any kind. The witch's flesh had a porcelain gleam to it; a ghostly white canvas of sprawling, faint blue lines. The woman's fingernails appeared polished but natural, if a tad long. The anatomical peculiarity left them both speechless. Sterling saw the tail ends of a strange pattern near her wrist. She gently raised the stranger's hand, pushing the sleeve up.

"What in the hell is that...?" Chase asked.

Sprawling scars were carved into the witch's flesh, disappearing under her sleeves. Sterling gently drew back the edge of the coat's neckline.

They were everywhere. Bizarre symbols and words strung together, just like she'd seen at City Hall. Despite being grotesque, the words were cut into the woman's skin with near surgical precision, a macabre masterpiece of flesh and art. Sterling guessed the elegant print covered most all of her body, and surmised the woman had known a pain so extraordinary it made her skin itch.

"Scarification?" Chase asked.

Sterling shook her head, spellbound by the inexplicable discovery.

"That's a thing, right? People cutting designs into their skin like tattoos."

"Hey," Georgia hollered back at the terminal. "What's the problem?"

Chase and Sterling exchanged a puzzled look.

"We're done here, Georgia," Chase said.

"Done?" she repeated. "What do you mean, we haven't even—"

"She doesn't have any prints," Chase clarified.

Georgia's eyes tripled in size as she crossed herself a second time, shuffling around the counter.

Chase turned to Sterling and said, "Everyone has prints, Boss. *Everyone.* Even if they burn their skin off there's still *something* there. But this,"—he studied the smooth contours of the witch's hand in disbelief, trying to make sense of it—"I've never seen anything like this before. She's like a doll or something."

"We may not be able to take her prints," Sterling breathed, "but we can damn well take her photograph." She ushered the witch toward the wall, where a plain white background was pinned. She directed the witch to an X on the floor marked with tape, then approached the SLR camera, which was mounted to the top of a tripod.

"You're up, Georgia," she said.

Georgia hesitated, paused behind the counter, her face painted with worry.

Sterling began preparing the camera but stopped, noticing Georgia hadn't moved from her spot. "What's the problem?"

Georgia breathed slow, eyeing the witch. "I just—are you sure that's a good idea? Maybe we'd do best to leave her be for now? Maybe see about raising the State Police once the storm clears?"

The fact that Georgia was spooked spoke volumes to Sterling. In all the years she'd known Georgia, she'd never seen her even remotely worried about a guest at the station. Be that as it may, though, she intended to see her last night through to the end. "She's *our* responsibility, Georgia. At least until the storm's over."

When Georgia didn't come forward, Chase extended a friendly hand, resting it on her shoulder. "Why don't you go see what Max is up to, Georgia. I'll take care of it."

Georgia turned to Sterling, whose disappointment was evident, then exited the room in disgrace. Sterling flashed back to her mother's face that night and felt a stab of remorse. Should she have gone easier on her?

"You should cut her some slack," Chase said.

"What's that supposed to mean?"

"It means that the storm raging outside along with all these new faces showing up is putting everyone on edge, *you* included."

"This is our job, Chase. We don't have the luxury of being able to worry. We have a duty. We act or people get hurt, simple as that."

"Maybe you and I... But Georgia? Rosa? They're not built like us, Sterling. They're dealing with this shit the best they can. Let's say we try and cut them a little slack, huh?"

Sterling shook her head. "Let's just get this over with." She cautiously maneuvered the witch in front of the white background.

Chase stepped in front of the camera and peered through the viewfinder, twisting it on the mount. "A little to the left," he instructed, squinting.

Sterling eased the witch about six inches over, then stepped out of frame.

"There," he said. "Perfect."

Sterling backed away another foot.

"On three," Chase said. "One."

She watched, half expecting the witch to spring to life and run at them shrieking at the top of her lungs like some crazed lunatic.

The tingle in her skin prickled to life.

"Two."

Her blood thumped like geysers in her ears, loud and heavy.

There was a *snap!* as Chase pressed the button.

A blinding starburst flared as if she'd looked at the sun, and then a clap struck her ears like two wet hands. The shrill ringing wailed inside her head, throwing off her equilibrium. She staggered drunkenly to the wall, the whole world tilting like the Earth had been knocked off its axis.

The screeching rose to a climax, building like a thousand wailing ghosts before finally cutting out with a violent tremble that wavered through her bones. The room spinning, she pressed her back to the wall to keep from falling to the floor. She found Chase on the ground at the foot of the tripod.

"Chase..." She heard her voice echo sluggishly in her ears, reverberating like she'd just been in a head-on collision.

She closed her eyes and waited for the disorientation to pass. The world began to settle beneath her feet, vibrating subtly.

Chase moaned.

She stumbled away from the wall, her arms held out to catch herself.

"Chase? Are you all right?" She didn't recognize her voice. It was low and stretched, like a toy whose batteries were dying.

Her head thrummed with pain, crushed in a bone vice as the earth shuddered one final time. Her legs wobbled beneath her and she folded to the floor, army crawling the rest of the way to Chase.

He groaned, "Maybe Georgia was onto something..."

Sterling let out a miserable laugh and smiled, patting him on the shoulder. "You're fine, big guy. You're fine." She winced, forcing herself to her feet and offering a hand to Chase. She pulled him up and together they looked to the camera.

Their mouths fell open.

On top of the tripod was a heart of charred, melted plastic. Ribbons of smoke rose in the air, and any hope they had of taking a picture of the witch was gone.

CHAPTER 16

"THAT'S THE *BEST* you've got?"

Sterling and Chase stood in front of a two-way mirror that shared a wall with the interrogation room. Georgia and Rosa were nowhere in sight, leaving Sterling and Chase to devise a plan.

"What other options are there?" Sterling asked.

"Have you lost it, Sterling? I mean, listen to yourself. You want to take this woman, who we know *nothing* about, mind you, and just leave her in there with nothing but a tape recorder? For Christ's sake, we haven't even attempted to interview her yet!"

Sterling turned, shaking her head, "Come on, Chase, that'd be a waste of time and you know it." She stepped forward until she was nose-to-nose with him. "We have got to start thinking outside the box if we want to get to the bottom of this."

"The bottom of *what*, Sterling?" Chase said, hands in the air. "This isn't some reality TV show where we chase around fucking ghosts and goblins. Someone's just playing a prank. A damned good one at that, but that's all it is."

Sterling stared determinedly at him until Chase let out a

frustrated breath. "So let me get this straight," he began, tossing a look at the window, where the witch waited on the other side of a brushed metal table, her cuffed hands resting in front of her. "You want to set a tape recorder in there and listen for *what* exactly? Spooky sounds? Voices? Don't you have any idea how fucking absurd that sounds?"

"I don't care *how* absurd it sounds, Chase. You saw what happened to the camera, and I've been hearing and *seeing* weird shit all night long. And that woman," she said, pointing a harsh finger at the pane, "has something to do with it."

Chase grit his teeth, looking at the witch. "It's just a costume, Sterling, that's all. A *costume.*"

"And her hands? The camera? Those scars she's got all over her body? Am I just imagining that, too?"

Chase's mouth pulled into a thin line, finally at a loss for words. Reluctantly, he nodded. "Fine," he said. "I will entertain this idea because I want to support you, and because we've got enough problems right now for you to be getting worked up over shit like this. So what do we do?"

Sterling held up a tape recorder. "Leave that to me."

She exited, swinging around the corner and letting the door to the interview room slam closed behind her.

The witch hadn't moved from the chair. She might as well have been stone; her pale, emotionless face staring into nothingness, her burning hot hands resting on the table before her.

Without saying a word, Sterling turned on the recorder and set it across from the witch on the table.

There was a moment of silence, then Sterling asked, "Are you hungry?"

The wind howled while they waited, and Sterling heard more branches surrendering to the earth. "The storm's getting bad, and it's going to get a hell of a lot worse before it gets any better." A pause, then: "My point being we've got a long night ahead of us, which means you and I are going to have plenty of time to get to know each other, whether we want to or not."

Sterling thought her words might elicit some sort of reaction, but the witch gave nothing.

On the table, the tape recorder hummed faithfully, etching her unhurried breaths onto film.

Sterling gazed at the witch, drinking in the darkness surrounding her brilliant, dead eyes. She let herself get lost in them, those shimmering mirrors, and before she could stop herself, a professional wall gave way in her mind. She reached out impulsively, almost out of instinct, and pressed her clammy palm to the witch's face. It was like touching a piece of marble, but her skin warmed as she held it there, lost in the witch's eyes. She remembered touching Heidi Harris's face the same way, feeling the same warmth on her skin, thawing the icy exterior of armor she walked around in day in and day out. Sterling knew she shouldn't have touched the witch, but her curiosity got the better of her in that moment. Searing electricity webbed from their connection, and Sterling's eyes fluttered in glorious, unbridled wonderment.

She drew her hand back as if she'd touched an open flame, horrified with herself.

On the other side of the mirror, Chase looked on in shock, his concern over Sterling's mental health soaring to new heights.

Sterling held her hand there in front of her face, suspended in disbelief in a dreamlike state, studying the limb as if it were some foreign organism.

What's happening? she thought, sick with doubt.

Chase beat on the window with his fist, breaking the spell.

Sterling turned and took a long look at the glass, where her broken, warped reflection stared back at her with profound disappointment. She frowned, imagining the look on Chase's face on the other side, then got up and walked out of the room.

She pulled the door closed behind her, stepping into the corridor.

Chase met her and said, "What the hell was that?"

Sterling practically floated like a cloud.

"Oh no. Don't you fucking do that, Sterling."

"I don't know what you're—" Sterling began to walk away, but Chase seized her by the arm, jerking her around.

Sterling was ripped out of the reverie. Her mouth hung open like a hurt schoolgirl while she struggled to get the words out.

"You've been acting weird ever since the diner, Sterling. Now ordinarily, I wouldn't find that cause for concern, but with this guy showing up, and this storm, and now this nut in there, something is really starting to feel off here."

"I said I'm fine."

Chase shook his head.

"I'm *fine*, Chase. I told you. Now take your hand off me before my good mood turns into a bad mood and wrecks your whole fucking night."

Chase held her glare for a second before releasing her. "I just want to make sure you're thinking straight and that you've got your mind right before you make any other ill-advised moves, like you just did back there."

Begrudgingly, Sterling nodded in agreement. "Yeah…I think I just need some air. Keep an eye on things for me until I get back."

Chase nodded, relenting. "Sure."

"Miss Sterling?" They turned to find Max standing at the door to the lunch room.

Sterling looked down at the boy and smiled. "Hey, Max. You staying out of trouble?"

The side of Max's face twitched nervously, like he was caught in a spotlight, then reluctantly pulled into a wry smile. He shrugged. "I guess. What about you?"

What about *you, Sterling?*

Sterling looked at Chase, then back at Max. "Right as rain. Just tryin' to figure this thing out, you know? Look after your dad for me while I'm gone, will ya? He's always been a little scared of the dark."

Max half hid behind the wall, chuckling quietly.

Chase said, "Go hang out with Georgia, buddy; I'll be there in a minute."

She watched Max nod with a subtle tip of his head, then disappear back into the lunch room.

"You're just immune to good advice, aren't you?" Chase asked.

"Maybe. But I'm still your boss, at least until tonight is over, and I'm telling you that I'll be back in half an hour. So do me a favor and make sure nobody goes anywhere near that woman while I'm gone. Can you do that?"

"Me?" Chase said sarcastically. "Whatever you say, Sterling. I just work here, right?"

And before he could say anything else, she was gone, back into the storm.

CHAPTER 17

GEORGIA WAS GONE.

Her eyes were glued on the television set in the break room, absorbed in a documentary about a paranormal bed and breakfast, a bowl of steaming hot ramen in her lap. Max didn't much care for those shows; they never showed anything good. Sometimes the silly people on the TV would call out to the ghosts, but the ghosts never called back. Doors would open and close, things would move around the room, but you never really *saw* a real live ghost, and that's where it just seemed pointless. Daddy said they were all make believe, and Mommy did too.

Georgia was fun, of course. She was good to Max and treated him like one of her own. She'd sneak him double fudge cookies and let him watch as much TV as he pleased, unlike Mommy and Daddy. They'd told him he needed to slow down on the sugar on account of the extra padding around his belly, so now the only time he got any sweets were on what Mommy called "special occasions."

Georgia kept on. "I told them. I told Sterling and Rosa, but nobody wants to hear nothing I say around here and now look what's going on."

Once Georgia got pulled into one of her shows, there was just no getting her out. She'd even babysat him a handful of times when Mommy and Daddy went out on a "date night" as they called it.

Max liked going over to her house. He'd sit in that big old comfy recliner with the patches on the arms, or sneak outside and play with the ducks that swam in the pond in the backyard. Georgia was sweet and fun, and she had a big, kind heart. She'd said to him, "Maxy, honey, there ain't a person not worth loving in this world, and the ones you don't want to love, the ones you sometimes hate, often need it the most." And that was exactly what he thought of when Billy had hit him in the arm at school. He was a mean one, that Billy Capshaw. But he did his best to remember Georgia's words, because she was one of the "good ones" according to what his Daddy said.

Max was getting good at adventuring. He'd already snuck out of the room once tonight and found Daddy and Sterling arguing out in the hallway about the witch lady. It reminded him too much of home, where Daddy and Mommy fought, sometimes all day. So he'd blown his cover to get them to stop. He didn't like seeing them fight, and he *really* didn't like the witch lady. She gave him the willies.

"Oh my Lord in heaven," Georgia gasped. "Can you believe the shenanigans going on in this world, child?" The show on the TV had finally changed; now a man and a woman in fancy clothes were talking about weird slimy animals washing up along the beach over in New York City. The news even showed one of them, but he didn't want to look. There were a lot of strange things on the news lately, even more than usual, but any time it would start to come on his parents would just change the channel or flip the TV off. That was just fine by him. He didn't want to see it anyway, no siree, bob. And besides, he still had a few sides left on his Rubik's

Cube to attend to.

Georgia said, "First haunted houses fallin' outta the sky, and now these things comin' right out the ocean! Old Marty Eisenhower said there's even a whole town built underground over in Vietnam somewhere. Some sort of fallout shelter for rich folks, they say. Boy, if Peepaw saw this, he'd be rolling over in his grave right this very minute! Next thing you know, we've got a spaceship flying right over good old Drybell itself, hear you me."

Georgia turned and looked at him, drunk on conspiracy. "Whatcha think, Maxy? You think the world done headed for its end?"

Max looked at her and shrugged. "You're silly, Georgia."

Georgia groaned, eyeing him suspiciously and making a click as she rolled her tongue around inside her mouth, "Eh, yeah, your daddy don't believe in it much, neither. That's all right, though, Maxy, you know why?"

"Why?"

"Because you're a good kid, and the only thing good kids got to believe in, in this life, is themselves."

Max smiled at Georgia and she let out a little sigh as if he was the most precious thing in the world.

"Georgia?" Max said. "Can I have a dollar for the vending machine?"

Georgia chewed the corner of her lip, mulling it over. "Just don't tell your pop that you got the money from me. You already loaded up on sugar during the party and you know how they are about you eating sweets."

Max's eyes lit up. "Boy, thanks, Georgia! You're swell!"

"*Swell?* Good riddance, child, where on Earth did you hear that? You born in the thirties?" Georgia chuckled, fishing a dollar out of her purse. Max snatched it out of her hand before she could even offer it to him.

"Heard it on *The Andy Griffith Show*. Cool, huh? Daddy says that's how things used to be before..." Max got a befuddled expression on his face. He shrugged, as if he'd thought about it too hard, and said, "Before now, I guess."

"Yeah, I know what you mean," Georgia said with a sigh. "The old days... But we ain't got it so bad here, now, do we, Maxy?"

Max smiled, warm with life, then hopped off the chair and beelined out of the lunchroom into the corridor. The vending machines were just around the corner, down by the grimy elevator to the basement. The journey seemed short in his mind, but standing there now, it looked a bit longer than he originally thought.

Max took a deep breath and puffed out his chest. He might not have been tough, but by god, he was going to at least pretend to be.

He started forward, putting one foot in front of the other. The floor was wet and sticky, and he listened as his Velcro shoes peeled off the concrete with each step. The air circulating in the corridor was damp and earthy, and the grungy walls looked like the color had been sucked out of the world, rendering them a sickly shade of white. He padded slowly past the interview room, where he knew the witch lady was waiting.

A chill passed through him.

Wait a minute...

Didn't he hear a story once in class about a witch that ate children?

That's right! A whole house made of candy, just think of it! Billy Capshaw had told him so last Christmas when they were making gingerbread houses in class. He'd made his right next to Max's, complete with a roof spotted with gumdrops and slathered with cream cheese frosting. He'd even made a mailbox using a piece of licorice, a Milk Dud, and a toothpick. But even despite rotten Billy Capshaw's best efforts, the teacher had still said she liked Max's best. And Billy Capshaw did not like that at all. He'd stewed there, across from him, for at least a whole minute. Maybe two. Billy had had the meanest look on his face Max had ever seen, and when Miss Dallas had walked away to survey the rest of the class's gingerbread houses, Billy decided to get his revenge.

Next thing he knew Billy was telling him all about the story of the evil witch that lived in a dark forest in a delicious candy house, just waiting to catch little children who were too greedy they couldn't stay away. Billy said that the witch had kept the children in cages, and cooked them in the oven for a snack when she got really hungry. Max wondered if the witch in that room lived in a candy house; wondered if she kept kids in cages for a snack when she got hungry like Billy said.

He picked up his pace, forcing himself to keep his eyes on the crook in the wall ahead as he passed the door to the interview room.

He listened to his own hushed breaths.

Behind him, down the corridor where he'd come from, Georgia's news program was spouting out scary things he didn't want to think about. Overhead, the glass tubes hummed, spitting with light. They made a hissing sound that he didn't much care for, and they sounded like they were going to turn off any second. Daddy was scared of the dark, Sterling had said. Thinking about the lights going off now with only a door between him and the witch lady made his heart race, and he felt the same fear of the dark in his heart.

After what felt like miles, he came to the bend and stopped. He eyed the way he'd been going, which Daddy said led to the place where they kept the bad people. The broken lights couldn't quite reach that far, so it might as well have been an entrance to an underground cave.

Stay away from there, dummy, he thought. *You don't have any business going near the bad people.*

He inched around the corner, hurrying down the hall. His face bloomed into one of elation as his destination arrived. The chromed vending machines sang in electric glory, glowing with light inside their bellies and filled with all the sweet treats he could ever ask for. He thought of the evil witch in her house of candy, but was relieved to find that he could see inside the vending machines through the glass window.

Nothing but candy, he thought.

He reached into his pocket and fished out the crumpled dollar bill, beaming with delight.

Snickers? he thought.

"Nah," he said, with a shake of his head. There! He wrestled the bill into the slot, and the machine ate it right up. He jabbed *E1* and then stood back to let the machine do its magic.

The metal coil began to unwind, the chocolate bar poised to escape to the slot below in a dreamy tumble.

His eyes widened, taking it all in, salivating like one of Pavlov's dogs.

The lights cut out. The electricity wound down like time itself, the spark in Max's eyes fading along with it.

Before he could begin to panic, the overhead lights moaned back on, pale as ever, but the inside of the vending machine remained dark, the coil frozen halfway there.

"Hey!" Max gasped, stepping forward and thumping his hands against the glass. "Ah man, my dollar!" He lightly banged on the window with his fist, letting his forehead thunk against the display. With his shoulders slumped, head hanging, he kicked the machine like a dented can.

Then, hands in his pockets, head heavy with defeat, he made his way back. He rounded the corner and kept on a few paces before stopping in his tracks.

Wait a minute, he thought. *What's that smell?*

He sniffed at the warm air and found it somewhat pleasant.

It smells like...chocolate?

His eyes slowly rose to find that he'd stopped right in front of the interview room.

The smell began to cultivate in his nose, rich and wonderful like a world of chocolate was in his head. His mouth watered, his head swimming in a river of chocolate the size of the Mississippi.

He kept his eyes down on his own two feet, doing everything he could not to look up at the thin barrier separating himself from the witch lady.

All of the scrumptious scents overwhelmed his senses, and his thoughts were lost among the plates of hot chocolate chip cookies and brownies.

Is she really that bad, though? he thought.

Maybe she's just a regular person?

Maybe she's nothing like the witch in the story?

Maybe she's a different kind?

Maybe she's just some funny lady dressed up like a witch who doesn't wanna talk to anybody.

No, that's not true and you know it! Don't even think it!

But the candy…

Are you crazy? You remember what Billy said, don't you? He said one day that witch will find you, and when she does, she's gonna eat you up!

Just when he thought he couldn't hold on anymore, his curiosity got the better of him.

He craned his head up and slowly lifted his wild, crazed eyes.

In front of him, the door groaned with a long creak, echoing up and down the hall. A cloying scent of every glorious homemade treat he could imagine wafted out of the darkness and breathed into his drunken face. His knees buckled and his eyes rolled back in his head.

And just as he felt a heat roll out from the darkness, he spun on his heels and ran.

CHAPTER 18

DRYBELL WAS ASLEEP.

Sterling had the air conditioner up in the car as high as it could go, blasting wintry air at skin that might as well have been on fire. She was flushed with fever; her cheeks red with blood, the wild hairs on the side of her face wet, pasted to her temples with sweat. Her wool uniform itched and was damp like she'd just stepped out of a sauna. She toweled her face off with her sleeve, raking the hair away from her eyes with her fingers and focusing on the road.

Maybe she was coming down with something after all? It'd been a lie initially, of course, to get Chase off her back. He was always breathing down her neck, sticking his nose in her business every chance he got. She didn't mind the extra attention before, when things were simpler. It had even seemed charming. But now? Well, this was just too much. She needed space. Needed to think just one coherent thought for a single second.

And when she finally could, she didn't have a clue what to think. Nothing about this night made even an ounce of sense. It was like everything she'd worked for her entire life was crumbling down in front of her like a burning house of cards.

Other people had vices. Smoking and drinking. Sex. Drugs. But what about her? What did *she* have? What did she really have anymore?

She thought back to her glory days. The friends she'd been so close with whom she'd never spoken to again after college. The support system. The comradery. The three bowls of angel hair pasta the night before a race (or sometimes Masala pasta if she wanted something with a little more kick). The clingy ex-girlfriend Heidi Harris, and her constant need for reassurance. But most of all, the feeling of her weight on the starting blocks just before the gun went off.

She stamped down on the accelerator, tearing over wet earth and soggy leaves across the stormy mountainside. She glanced out the driver's window at the black, gloomy storefronts. Fog was thick in the air, coddling empty wooden benches that reminded her the world was fast asleep, drunk on dreams and brighter days. She was thankful that the rest of the town could go on none the wiser, chasing their fantasies in a place where anything was possible.

The snowman perched on Grayson's Market leered at her as the cruiser fled past. The gigantic striped scarf fluttered in the gale, and she wondered if the snowman would survive the storm.

She hoped it didn't. She never wanted to see that hideous thing again in her life.

As she made her way through town, she was disappointed to find that she couldn't come up with a single thing she did for herself, and the horror that she'd disrespected Ovi's grave words was gut-wrenching. His voice echoed in the darkness.

"Be true to yourself, love."

Sterling Kaur Marsh, British Indian love-child of Ovi and Anna Marsh, had failed. Again. She felt herself withering away, glad to be so far away from her extended family with an ocean between them.

The sound of a gun went off, ringing in her head in a blinding flash.

A horrible thought came to her then: she was standing over a man with the Glock in her hand, the glowing barrel red-hot with ribbons of smoke. She stood watching him die, a flower of blood blossoming beneath his starched white dress shirt in the middle of his chest. The man panted weakly, gasping for air.

"Please," he'd begged. "Help me…"

He'd asked her for mercy, but she'd had none left to give. Her mouth was pulled into a thin line, eyes narrowed, the blood rushing through her body like red rapids. The truth was, she'd wanted to see him die and, against her better judgment, had intentionally waited to call the paramedics. She'd waited there, watching his life leave him like a dying fish because she had to know, beyond a shadow of a doubt, that he'd never be able to hurt anyone again the way he had hurt them; that she'd never have to worry about others being afraid of him, and the things he did.

Until that day, he'd fooled everyone else. Tricked them into believing he was a decent human being. That he was one of them.

But he hadn't fooled her.

Just because he wore a silk tie, drove a fancy car, and was called a pharmacist didn't mean he wasn't something else below the surface, something that other people couldn't see.

His wife did, though. She knew all too well what he was really like, under the skin. She knew there wasn't only a man there, but a monster, too. He'd said he loved her, sure. And he was always eager to show her just how much with his fists and a strip of leather he'd kept in the closet on the back of the door, where he'd see his own reflection in the mirror every time he'd taken it. His wife never wanted to believe it, no matter how many beatings she'd taken, and she died still thinking there was a good man inside him somewhere.

Just one more fairy tale, Sterling thought cynically.

A flash of hot rage turned her vision red, and her hands

tightened around the wheel.

He deserved to die. And she'd do it all again. Because she would do anything to protect the people who couldn't protect themselves.

And it all led back to here. To *this* moment. The end of her. Of her life. Her dreams. All taken away in the blink of an eye, the pull of a trigger. Some bad cartilage in her knee had taken away one future, and now she'd ruined the other.

Her resignation was the only option left. The only way to move past it, and Chase, and all the bad things that had happened.

The letter… she mused.

How could she have been so careless? She thought back to that moment in the house, where she'd held the letter in her own two hands and read it one last time. Hadn't she put it in her coat? She could hear her mother's chiding voice in her head, "You care so much about keeping every little thing neat and tidy. You only want this, and that. Always so obsessive about controlling everything happening around you. But what about *you,* Sterling? What about *your* life? What's the point of pouring all that energy into everything around you if you can't get yourself right?"

Not now, Anna, she thought.

It wasn't her fault she forgot. The familiar buzzing came back, hissing behind her eyes like rusty nails. Thankfully, this time it left just as quickly as it came.

She remembered now. It was the TV. The thing had jumped to life with those god-awful sounds she'd been hearing all night, and she'd been so unscrewed by it she'd forgotten to slip the resignation letter into her coat.

How could you forget it? she scolded herself. *After everything that's happened?*

She shook her head.

What difference does it make? No use worrying about it now, just get it and get back to the station, before they find out the truth.

She questioned why she had to have it this instant and knew

it was because she needed to say goodbye, needed to sprinkle dirt on the coffin like she should of.

Because she needed it.

Because I need it, she repeated in her head.

Chase's face came to her then, like a vision.

Need. The word made her cringe.

And as she thought about what *she* needed, Chase gazed at her longingly, and she at him. There was safety there, in his strong arms. She had tried to tell herself repeatedly that she didn't need him, but she knew that wasn't true. Or maybe she didn't really need him, only needed *someone.* Someone that could be her hope in the face of hopelessness.

Glimpses of that unrestrained memory flashed before her eyes like a forbidden film. The night had carried her away to twilight, long after that monster's body had been collected and taken away by the coroner. She was at the station in her office, racked by sadness and anger, handwriting reports with the same hand she'd used to murder the man in cold blood hours earlier. Her mind was broken by chaos and disorder, and for the first time she'd become truly frightened of herself, of the person she'd discovered underneath.

Chase had come to her then; he'd seen the plum bruise on the side of her face, the despair in her eyes. It was a pain he'd never known and would never understand, and in one innocent act of kindness toward someone he'd come to know as both a friend and a partner, Chase had put his hand to her tender face the same way she'd put hers on the witch. He'd smiled regretfully, looking deep and long at her. She lost herself there, in those beautiful blue eyes, and knew that she was never coming back.

And for the second time that night, she pulled the trigger.

Chase took her in his arms then, his breath hot and heavy. Their tongues explored each other's mouths, and they ripped into each other's clothes as if the world wouldn't be there come sunrise. Before she knew what was happening, their naked bodies were pressed together against the wall, slick with sweat, moving to a song she hadn't heard in years, and with a man no less. And what had started out as something tender and gentle devolved into something vital and urgent, as if nothing else mattered or ever would.

Afterwards, they'd laid together on the floor behind her desk with his arm draped over her. She'd felt his warm breath on the back of her neck and their tortured hearts beating in unison. She'd closed her eyes and made the decision to let herself feel everything, soak it up while she could, because happiness was a fairy tale, just as much as the witch herself. Sterling stayed huddled there with him until sunrise, nestled safely away from all the horrible thoughts swimming around in her head, with a man who could never truly be hers. A symbol of the life she could never have. A dream that would never be realized. And against all better judgment, she'd said the words she'd promised herself she'd never say.

"I love you."

There was a heavy whirl, like the force of a semi-truck passing by, and the memory ripped away around her like cheap wrapping paper, leaving her back in the patrol car.

She was parked in front of her house, hot tears rolling down her cheeks. She quickly squeezed her eyes shut with a muffled sob, willing her memories of him and all his broken promises away. She let out a frustrated scream, wailing on the steering wheel with her fist until her skin was bruised.

She threw open the front door and it slammed into the wall, the deadbolt leaving an imprint in the drywall.

She didn't bother to close it.

The wind fluttered the drapes framing the window, like the house had suddenly awakened. The ghostly headlights from the patrol car shone through the living room window, leaving motes of dust swirling in the air. Sterling was crying so hard she was practically laughing now, weeping for her lost dreams and shattered life.

She remembered the way Chase held her, the way his heart felt, calmly beating against her naked back. But most of all, she remembered the escape. The fleeting glimpse into a dream that would never be.

Her chest heaved as she staggered through the beams in the living room, her breaths labored and broken. Her body shuddered as she was racked with sobs, drunkenly making her way to the bedroom.

She remembered the way Chase's body moved and the way she moved with him, remembered the way it numbed the bad thoughts and warmed her inside.

She stumbled through the doorway, a sharp, agonizing cry escaping her throat. She turned and beheld what she'd become in the mirror of the vanity. The distorted, doomed reflection confirmed everything she knew about herself in one ephemeral glimpse. A heat began to pour up her throat, building. Powered by rage, she seized the snow globe from her desk that Chase had won her at the fair and hurled it as hard as she could. The glass detonated like a hail of a thousand exquisite diamonds, and the infinitely loud clatter was like music to her ears.

The heat was boiling now, searing her insides. Smothered by a mountain of rage and fury that had been building for a lifetime, she threw off her jacket. Her fingers worked the buttons on her sticky shirt, peeling it away. She unfastened her belt and pants, shoving them down and feeling a rush of heat from her freshly exposed skin.

She remembered the way Chase felt inside her, the way his hands had explored her and taken her as if she was all that mattered in the world.

She was on the bed now, nerve endings on fire, writhing with an urgency that utterly engulfed her, concerned with only her most primal desires. Tears slipped from the corners of her eyes as her hands slid over her flushed skin, continuing down to her thighs.

She shuddered as her cool fingers slipped further, and when

she finally reached the place she'd craved so badly to be touched again, she found that it wasn't Chase's face she saw there in her mind's eye, but the witch instead.

CHAPTER 19

IT HAD BEEN long enough. Chase had done like she'd asked, let the tape recorder wind down while the witch sat there mockingly. He'd stood right on the other side of the two-way mirror and studied her for a good twenty minutes, just hoping to catch even the smallest hint of a microexpression. A nose scratch. A sneeze. An eye twitch. Hell, even a blink was better than nothing at this point.

But no. In the end, the witch had prevailed. She'd just waited there silently, face blank, more lifeless than the paint on the walls. And the worst part wasn't that she didn't move or speak, as unsettling as that was. It was that Chase had a gut feeling that if they'd left her there, locked in the station, and come back in twenty years, she'd still have been in the same position, staring off into eternity with those empty silver dollar eyes. But he'd never tell anyone that, because that would mean admitting that there was even a minute possibility that the witch was actually real.

And the supernatural didn't exist. Not unless you believed Rosa's stories of healing taking place at Drybell's very own Our

Lady of Mercy chapel.

God, what a shitty night. First Jennifer had caught them together at the diner and gone apeshit, and now Sterling was losing her nerves on tonight of all nights when she should have been focused on how to save her job. The realization hit him that Max was this very second being looked after by a woman who believed her reincarnated grandmother was a stray cat she fed a can of tuna once a day. He loved Georgia, but good god, she was out there. You wouldn't find a more loveable conspiracy theorist this side of Connecticut. But she loved Max just as much he and Jennifer and that was enough for him.

Max… he said to himself.

How long had he been standing here?

He checked his watch.

"Fuck," he muttered. "Good job, asshole."

He let himself into the interview room and calmly sauntered over to the running tape recorder, switching it off. The soft hum of the cassette abruptly stopped, leaving them in silence and letting in more of the storm outside.

He considered the tape recorder thoughtfully, then looked at the witch and scoffed. "We're just rolling out the red carpet tonight for you, aren't we?"

When the witch didn't answer, Chase walked up, looming over her, his golden hair hanging down in front of his eyes. "I don't know who you are, and I don't *care* who you are, but you've been causing a whole lot of trouble around here tonight.

"You see, for one reason or another, people seem to feel a little uncomfortable with you wandering around Drybell looking like that. Can't say I blame them. Truth is, your little prank seems to be getting under everyone's skin around here, present company included. You should really think this through, because if you don't start cooperating, you're going to be up to your ass in trespassing charges come morning. Breaking and entering. Vandalism."

He paused, leaning down and getting right in her face. "You might have everyone else fooled around here, but you don't fool me." Chase lingered there, glaring at her. "Now, we ready to talk?"

Crickets.

"Damn." Chase shook his head. "I'd hoped you were smarter than this." He rolled his tongue along the inside of his cheek with a clicking sound. "Fine, have it your way. Just remember that I gave you a chance to do the right thing."

He got behind her, and before his hands could touch her body, she rose from the chair. Chase stopped, confused, then said, "Walk. *Slowly.*"

The witch sedately marched ahead of him down the corridor, passing under the flickering lights.

He knew it. She understood him. She had to. Why else would she be following his orders? She wasn't catatonic, just difficult.

She just wants to get a rise out of everyone, that's all.

"Wait here," he directed.

The witch stopped.

He moved around in front of her, opening the door to lockup. "In," he said, and she went.

"You in the cell, step away from the bars," Chase announced. The man's hands withered away like a dying flower as the witch shuffled past his cell like death incarnate.

Before Chase could instruct her where to go, the witch stopped in front of the second empty cell.

As he unlocked the cell door, he noticed the man in the neighboring cell shrewdly observing them from the shadows, seemingly fascinated by the witch's presence.

Chase stepped aside and the witch floated past him like a ghost.

A warm draft caressed his face like spidery fingertips.

His eyes fluttered drowsily, a projector whirring to life, reeling in his head. He heard it click, purring in his ears. Gingerbread and eggnog. He could smell it, just like the party.

Laughing. He was in his own kitchen, back at the house. The kitchen table was a mess of candy. Rusted baking sheets covered every flat surface, some teetering on the verge of a dive to the linoleum. Jennifer had Max in her arms at the table, giggling, her head resting on top of his own. Chase stood there watching them from the doorway while Max squeezed out frosting from a piping bag.

Gingerbread...

They'd baked over fifty cookies that weekend for the Christmas Banquet at City Hall. Jennifer had been nominated to bring desserts that year, and Chase had volunteered to help. He watched them laugh and smile, when Jennifer turned to him and said, "Are you going to stand there all night and stare, or are you going to help us?"

ARE YOU GOING TO HELP US?

"Hey!" The voice cracked the memory like an eggshell, and he found himself back in the jail.

"You all right?" the stranger asked.

Chase blinked rapidly. "What?"

"You were just standing there," the man said. "For *ten minutes*. You weren't moving."

Chase looked at the man in a daze, then checked his watch.

He's right.

"Sonofabitch..." he muttered.

The stranger said, "You don't look so good. Where's Marsh?"

Chase cast a dubious glance at the witch, who stood dead center in the cell. He started to walk away, then said, "I'm fine."

"Wait a minute," the man said. "Chase, right? Just think about this for a moment. Something about this strike you as odd?"

Chase stopped short of the door, looking over his shoulder.

The man in the cell had his hands up in the air, trying to reason with him. He tipped his head toward the witch's cell. "Something is not right here," he said soberly. "Where's Sheriff Marsh? I need to speak with her now."

"About what?"

The man was silent.

"All right then."

"Look, I can't explain it right now. If you can just get her—"

"She's busy."

"It's *important*," the man said.

"Anything you got to say to her, you can say to me."

There was a minute of silence.

"That's what I thought."

Chase stepped through the door.

"Please," the man said, more pressingly.

Chase turned back and looked at him ominously, then slammed the door behind him.

He could hear the man shouting from the other side.

CHAPTER 20

BROKEN GLASS CRUNCHED as the patrol car rolled to a stop.

The door swung open, and Sheriff Sterling Marsh stepped out into the night. The mist was considerable here near the river, concealing the lower forest and surrounding the car. The rain was light, barely there. Her breath was white smoke in the night, and the forest lit up as lightning quietly seared the sky. A red and blue cyclone whirled on top of the car, and as Sterling threw the door closed a heavy dose of thunder grumbled beyond the Painted Mountains. High above her, the storm was nearly idle, a fickle beast holding Drybell hostage, threatening to awaken at any moment. The wind had calmed substantially, and the steely clouds had pulled apart, venting downcast moonlight.

The car was parked at the entrance to Old Ferry Bridge, a two-lane pathway about a hundred yards long that ran over the Connecticut River. Ironically, Old Ferry Bridge had recently been repaved and was currently littered with a fleet of derelict construction vehicles. Heavy machine equipment was strewn about the shoulder, overlaid with clear plastic tarps to stave off the long winter.

Sterling turned on her flashlight and treaded beside the high beams.

Jackknifed at the entrance was a heap of scorched steel and rubber. Beyond that, a hedge of fog obscured whatever lay on the other side of the river. The wreckage was substantial, blocking virtually the entire length of the bridge. Access would be impossible.

We're trapped, Sterling thought to herself. She recalled her conversation with the man at the station. "No one goes in; no one goes out," she'd said. The words seemed infinitely more serious now.

The cab of the semi was mangled beyond recognition. Most all of the black paint had melted away, save for a few select patches, and both the interior and exterior were burned down to the bare metal. Sterling approached the cab, grabbing hold of the blackened step bar and climbing onto the side. She pulled herself in and combed the beam through the cab, finding nothing but the charred remains of the interior.

She exhaled, undeterred, and craned her head toward the rear. She shifted on the side of the wreckage, switching the flashlight to her other hand and leveling it at the trailer.

She leapt off the side and landed back on the highway, pacing along the trailer.

Miraculously, the cache had survived the worst of the fire. The center was badly split, and the rear half teetered over the side of the bridge. Sterling traced the remains with the light, following it to the rear.

She reached the far end, where the rear doors hung open on creaky hinges, lightly swaying in the wind. She placed her hands on the guardrail and tugged as hard as she could, testing its strength.

Satisfied, she delicately leaned her weight on the bridge's railing, reaching out with the flashlight to get a glimpse inside. The dim beam shifted into the darkness, unveiling a panel of blown electronics and destroyed machinery. Bushels of wires and metal cluttered the inside walls. There were two lengths of gnarled metal bent severely that Sterling guessed were from a railing system of some kind. The mechanism was mounted to the floor and led into the darkness beyond. She gathered that the truck must have been transporting something substantial.

The guardrail groaned.

She froze, her upper body extended out over the black river. She eased her weight, carefully shrinking back. "Damn it..." she muttered, lightly tapping the flashlight on the metal.

An idea came to her.

She moved away from the railing and back to the road, following it to the shoulder. She swung the funnel of light to the edge of the dirt, where a natural path sloped down the hillside.

Below, the trail wound down the slope, curving into the night.

She looked around, as if expecting someone to be there, but found no one. The trees hypnotically swayed together, and the smell of running water wafted past her face. Damp mist floated by like a stream of ghosts; she felt it kiss her skin as it passed.

Intrigued, she started down the hill, steadying herself with her free hand as the beam from the flashlight revealed more of the trail.

The sound of rushing water grew louder. As she descended, the mist dissipated, leaving behind crisp, fresh air, like wet earth and pine needles. It made her grateful to be in nature, away from the witch and her own devices.

She stopped as the light wavered over a patch of disturbed mud. She shifted her weight toward the mountain to hold her steady, then crouched on her haunches, studying the hillside.

The gravel and foliage were peeled away like a wound, revealing a deposit of fresh soil below. She moved the light further down the incline, where more layers of the earth had been crushed and pared back.

Something fell, Sterling thought. *Something heavy.*

She rose, then turned and looked up, where she could see the rear of the trailer dangling from the ledge high above her, the doors creaking on their hinges.

The water...

Sterling stepped off the beaten path, practically on her side, sliding over the grass and dried pine needles.

Her boots slid through wet mud.

She began to pick up speed.

Her feet shot out from under her, her body arched, and her butt crashed onto the rocky hillside. The sky fell into a blur, the darkness rushing by as she tore down the hill through the mud, plummeting.

Her body launched through the air, bucking around. The air gushed from her lungs as she landed on smooth rock with a grunt.

Her eyes opened weakly.

The flashlight lay on the rock in front of her, angled at the river.

She sluggishly traced the beam with her eyes.

Her pupils dilated and her breath hitched. She coughed, spraying up a cloud of dust, and groggily pushed herself to her feet. A dull throb stirred in the back of her head and her back was bruised to hell, but other than that she didn't have a scratch on her.

Trapped in the glow of the flashlight was a massive coffin-shaped pod. The contraption was half-buried in the wet sand, sticking out like some forgotten effigy. The black river lazily washed around it, feeding down the mountain.

Sterling fished the flashlight out of the sand and cautiously walked toward the vessel-like buried treasure.

The thing was like a tomb fit for a giant. It was easily eight feet tall and three feet wide, black with a dulled golden exterior that glinted when the light touched it. The side panels were a network of intricate cogs and steel wheels that reminded her of the inner workings of a clock, with rounded two-inch bolts that dotted the seams.

Whatever it is, it's built like a vault, Sterling thought.

She took a step forward and swung the beam up, noticing a small digital readout on the side. An array of bars spiked erratically, and a small red light flashed to the side of the display.

A warning.

She took note, then trudged into the river, holding onto the massive container as a makeshift buoy. The icy water flooded over her skin, soaking into her pants and boots. She grimaced, biting down and disregarding the cold, then waded toward the front of the pod, pulling herself along the long rails fixed to the sides.

A weak light grew as she drew herself closer. She heaved her body to the side of the object, letting herself rest. She took a deep breath, watching the pitch blackness engulf her. She readjusted her grip on the flashlight, then pushed herself further into the river. She could see that the front of the pod was wedged open, held that way by the current and anchored in the mud by its own hulking weight.

The freezing river rushed past her waist. She jammed the flashlight under her arm and shimmied around the corner, rounding the opening.

The sight staggered her; her mouth fell open, her face glittering like copper in the weak amber light. She nervously fumbled the flashlight from under her arm and thrust it forward, lancing the hollow of darkness. She gasped, recoiling as the cavity flared to life in a brilliant gilded light.

The interior was incredible; a tomb composed entirely of tarnished gold like an ancient Egyptian sarcophagus. She ran her fingers along the inside walls skeptically, caressing a texture not unlike melted wax.

Her mind began racing, trying to piece together the accident.

The truck.

The prisoner.

And now this.

And at the end of the long chain of coincidences, there remained only one at the center.

The witch.

That dangerous heat warmed her skin, familiar and rousing, and she shuddered thinking about what she'd done no more than a half hour ago. And not only that but *who* she'd thought of in the heat of the moment.

Sterling went to take another step and her foot hooked the edge of a flat surface.

She toppled forward and the flashlight splashed into the water with a *gulp!* She tightened her grip on the pod, noticing the faint glow of the flashlight under the murky surface. Mesmerized, she held onto the vessel with one hand and used her other hand to dip her fingers into the river, brushing a hard object with her fingertips.

The witch has no fingerprints, she suddenly remembered. *No identity.*

She squinted, using her foot to pry the object, freeing it from the bed of sand.

Her fingers tightened. It was heavy, whatever it was. She jerked hard and thought it might slip from her grasp but it didn't.

The object broke the surface with a splash. She threw it under her arm, inching back around the pod. She carefully held it tight, heart hammering, and when she'd reached the safety of shallow waters, she took it in her hands, wading out of the water to the shore and setting it on dry land.

She got down on one knee and unzipped her jacket, throwing it to the side. She lifted the flashlight, casting a bright glow on the object.

It was an elongated container, at least seventeen or eighteen inches long, and heavy. Sterling laid it down in the sand and leaned over, maneuvering the light closer.

The capsule was similar to the first in construction but on a much smaller scale, though equally fortified. Unlike its larger sibling, the capsule had a clear pane on the front, allowing a glimpse of the interior. The glass window was edged with sequences of unusual words that ran from one side to the other. She'd never seen anything quite like it.

Sterling shone the light through the glass and it sparkled like a tiny room full of treasure.

"Gold..." she whispered to herself.

Inside, a long black object was fixed in place, fastened with two catches. Sterling shifted her position, getting down on her knees and attempting to make out the details.

She feverishly felt along the edges for a latch but found nothing. When that failed, she attempted to pry the seams apart with her fingers.

Defeated, she gathered it up in her arms and began the trek back up the hillside.

CHAPTER 21

GEORGIA WAS STILL watching her show when Daddy appeared in the doorway. They'd been sitting there for so long now he'd lost track. He could tell she was feeling better; her face didn't look quite so tired now, and she was talking more. She'd said a few weird things that he didn't understand, but she seemed like her old self again more or less. They'd even played a couple games of Which Witch?, although he'd easily won each time. After that, curiosity had gotten the better of her and she'd switched on the TV again. "I'm just gonna let my batteries recharge for a minute or two," she'd said. So while she got sucked into her weird television shows, he'd worked on his Rubik's Cube some more. He aligned two more of the faces, the blue and orange, but there was plenty more work to be done and his eyes were starting to hurt by that point.

He sat at the base of the Christmas tree, watching the tiny model train do laps around the tiny town Rosa had painstakingly set up, and wished he could shrink himself down so he could go inside and become one of the passengers. He imagined it would be nice and cozy, and he'd have the whole train to himself while he watched the giant bulbs from below like twinkling stars. He had an assortment of cookies on his plate, as well as a few more he'd stashed away in his satchel for later. He grabbed a nice frosted gingerbread man and bit off the head with a snap, then felt his hair falling down in front of his eyes and combed it back with his fingers.

"You sure that's the best thing for Max to be watching right now, Georgia?" Chase said.

Georgia turned and her jaw went slack like she'd been caught red-handed. Her jowls quivered as her mouth hung open. She sprung to life, scrambling for the remote. The TV screen flashed and an old Disney cartoon with Donald Duck and a gorilla came on.

"Oh! There you are," she said. "We was getting worried, weren't we, Maxy?"

Max hooked an eyebrow.

Georgia grinned.

"Cable's working?" he asked.

Georgia held the remote up. "Nah. Just some things I had saved on the DVR from last week. You know, lots of strange goings-on in the world, can't afford to miss a thing these days."

"Oh. How you two holding up?" Chase asked, slipping into a chair next to Max.

Max shrugged. "Kay, I guess."

"He's been keeping me busy all night with these games," Georgia replied. "Needed to let my melon recharge a bit before I let him beat me some more. Felt like I was playing my sisters all over again, have mercy."

Chase looked over at the closest table, where Which Witch? was still setup. Chase took the lid in his hands, studying the picture. "*Which Witch?* Never heard of this one before."

"Georgia says it's *old*," Max said with a hand to the side of his mouth.

Chase shook his head. "Fitting..." he said under his breath. He tossed the box back on the table.

"That woman: is she a witch like them?" Max asked, pointing at the cover art. Georgia cast a glance over her shoulder and frowned.

"There's no such thing as witches, Ace," Chase said.

"Then why is she dressed like that?"

"Because she's trying to play a joke on us, that's why."

"Georgia says witches are real. She says they turn kids like me into rats and eat them."

Chase's ears nearly started bleeding. He glared at Georgia and she quickly snapped back to the TV before she could behold the irritation on his face.

"You see, Max," Chase began, "when people like Georgia start to get *old*, sometimes they get confused about what they say and their imaginations get so big they start believing in things that aren't real."

Max's forehead crinkled as he considered this. "Like the witch?"

"Like the witch."

Max sighed, relieved that the witch stories weren't true. But if she wasn't a witch, then who was she?

"How much longer until we go home?" he asked.

Chase exhaled, running a hand through his hair before massaging tired eyes. "Storm's been getting worse, Ace. Lots of rain. And with all these strangers showing up tonight, Sterling needs a little extra help around here. I haven't been able to get a hold of your mom, so it might be a while before I can bring you home. You think you and Georgia can stick it out for a little while longer?"

Max bobbed his head.

Georgia's voice piped up in the background, "Yeah, we've got lots of games to keep us busy, and I'm just about getting a second wind here..." she said, chased by a long yawn.

Chase rolled his eyes, lured into an unexpected yawn himself.

Max watched the tiredness soak into his Daddy's face like warm sunlight. He had an idea. He reached into his satchel, rummaging around. After a moment, he removed two homemade chocolate chip cookies he'd stashed away for later, part of his emergency supply. "Here. To help so you don't fall asleep."

"Thanks, Ace." Chase smiled. "You're a good kid, you know that?"

Max smiled.

Chase patted him on the shoulder and wedged a cookie between his teeth before standing up and stretching his back with a protracted groan.

"Georgia?" he said.

Georgia looked over her shoulder, keeping one eye on the TV.

"We still haven't been able to get outside the valley. I'm thinking we don't get a call out until this storm passes, but Rosa's going to keep at it in the meantime. She's been trying to get through to State Police all night. Keep trying on your cellphone just in case, though."

"Sure thing, sugar pie," she replied.

He started away, then stopped beside her chair and quietly said, "And how about a new game? Maybe one without something that's gonna give him nightmares?"

"I am *so* sorry," she whispered. "My brain is fried and I didn't even think—"

"It's fine," Chase said, cutting her off. "Just...get something else. Okay?"

Georgia nodded. "Consider it done."

Chase turned back and said, "Love you, Ace. Be good."

And then he was gone.

"Well then," Georgia said, wrestling herself free from her chair and clapping her hands together. "Battleship, anyone?"

Battleship hadn't lasted long. That game was more boring than watching Mommy load the dishwasher. He could tell Georgia was equally bored. He'd watched her keep looking over at the TV, drumming her nails on the table, eyes barely open.

After the third game, he'd asked Georgia if they could take a break. At this rate, if he played another game his brain was liable to shut off because it was so bored. His plan worked like a charm. Georgia agreed, retreating to her chair in front of the TV, where a man was making his way through a dark house with a flashlight calling out for someone who wasn't there.

Now he could do what he really wanted to do and go have a look around. Give the station his own personal inspection.

Georgia was snoring the way his Daddy did sometimes. The corner of her lip made a funny sound, sputtering like a boat engine, and her eyes were closed shut with her head tilted up at the ceiling. He saw her eyelids moving and guessed her eyeballs were rolling around underneath them.

Max tucked his satchel behind him and tiptoed to the closet, opening it and quietly unfolding a wool blanket that was tucked away. He watched Georgia sleep a moment as the train slid around the Christmas tree in loops, finding joy in the moment like he was at the North Pole in Santa's Workshop. He smiled, then carefully draped the quilt over Georgia before making for the hallway.

Out in the hall, things were quiet. The horrible white lights brought an ache to his eyes, and he wondered if they were making things just a little bit colder in there than they were before.

He glanced both ways, finding nothing but ugly brick walls trailing in both directions. He listened to the rain trickling down the windows, the thunder crashing like fireworks and unsettling the walls.

He swallowed, tugging the strap of his bag, readjusting it.

Daddy's door was closed.

So was Miss Sterling's. But he could hear voices talking on

the other side.

The witch was gone. He knew that much for sure. He'd heard Daddy take her away to the place where they kept the bad people. He was glad she was gone. He didn't want her around, and he didn't think Georgia did either.

There's no such thing as witches. He listened to the words play over and over again in his head like the records. Only the words stayed. Lingered. They looped around in his head like the train, only instead of a Christmas tree in the middle, the witch was there instead, horrible and awful and scary.

He had to be sure.

He started down the hall, pressing himself flat against the wall outside Miss Sterling's office.

He heard Sterling and Daddy arguing again, talking about grownup things. He thought hard about the last time he'd seen him with Mommy, smiling, and couldn't. Had it been so long?

It was time to go.

He slipped past the office, listening to their voices fade away.

He passed by the threshold to another room and smelled burned plastic.

What's that?

He wrinkled his nose, sniffing the air.

Boy, that stinks!

He poked his head into the office.

The room was bathed in cold moonlight.

He knew this place: this was where they brought the bad people before they took them away to jail. A few times he'd even watched Georgia and Daddy take their fingerprints when they weren't looking.

Daddy would have been furious if he'd caught him, but he was usually pretty careful.

He slinked forward, a hand pressed to his leather bag to suppress any crinkling leather. His cheeks puffed up with air, his breath held tight. He wandered around in the darkness with his hands out in front of him, fumbling in the shadows.

After a moment, he couldn't hold it anymore; he exhaled sharply, and the air gushed out of his lungs just as his forehead knocked into something rigid. "Ow!" he said. Horrified, he clapped a hand over his mouth and listened.

The rain droned on faithfully.

Nobody heard, he decided.

He was at the foot of a set of tall black poles.

He ran his fingers along the smooth metal, finding it rough and warmer toward the top.

The smell intensified; this had to be where it was coming from.

There was a break in the clouds. Bluish light filtered into the room, giving him glimpses of the thing on the poles. It was black and crispy, whatever it was having melted into a blob.

He touched the surface and felt heat.

"Yikes…" he muttered.

A clap of lightning lit up the room, and a dark shape sprang out beside him. He gasped, stumbling into the tripod and knocking it over with a crash. His butt hit the tile, and he scooted back into a chair, nearly knocking it over as well.

When the shape didn't move from its spot, he squinted in the dark, letting his eyes peel away the layers of shadows.

The witch's hat!

He chuckled, putting a hand on his heart and shaking his head. It was only the dumb witch's hat. He giggled some more because he'd nearly felt his heart explode, and then pushed himself to his feet. He walked over to the counter where the hat was perched. He carefully picked the thing up, looking it over.

Man, it was weird. The hat had patches all over it like the kind Mommy used on her jeans when they ripped, only these ones were uglier. Some of the squares were the color of mud and others were black as coal. There were even a couple that were lighter, and when he looked at those parts closer, he realized they were almost the same color as his skin.

His head went heavy, like he wanted to lay down right there and take a nap, or maybe listen to the rain tap on the window in the dark. The corner of his mouth hooked into a smile as he stared down at the thing in his hands. He let himself sink to the floor, folding his legs under him and holding the hat out.

It was almost like the hat was breathing. The thing shuddered in his hands, caressing his sweaty face with a breeze of cold air. He looked down inside the hole, and it was like looking into the well in their backyard, this deep, dark pit that might as well have gone to the center of the Earth. He wondered what was waiting there in the darkness and his mind reeled at the possibilities. One thing he knew for certain: Mommy and Daddy weren't down there, and neither were their voices, which meant he'd never have to listen to them fight ever again. The idea was more tempting than he wanted it to be. What kind of boy would want to leave his parents behind? Not a good boy, and that was what he was.

He couldn't say why, but in that moment he wondered what it might feel like to be a witch, to put the hat atop his head and see the world like she did. Maybe she was just misunderstood? Maybe she just *looked* scary, but really wasn't. After all, Daddy said there was no such thing as witches. And Daddy would never lie to him.

He felt the cold on his face, blinking hard as it glazed over his eyes. It cooled his feverish skin and freshened the stale air in the station that he'd been breathing now for hours on end. He cocked an ear toward the hole and listened, and he could have sworn he heard a faint grumble like a hungry stomach deep inside.

There was a funny wet sound, like when he rolled his tongue around inside his cheek, and his eyes widened in anticipation.

The hat wasn't so bad, he decided.

He smiled, stretching the brim in his fingers, pulling the hole wide as it could go.

He lifted it high in the air, slowly lowering it down onto his head. He felt it shift in his hands, like it was waking up, and the sound inside grew louder, moaning like an old man.

The buzzing in the room grew louder and it was like the flies were right next to him, swarming around his head like a black cloud.

The hat was ripped out of his fingertips.

The light slammed on.

Max gasped, recoiling like a vampire caught in the sunlight.

"Good lord, child, you about gave me a heart attack!" Georgia cried. She realized what she held in her hand and grimaced, chucking the hat onto the counter. She stormed over, reaching down and jerking him up by the wrist.

"But Georgia!" he argued.

"One minute you're there, the next minute you're gone. I must be out of my mind!"

"But the hat! The witch!"

Georgia stopped in her tracks and shuddered like she had bugs crawling over her. "You *cannot* just go running off by yourself anytime you feel like. I'm supposed to be watching over you, Maxy."

"But I was trying to see if the witch—"

"Stop!" she snapped.

He froze. He'd never heard her talk like that in his life. She'd never lost her temper or yelled at him before, not even after the time he'd broken that glass ballerina she kept by the window. Not even when he'd spilled paint all over her kitchen floor, or accidentally caught her favorite skillet on fire.

Georgia looked at him and he could see the worry. "Just stop, Maxy. Okay?"

Max was silent, tears pooling in his eyes.

"Sterling and your daddy have a lot of problems they're trying to sort out right now. Bigger problems than having to worry about you running around by yourself."

Max sniffled, wiping his eyes.

"We're friends, you and I, and friends don't run off without telling each other where they're going, right?"

Max stared at her.

"Right?"

Max nodded.

"I do not know what I would do if something happened to you, do you know that?"

Max nodded again.

"Good." Georgia kneeled down, pulling him into a hug. His body was limp, but after a moment he slipped his small arms as far as they would go around her and squeezed tight. She looked him in the eye and winked, tussling his hair.

As she pulled him through the door, back into the hall, he turned and peered over his shoulder. He could have sworn he saw the hat move, but he couldn't be sure.

CHAPTER 22

STERLING AND CHASE stood in her office on either side of the desk, the unusual container from the river resting between them on the surface.

She'd snuck in unseen after returning from the bridge and changed out of her wet clothes in the locker-room into a fresh uniform, but she could still smell hints of the earth on her skin. The minerals from the muddy water and the damp soil absorbed straight into her flesh, but she didn't mind it. It made her think of home, the only safe place there was left.

A fresh pot of Hallowed Grounds Coffee spiritedly percolated on a metal side table (the bag a gift from a former colleague working in Winterview City), and on the corner of her desk sat a framed photo of Sterling and her mother and father at the Madison Turkey Trot from New Haven three years prior, a layer of dust coating the border.

Chase examined the object in front of him, his face pulled tight, a narrow pinch in his brow. He combed a hand through his hair and said, "I give up. What is it?"

"I don't know."

Chase cocked an eyebrow. "Where'd you find it?"

Sterling looked at him straight-faced, biting her lip, then flattened her hands on the desk, leaning forward. "Old Ferry Bridge."

"*Old Ferry Bridge*? You went there? Alone?" Chase shook his head, heatedly pacing away. "What am I saying, of course you went there. You are going to have to help me out here, because I am having a really, really bad case of déjà vu, Sterling."

"I'm sorry. I needed to work some things out."

"You know—you *could* try talking to me. But to be honest, I don't even know why I try anymore."

"Chase, *listen*."

Chase glared at her, the whites of his eyes showing.

"I found something."

"Yeah? What?" Chase said shortly, as if not even caring to listen anymore.

"There was a truck, just like Spencer said. A semi. Jackknifed at the entrance, burned all to shit."

"Yes, information we got *hours ago*. Come on, Sterling. A semi crashed, so what?"

Sterling stared at this man she didn't recognize. Somehow all of the intimacy they'd shared once upon a time had eroded into this hollow, dead thing. The snapshot she kept in her head of them from that fateful night caught with a flame, slowly burning away.

Leaving her.

Chase waited for her to speak, but she could only look on at him, this man she thought would be so important to her one day. And the truth was, another thread had unraveled somewhere inside her. She was wounded, but she'd never tell him that, never let herself become a victim.

The sadness molted into white-hot anger. Chase started to walk away and Sterling snatched his arm, jerking him back. "Goddammit, will you just listen to me for a minute?!"

"What the hell, Sterling?" he snapped, ripping his arm free.

"It was a *transport*," she replied.

Chase scowled, looking at her like he didn't recognize who she'd become, but he stayed there all the same, listening.

"It wasn't just some run-of-the-mill delivery truck, Chase. This wasn't like any truck I've ever seen. It was a transport," she said, almost in a whisper. "It wasn't military…but whatever it was, it was something big."

Chase waited for her to finish.

She continued, "Down near the river on the shore, there was something lodged in the sand."

"You're talking about this thing?"

"No," she said firmly. "It was bigger. Built like a fucking tank with some sort of railing system, and it looked like a giant, futuristic coffin or something. It had all these gold parts and these weird symbols. I don't know. It was like nothing I've ever seen." She paused, then said, "It was open."

Chase threw his head back and laughed. "Fine, Sterling. Fine. We've already had every other fucking weird thing happen tonight that could possibly happen, what's one more?" He folded his arms across his chest, unconvinced. "So what was in it?"

"That's the thing: it was empty. I went down there and looked inside. I don't know what I was expecting to find…maybe money. Gold bars. Maybe a cache of weapons, or some type of illegal equipment or something. Only there wasn't anything in there. It was empty."

Chase chewed up the information, then eased back on the desk, doubtful. "Empty?"

Sterling nodded.

"So you think, what? That whatever was inside spilled into the river?"

Sterling shook her head, "No. No, I don't think it was anything like that."

"Then what?"

"Look, I know how this is going to sound, so just hear me out, okay?" she said, rolling the wooden chair forward and easing onto the edge. Georgia would have been laughing her ass off if she'd seen her like that: bent over, eyes hungry with speculation, hands in the air like a storyteller passing on legends of days gone.

Chase's arms tightened over his chest.

Sterling began, "Don't you think it's a little bit of a coincidence that *she* shows up in Drybell right after that big rig crashed here?"

"She who?" The wheels spun for a few seconds, then his eyes blew up double their size. "The witch?" He almost shouted the word. "Come on, Sterling. I told you, it's a fucking prank! Someone's trying to pull one over on us. You know how it is now with YouTube. Every nut out there is trying get their fifty-seconds-of-fame, and Drybell is the perfect place for them to pull this type of shit." He sauntered to the window and split the blinds with his fingers, peeking into the darkness. "They've probably got cameras set up all over town filming our reactions."

"Okay," she said, exasperated, "where did she come from then? I've worked here ten years now and you've been here most your life. We know every one of these people, so how come we've never seen her before? I know *I've* never seen her before. Have you?"

"Well, no, but—"

"Then where?"

Chase rolled his shoulders, raking a hand through his shiny blond hair. "How the hell should I know? She probably went to the nearest costume shop, bought some contacts and a fucking witch costume, and *poof* here she is. Wicked Witch of Drybell just dropped out of the fucking sky. Who knows, maybe she rode a tornado in!" He was practically shouting now.

Sterling stepped closer, her voice low. "Are you telling me that you don't even get the slightest sense that something is not right with that woman?"

Chase stared at her for a good ten seconds, and Sterling could see that the words were on the tip of his tongue. But it was no use, he was too worked up to agree with her about anything, even if he *did* actually think she was right. And he'd play stubborn just on principle to spite her, because Chase could be petty like that.

If only he'd seen City Hall, she thought. If only he'd seen the symbols smeared over the sterile walls, heard the screams coming from the darkness.

Chase placed his hands on her shoulders and brought his face close. She could taste the stale coffee on his breath and smell the salty, woodsy cologne she'd wasted seventy dollars on during that daytrip to Hartford before the fair.

And as calm and composed as he could, nearly to the point of fraudulence, Chase said, "She is not real, Sterling. None of this is real."

"And what if you're wrong?"

Chase looked at her with pity, his nerves calmed, replaced with dread. She could see that in his mind, the real horror wasn't the witch, it was what was happening to her. What *had* happened already, and was only growing worse.

Chase smiled halfheartedly. "Then I guess I was wrong about two things."

"You're unbelievable," Sterling scoffed, turning away. "I found this next to that thing in the river." She pushed the box across the desk.

Chase picked the weighty object up, bringing it closer to his face. "Can't really see all that much. Maybe we can pry it open?" He grabbed the edges and tugged.

"I already tried that. It's practically welded shut."

"What's all that writing on the glass?"

Sequences of frosted script covered the small viewing pane and intricate scrollwork ran along the edges.

"I can't read it. It's written in some other language," Sterling replied. "Maybe Italian?"

"No," Chase said, shaking his head, "it's not Italian…"

Sterling looked at him, surprised.

"I took some Italian in college before I dropped out."

"You never told me that," Sterling said.

Chase carefully spun the container in his hands, inspecting it. "Back before the academy, I was working on a Bachelor's in Linguistics. Thought I might go abroad for a while, maybe see something else besides this stinking town."

"Why didn't you ever tell me?"

"Because you never asked me." He smiled wryly. "I guess there's a lot of things we didn't tell each other, huh?"

"Sterling—you're back," a voice said.

Rosa stood in the doorway.

"Hey, Rosa," Sterling greeted.

"When'd you get back?"

"I just got here," Sterling replied. "Had a couple things I needed to take care of."

"What's that?" Rosa asked, noticing the strange box in Chase's hands.

"Oh," Sterling said, "I found it over by the crash site." She took it from Chase's arms, holding it out.

Rosa quickly examined the case, eyeing it suspiciously. She leaned forward, attempting to peer inside the window. "What is it?"

Sterling shrugged, deferring to Chase.

"Haven't quite figured that out yet," he answered.

"I don't see anywhere for a key," Rosa added.

Sterling turned it over in her hands. "I don't think there is one."

Rosa's eyes fell, her face hardening. "Maybe it's for the best. I mean, it's locked for a reason, right?"

"Right," Sterling agreed. She set the container down on the desk. "Have you been able to reach anyone?"

"No," Rosa said, slowly shaking her head. "I've been trying

all night, but so far I can't get anyone outside the valley."

"So we're cut off..." Sterling murmured.

"We have been before," Chase added. "Just a little storm, guys. Nothing we can't handle."

A faint vibration rattled from Chase's chest. He reached into his jacket, pulling out his phone. He looked at Sterling and said, "Pray this goes through," before promptly exiting the office.

Rosa watched him leave, then poked her head out the door to make sure he was gone.

"I've been looking for you all night," she said, letting her cool demeanor fall away. "I've been freaking out, Sterling. I was worried when you disappeared. Chase and Georgia were asking questions, and you still haven't told me anything. What happened?"

She'd seen this coming. She'd been dodging Rosa since she'd brought the witch back from City Hall, even going so far as to avoid dispatch. After all, ignorance is bliss. That's what she'd said to Anna during their last conversation, but her warning only fell on deaf ears.

Sterling swallowed. "What do you mean?"

Rosa's face pinched. She cocked her head to the side. "What do you mean 'what do I mean?' *City Hall*, Sterling. That call we got?" Her voice was hushed, anticipating Chase appearing in the entrance to the office. "What happened? Was Jennifer there?"

Sterling exhaled, leaning against her desk. Her head fell, eyes red-rimmed with tears. "She's dead, Rosa."

Rosa instinctually raised a horrified hand to her mouth, taking a step back.

"She hung herself," Sterling said, and the reality hit her harder than a cinderblock falling out of the sky. Tears rolled over her cheeks and she looked up to see Rosa's face, the usual cold demeanor twisted into shock. Up until that point, the whole thing had seemed almost surreal, like a dream she only remembered pieces of. The walls of City Hall vandalized with bloody, ancient symbols. The screams and voices carrying to her from locked corridors and dark places. She wondered what she would have found if she'd explored the rest of City Hall, and her skin prickled at the thought.

"Oh my God," Rosa wept, hands on her face. "Oh my God, Sterling. But Chase…"

Sterling was off the table in an instant, attempting to quell Rosa's state of mind. "He doesn't know yet," Sterling explained.

"We have to tell him," Rosa cried.

"We *can't*, Rosa."

Rosa gaped at her. "What're you talking about, Sterling? We have to tell him. He has a right to know!"

"Do you really think now is the best time to tell a man that his wife, the woman he's spent his *entire life* with, is dead? Think about it, Rosa. If we tell him now, we're going to be down one more person around here, and with everything happening out there, things are only going to get worse. And he's not the only one. What about Max?"

"So…what, we just pretend like everything is fine?" Rosa said, wiping her eyes with a Kleenex.

"Rosa, I have a duty to protect this town and everyone in it, and that does not work without Chase. He will be a lot more useful to us if he's thinking straight."

Rosa stared at her incredulously, and Sterling could see that she loathed her in a way few people did. "I won't lie to him," Rosa said defiantly.

"You don't have to," Sterling told her. "I promise I will tell him the second this storm has passed and we're in the clear. But until then I need him functioning and with a clear head."

Rosa gaped at her, furious. She stormed out of the room with a huff, and then Sterling was alone again.

CHAPTER 23

"THERE'S SOMETHING YOU need to see."

Chase spoke low, his voice tinged with a clandestine distress. A great crash boomed beyond Sterling's rainy office window, and a web of dead light lit up his face.

She almost gasped seeing him there, the same man she'd lusted for so many times, now a stranger. He looked ten years older than when she'd last seen him. A harsh five o'clock shadow darkened his chiseled jawline, and his eyes were sunken into his skull, the blue irises the sheen of a dirty pool.

Something had changed.

The time was about a half-hour after her disagreement with Rosa. She'd hoped Rosa wouldn't tell Chase, and as far as she could tell that hadn't happened. She felt as dirty as a locker-room floor, denying life-changing information the way she had. Hated herself for it, and she could tell by the way Rosa looked at her that she hated her too. But feelings didn't have a place here. She had to be objective. Had to think strategically. The situation was already elevated through the fucking roof, and then some. She hadn't lied to Rosa about Jennifer's death, and she hoped that bought her some morsel of accountability. If Chase found out the truth, there was no telling what would happen.

She'd taken the chance to regroup and let the chaos settle, seizing the opportunity to guzzle down two cups of scalding black coffee. She'd forced herself to wolf down a questionably brown banana while boxing up the few possessions she kept at the office in brown packing paper. Each item she'd wrapped and boxed felt a like a small piece of her soul being locked away and doomed to an eternity of darkness, systematically rendering her presence at the station futile and transforming her into to a useless, powerless thing.

Afterward, she'd sat down in her office chair and taken her mother's gold ring out of her pocket, using her middle finger to twirl it across the bare desk like a graceful ballerina trapped in a hypnotic dance.

Then Chase had walked in and the ring folded under her finger, smacking against the desk.

"What is it?" Sterling asked crossly, rising from the chair.

Chase swallowed, unbuttoning the top button of his shirt and pulling it apart like he couldn't get enough air to his lungs. He ran his tongue over his cracked lips. "It's easier if I just show you," he offered, down to business. He waved at her to follow, and together they proceeded to the interview room.

The air dropped at least ten degrees in the hallway. The fluorescent lights looming above flickered uneasily, and she glared at them as if they were alive. She always hated them. The washed-out white light reminded her of neglected hospital wings, where people lay dying slow, painful deaths, confined to their beds like prisoners, muscles too weak and sick to step outside and let the warm sunlight touch their face. She liked to think if they did, they'd burst into flames, rising like phoenixes from the ashes, ascending into a world that loved them.

Ovi. It was a whisper, breathed into her ears like dandelion spores.

Suddenly she was there. The doors were all the same, the maze of hallways all impersonal and disturbingly sterile. Too white. Too empty.

And that smell... she thought. The smell crept into her nasal cavities, swirled around inside the fleshy tissue there.

Antiseptic.

Cleaners.

Hospital scented soaps.

Urine.

She felt lightheaded.

She dug deeper, further.

There was a flutter, and the scent of death was gone like a murder of crows into fog.

Sunflowers.

She remembered the sunflowers. The way they were the only thing in that cursed place that retained color. Golden yellow petals as long as her fingers. She remembered how she had been the one to bring them there, injecting life and color into a place where dreams ended and hope followed along after.

Ovi.

He was a shadow of himself that day. Just this thin, frail man with patches of hair who could barely support his own weight. She'd stayed there all night with him, holding his hand until the sun had come up.

And then...he was gone, and she had felt like the goddamn world had ended. Because it had. At least for her.

In a twist of fate, she'd come back years later, riding with the man after she'd put a bullet in his chest. She'd stayed by his side in the ambulance the way she'd stayed by Ovi's side. She remembered watching him in shock as he'd choked on his own blood, and she remembered she'd prayed to the darkness to take him, to remove him from the world because he didn't have a place in it.

Will that be you someday, Sterling Marsh? a voice in the back of her mind asked. *Feeble? Weak? Dying?*

Will you die there, too?

Or are you already dead?

She slowed, the joyless light skipping off her face.

"Sterling?"

Chase's voice. Soft. Worried.

She was standing in the middle of the hall. She came to, quickly wiping her eyes.

"You all right?" Chase asked.

"Yeah. Let's just get this over with."

As they passed dispatch, she glanced inside the shadowy room to find Rosa perched in her usual spot in front of the computer terminal. Rosa's face was vacant, blankly watching the glowing green screen, and she wondered what the girl was thinking. Wondered if she might tell Chase the truth.

A few doors down, a pair of composed voices conversed about the weather, but oddly enough made no mention of the spell over Drybell. She glanced inside and saw Max and Georgia inside the lunch room; Max's attention glued on his Rubik's Cube and Georgia leaned back in her chair, arms folded over her chest, eyes shut. She wheezed softly, lost in the dream world. Max looked up as they passed and Chase smiled out of the corner of his mouth, but Max didn't smile back.

They arrived at the interview room and Chase quietly latched the door behind them. The tape recorder was in the same place she'd left it.

Chase was pale under the harsh light, his normally silky blond hair greasy and deflated, eyes hollow and red.

"What's it still doing in here?" Sterling asked.

Chase walked over to the table where the tape recorder waited like an elephant in the room. "I don't know," he said humorlessly. "Felt wrong taking it out of here. God only knows what Georgia would say if she heard it. Figured this was the safest place for it."

Sterling moved to the table, standing alongside him.

"I listened to it a few minutes ago. It's..." his voice trailed off and Sterling looked at him expectantly. "Well, you'll see. Just play it."

Sterling held his eyes for a moment, then picked up the tape recorder and hit play.

There was a *click!* and the tape inside hummed to life.

At first it just sounded like a soothing variety of ambient noise, a stream of the barely detectable sounds that replaced the utter silence, making it bearable. After a few seconds, she detected the low rumble of thunder and the shrill call of the wind-torn wilderness. But beneath the tumultuous layers of the storm, she heard something else.

She couldn't make it out at first. It was barely there, just this faint shift in the wind, as if it had become sharper somehow, more severe.

Chase's hypnotized face was grave, cold with fear, and she knew that whatever was on the tape had finally been enough to get under his skin. Break through. She took a deep breath, comforted just the tiniest bit knowing that she'd finally have him in her corner again.

The sound began to climb, soft and erratic.

She turned an ear to the speaker, leaning closer.

Voices.

That's what it was. They were whispering. At least a dozen of them, shuffling about the room, changing in tone and pitch. All female, as far as Sterling could make out. They spoke unnaturally fast in a language she'd never heard before, their sound rising unevenly in her ears.

She looked at Chase and noticed he had withdrawn away a foot or two, his posture rigid as a flagpole and his forehead damp with sweat.

The ghastly murmurs continued their disturbing colloquy, all speaking rapidly out of turn at once, as if completely oblivious of each other, hissing bizarre, archaic words that cut through the empty room and ricocheted off the walls. She imagined a void of darkness, the entities like rabid animals snarling at each other, mad with rage.

"Chase? What the hell is this?" Her voice came out as a whisper itself, lost among the violence pouring out of the speaker.

Chase's eyes were wild now. He shook his head grimly, as if he could see what was coming, and began to step back. He shivered with fright, like whatever was set before them was beyond his understanding, beyond what he was capable of processing.

The whispers volleyed in time and space, climbing in a possessed crescendo. They snapped like hungry mouths, dissolving into guttural, animalistic wails that skittered over her skin and into her ears like vile centipedes, filling her head with horrible thoughts.

The voices abruptly began to cut out one at a time, as if a series of doors were slamming closed one after another in a long, black corridor from some dark corner of the universe that had been lost to eternity.

One by one, more and more of the horrible voices choked off, and the ones that lingered grew louder and more vicious, degenerating into something demonic. Something ancient.

Sterling's skin prickled with goose bumps; her stomach sucked up against her spine. Her hands were shaking now, and her face was wet with cold sweat.

Another voice dropped away, fluttering into the abyss.

Then another.

The last one was practically screaming now, like some stark mad raving lunatic locked in a walled off, forgotten room.

The viciousness alone made Sterling's blood run cold, and she noticed that her nails were digging into her palms, on the verge of drawing blood.

The crazed entity hissed a rapid-fire of unintelligible, commanding words, sinking octaves deeper until there was nothing human left in the voice.

Chase had backed into the wall now, and Sterling's own

hands were trembling violently as if she'd just swum through a lake of ice. The lights flickered with blackness, struggling to stay on. An impending doom swirled from the speaker like a deadly poisonous gas, and the voice kept on in a flurry, preaching the word of the damned.

She'd heard enough.

Sterling leapt for the tape recorder, seizing it from the desk. Her thumb on the button, she went to hit stop just as the erratic, fevered voice pulled tight as violin strings to composed, cold dead silence, and whispered,

"*STERLING.*"

The power snapped off, leaving them to their fates in a dark new world.

CHAPTER 24

THE SECOND CALL of the night.

Her face lit up like she'd just walked through the doors of Our Lady of Mercy, uncomfortably giddy with anticipation.

Thank God! Rosa thought to herself. *Finally, a distraction.*

Anything was better than sitting here all night with nothing to do but keep everyone's secrets. She thought about Chase, how he was walking around the station this very minute thinking everything was fine.

It was immoral. She wanted no part of it. The only reason she hadn't reported Sterling yet was because there was no one higher to report her to. At least not until the Chief got back tomorrow, and Sterling would be gone by then.

And the worst part? Chase didn't have the faintest idea what had happened, no clue that his wife was lying dead somewhere. Her hands were itchy with time. With lies. It was wrong what Sterling and Chase had done, and when she'd heard about what had transpired her heart had ached for Jennifer and Max.

The call.

"911, what's your emergency?" Rosa asked calmly.

She listened to the light rustling of the wind and the thunder on the other end of the line. Immediately she pictured the old payphone sitting on the outskirts of town, Maria's horrible contorted face looking up at her from the inside of the booth.

Though marred by the elements, the booth was in relatively good shape as far as phone booths went: a time machine constructed of brushed aluminum and faded blue panels, the only shortcoming an absent folding door. The thing had always given her the creeps, even long before she'd found her sister dead inside.

Rumor was that back in the early nineties, AT&T had come to collect the thing just like hundreds of other phone booths all over the country, but then Mayor of Drybell, Denton Farrow, had insisted that it not be touched, citing the eyesore as good luck.

Deep down she knew that wasn't the real reason. The fact was, the townspeople sort of got used to seeing the booth around as the years passed, and since superstition was as much a religion in Drybell as the Winter Festival, it was no surprise residents wouldn't dare take a chance in removing the thing from its sacred resting place.

But then why did the phone ring, way out where there was never anyone around to answer it? What was the point in having it so isolated? She'd been forced to drive past it every time she entered or left town, and it was like a scab being ripped off each time. Rosa wondered whose idea it had been to install it there in the first place, more than a mile outside of town. It just seemed like such a strange thing to do.

She'd hear it ringing sometimes when she arrived back in town after an afternoon visit to New Haven to see her mother, Guadalupe. It was always at night, and she'd pull across Old Ferry Bridge and see that eerie green glow draw nearer in the distance. The ringing would grow louder, and she'd twist the dial on the radio to drain out the sound and her dead sister's face. And then she'd see it there under that god-awful pale light, daring her to step inside and find out what happened to her sister.

The call!

She shook off the nightmare like water, composing herself in the chair like she always did. "911, what's your emergency?" she repeated.

The wind lulled to sleep on the other end of the line, and she heard nothing but the sound of rain. Intuitively, she knew it was the phone booth. She tried to fathom who would dare be out there in the storm on this night, but she knew there was no one.

Agitated, she said, "Hello? Is someone there?"

She listened vigilantly, patiently waiting for a voice, and prayed it wasn't her dead sister.

"Please, if you're—"

A sound so unbearable she couldn't find words to describe it screamed from her headset like a banshee. There was something horrific there, like getting a collect call from hell, and in a flurry of panic she wondered if that was where she would end up when she died.

She leapt from the chair, ripping the headset free from her hair and some of her roots along with it. The sheer intensity had nearly blown out her ear drums, and she checked her ears for blood.

She winced while the pain cleared, leaving only the ringing.

Ringing just like that phone.

The sound reverberated between her ears, clawing around inside her brain, her skull wobbly and heavy like a bobble head. She felt herself begin to shrink away in fear, shriveling away like a piece of rotten fruit. She tried to shake it off, carting the chair back to her station and sinking back into the seat.

She could still hear it lingering there, shrill and impatient as a fire alarm trapped in her skull. Her fingernails raked over the leather armrest, leaving long gouges. She spied small tufts of cotton jutting out.

She grabbed the cord, tugging the headset off the ground and cautiously holding it closer.

The sound was gone. She couldn't hear it: the storm, nor the rain, nor the ringing.

Her heart slowed and her mouth warmed into a smile.

The power moaned.

Rosa looked up at the ceiling, watching as the light panels in the ceiling shot off one by one with a series of loud knocks, leaving her standing in the darkness.

Out in the hall, a phone rang.

Her smile fell away like sand; the hopeful glint in her eyes dulling like oxidized metal.

Out in the hall, the phone continued to ring. She felt it rattle the bones in her body, jarring the fillings loose in her mouth.

No, she thought, shaking her head distrustfully. *It's just a coincidence.*

And yet it persisted, carrying on in the still of night.

She sat in the darkness for a moment, as if expecting the power to return. Her eyes darted about the room, taking in the dark corners and imagining something waiting there.

"Georgia?" she called out. She slowly rose from her chair and padded through the darkness to the doorway. The hall was a black tunnel. Empty. She poked her head out, squinting in each direction.

"Sterling, is that you?" she called out. "Georgia? You there?" her voice repeated, vanishing down the corridor.

The unnerving ringing kept on.

But where was it coming from?

There!

Rosa quickly traced the sound, powerwalking toward Sterling's office.

She turned the corner and flung open the door to find the room cleared out, everything carefully tucked inside a cardboard box on the side of the desk.

There was a simple white phone placed on the middle of the

desk. She eyed the thing suspiciously, cautiously stepping closer.

The phone wailed on, relentless.

When she finally couldn't take it anymore, she rushed over, snatching it from the cradle.

"Hello?!"

The wind greeted her again, lazy and carefree. She listened as it breathed against the receiver like crackling plastic.

"Who is this?" she demanded. "Answer me!" she said, voice climbing. There was a pause while she listened. "Please—say something."

The wind died down.

Someone was there.

Breathing.

They were on the other end of the phone, listening to her.

Her eyes snapped open and her face chilled with cold.

"Is someone there?" She barely heard her own voice. It was like she was immersed in an old black and white movie, the tension nearly unbearable now. The room felt like an ice locker. She saw her breath come out in small bursts of smoke. She looked at the window and saw the glass was thick with a layer of frost.

The person's breath hitched on the other end of the line, then sluggishly exhaled, like they were purposely trying to scare her. Rasping like a dying woman. The fine black hairs on her arms stood on end.

She began to pull the phone away from her ear and a woman's voice broke the silence. "Rosa!"

No. It couldn't be. It was impossible.

The phone slipped from her grip, thumping down on the carpet. She heard the voice shouting for her from the receiver, begging her.

She dropped down and scrambled for the phone.

"Please, Rosa! Please," the voice cried. "We need you!"

"Who—who is this?" she stuttered.

"Rosa, please! You have to hurry, there's no time. Please!" the woman screamed.

"Ma…Maria?" she gasped.

The woman on the other line hushed.

"Maria?" she said, clearing her throat. Her face was wet, and she realized tears were falling from her eyes. "Maria, is that you?"

She heard the woman snicker on the other end of the line, and it was one of the most awful things she'd heard in her life.

"Please," Rosa pleaded. "For God's sake, say something. Answer."

"I'm here, sister," the voice said callously. It was her, the voice clear as day, and she began sobbing into the phone.

"Maria, oh my god. Please, speak to me. Tell me where you are."

There was a string of steady wind on the other line and she knew her sister was in the booth. "I'm waiting for you."

Rosa swallowed. "Where? Please, tell me where!" she begged.

And the voice said, "In hell."

The line went dead.

Rosa clutched the phone in her trembling hand, her eyes huge and terrified, and she went to touch her crucifix and it was gone.

Another phone began to ring.

She let the handset fall to the ground and ran into the hall.

She followed the ringing to the break room.

Georgia and Max were gone, the chairs empty, the television hissing with white noise.

Where was everyone?

The phone wailed. She spun around, snatching it off the cradle.

"Maria?" she shouted, palms sweaty, face flushed with blood.

The woman cackled into the phone like a lunatic and Rosa's blood ran cold.

The line went dead.

Before she could set the phone down, two more phones began ringing elsewhere in the building. Her eyes darted to the open doorway, where the sound carried back to her from all over the building.

What's happening?

Her mind was racing, thoughts flying through her head so fast she couldn't fully process them all.

More rings assaulted the quiet night, and soon the sound was everywhere, coming at her from every room in the building, clawing at her ears and skin while the crazed laughter echoed in her ears.

I'm waiting for you, sister. In hell.

She sprinted into the hall, desperately racing through the building.

"Sterling!" she shouted. She slowed as she passed Chase's office, then the locker room. She threw open the doors to the restrooms. "Chase! Georgia! Max!"

Where were they all? Where had everyone gone? She began to pick up her pace again, jogging down the halls shouting for someone, anyone.

"Please help! Anyone!"

The phones continued to ring.

She burst through the door to the lobby and slid to a stop on the tile with a screech.

In front of her, beyond a wall of glass cold with rain, was a panoramic view of the most powerful storm she'd ever seen. Lashes of white-hot light webbed through black clouds in brilliant flashes, and she thought the sky looked like it'd cracked open like a black eggshell.

The ringing was only coming from one place now: beyond the entrance.

She looked over her shoulder, where she knew all there was was an empty, abandoned building.

They'd all gone. Left her alone.

She swallowed, her chest taking in long, shallow breaths. She slowly jogged toward the entrance, a pane of dazzling electric light, and placed her hands on the door.

As the door released open, the storm roared to life, blaring in her ears. She heard her pulse; felt the blood pounding with vigor and terror.

Down the wet concrete steps, in the middle of a black sea of asphalt, was the phone booth.

The chaos in her head grew louder, more intense, the thunder booming like bombs being dropped, and the flashes lighting up the dark sky like the sun was colliding with the Earth.

It was impossible, yet there it was.

The phone booth called to her from the distance, crooning and violent at the same time, like a woman gone mad.

She sunk into the pool forming at the bottom of the stairs. She couldn't feel the bite of the water; the ringing was the only thing that mattered anymore.

Her sister was calling her, and she knew she was the only one that could save her.

She was the only one that could end it.

She stopped short of the booth. Her eyes traced the entrance as the phone inside rattled on its cradle, beckoning her in.

It would stop soon. She didn't have much time.

She sucked in a deep breath, grabbed the cool metal edges, one with each hand, and stepped inside.

CHAPTER 25

THERE WAS A scream.

It was faint, but she heard it. Sterling shot up from the basement floor, a collection of faded manila folders gripped tight in her hands. Chase whipped around from the tall shelves of evidence bags, the witch's hat clutched in one hand, a tag in the other.

After she'd finished boxing up the few things left in her office, she and Chase had collected the witch's hat and the tape recorder and taken the stairs to the basement: a drafty subterranean archive of forgotten objects sealed away from the world in hefty evidence bags. Each item had been meticulously labeled and organized using a system that went as far back as Drybell's tradition itself.

"Did you hear that?" he asked uneasily.

Sterling swallowed, nodding.

There was a jolt and the door to the basement flew open.

Max emerged through the other side shouting, "Dad! Sterling! Come quick, something's wrong with Rosa!"

Sterling shoved the files back in the cabinet and slammed the drawer closed as Chase tossed the hat on the counter, both of them rushing to the boy's aid.

"What happened?" Chase asked quickly.

They each took a knee, crouching down in front of him.

"It's Rosa—she's gone crazy!"

"What do you mean crazy? What happened?" Sterling said hurriedly.

The boy's eyes were wild. He took a step back from them, animatedly waving his arms as he explained what had happened. "After the power went out, I had to go to the bathroom. Georgia was asleep, so I went by myself."

Chase exhaled in disapproval. "Christ! How many times have we talked about this? I told you not to go anywhere without —"

"Not now, Chase!" Sterling interrupted.

"I know, but I had to go and she was sleeping already!" Max defended. "I didn't want her to wake up. After I came out of the bathroom, I was walking back and I saw Rosa running down the hall."

"Running?"

Max nodded his head. "Yes, ma'am. She was running into all the rooms, shouting at the top of her lungs. She was scared."

Sterling and Chase exchanged a befuddled look.

"She said, 'Sterling! Georgia!'," he mimicked, his face pinched in bewilderment. "I tried to talk to her, but it was like she couldn't see me or something, so I ran to get Georgia. She tried to calm Rosa down, but she's gone crazy!"

Sterling got up, taking the stairs two at a time, Chase and Max's footfalls trailing behind her. She sprinted into the hall, tackling open the door to the lobby.

"Rosa, please!" Georgia's voice was muffled. "What the hell is the matter with you, girl, get away from it!"

Georgia was standing just beyond the lobby doors, hollering at the top of her lungs into the storm. Chase stopped short behind Sterling, throwing an arm across Max. "Go back to my office!"

"But, Dad!"

"*Now!*" Chase ordered.

Max looked at Sterling with hurt eyes, willing her to come to his defense. Instead, she nodded in agreement, turning away.

Max, betrayed, turned on his heels and stomped away, glaring at Chase.

"Rosa!" Georgia hollered.

Sterling rushed forward, throwing the doors to the station open.

The world whirled to life, the sky shrieking as it was lashed with whips of brilliant lightning, the terrain transformed into something alien.

Georgia twisted around, helpless and panicked. The makeup smeared around her eyes and lips made it look like her face was melting. "Sterling, thank God!" Georgia was breathing hard, on the verge of tears, struggling to stay upright in the wind, her shawl flapping around her wrinkled throat. "I don't know what's gotten into her. I tried to stop her, but she just pushed me away and kept going."

Across the parking lot, Rosa stood stock-still in a hail of windswept rain, completely drenched, body shivering.

Sterling and Chase surveyed the scene, watching Rosa as she stood at the throat of the storm. Georgia cupped her hands to the sides of her mouth and shouted, "Don't move, Rosa! Just stay still!"

Sterling's stomach turned, her eyes widening in horror.

Now she understood why Georgia was so panicked.

There was a massive dark shape in front of the girl, easily twice her size. "Oh my god," she muttered.

"Georgia," Chase said, forcing the calm in his words, "*tell me* that's not what I think it is?"

Without warning, the shape roared so loud it drowned out the thunder and rain and the sound of Sterling's own beating heart. They watched as the impossible shape doubled in height, holding itself there a moment, an immense shadow towering over Rosa and dwarfing her like a planet.

Sterling found herself stepping forward in horrified anticipation, her shaky hand on the Glock.

Georgia shrieked as the titan began to fall forward.

Sterling gasped as Rosa folded under the thing's enormous bulk, pancaked on the wet concrete with a heavy thud and a splash.

"*Shit!*" Chase yelled.

Sterling sprang into action, using the railing for balance as she flew down the wet steps two at a time, stumbling into the cold pool at the bottom. The parking lot was a lake, the water creeping up the tires and speed bumps.

The beast snarled and Rosa let out a bloodcurdling scream.

"Rosa!" She heard Chase's voice erupt from behind her, riding the vehement wind.

Up ahead, the frenzied shape violently mauled Rosa, the black mass tearing at the woman trapped beneath and the two thrashing against each other in one disturbing vision.

Sterling felt her feet begin to glide beneath her. Her right leg shot out from under her and she went down hard on the wet pavement with a painful grunt. The gun tossed from her hand, sliding through the water under a car.

Rosa screeched, her voice cutting in and out as the mass viciously tore at her. Her shrieking voice abruptly cut out, and Sterling dizzily slid under the car, seizing her firearm. Chase rushed over, helping her to her feet.

She wanted to scream to Rosa, tell her that everything would be all right, but the events were happening so fast she could barely get enough oxygen to her lungs.

They stopped short of the crazed, writhing bulk.

Covered in spikey, wet hair, the black bear must have easily been over four hundred pounds. She could barely see Rosa's body beneath the mad animal, only a motionless arm and mop of wet hair sticking out from under the creature.

Veins of blood fed the pools of rainwater that collected in

collapsed sections of the pavement.

Sterling quickly lifted her gun and took aim.

The gunshots exploded in the night like flashes of lightning. Chase stood beside her, discharging his pistol in cracks of white flame, unleashing hell on the possessed animal.

The bear barked, then backed away a foot or two from Rosa's lifeless body. The monster growled, baring its fangs and standing upright, rising to its full height. It bellowed furiously, howling as the bullets peppered its hide in small sprays of blood.

Sterling and Chase moved in together, unloading their magazines into the savage creature.

Click!

Sterling frowned, the bear still on its feet, manic with rage. She fluidly drew another magazine from her belt, ejecting the empty one and locking it into place.

They stood beside each other, guns in the air, and the bear loomed over them, its red eyes blazing with a murderous frenzy.

Then, the strangest thing happened.

The bear's mouth began to relax, the nightmare of pink-stained teeth peacefully falling closed, the primal roar slowly snuffed out by the wind, and the animal's possessed eyes widened, as if waking up.

And for just a fraction of a second, Sterling recognized something familiar in that creature's eyes: helplessness. The feeling of being possessed by something you couldn't ever hope to understand. A force that crept through the inky darkness with vile thoughts, whispering in your ear, seducing you when you're most venerable. Telling you that the bad things are okay. That the good is nothing more than a fantasy. The voice that spoke to you when you're on the edge, telling you how much easier it would be to jump.

Sterling thought back to what she'd done in her own bed earlier that night. Who she'd been thinking about when she'd lain there alone, tears streaming down her face, her shattered soul bared

to a heartless world that had turned its back on her and cast her into the cold, cruel streets.

The one who had never left her; never would leave her.

The witch.

The woman with the beautiful, dead eyes and the pale, fevered skin. Disgust bubbled up in her chest like acid, and her face contorted to a scowl.

She didn't pull the trigger, the hate did it for her.

The shot cracked in the air like a whip.

The bear's head rocked back, its enormous weight knocked off-kilter.

Chase startled, turning to see Sterling with the gun aimed down at the earth, her eyes blazing, wisps of smoke curling from the barrel.

The bear wavered, wobbling in the tempest, then drunkenly staggered back a step, fighting to hang on. The mass of blood and fur abruptly crumpled like a hundred rocks, its ravaged body colliding with the rear of a car before falling to the parking lot with a weighty splash.

Chase stared at her in awe.

Sterling shoved the gun back into its holster. She fell to her knees beside Rosa's head, then recoiled in disgust. Her hands hung there in the air, as if an invisible barrier had formed between them.

Chase waded over, flinching at the sight of what was left of the woman. "Rosa?! Oh my god, oh my god," he sniveled. "Is she dead?!" he asked frantically, falling on his knees beside her.

Sterling gently turned Rosa's head, looking for any signs of life. "Come on, girl, don't you fucking die on me!" Her hands slipped into something hot and sticky, and she realized Rosa's throat had been torn completely out, leaving jagged flaps of flesh dangling like wet parchment.

"Jesus!" Chase yelped in shock, falling on his ass.

Sterling moved her hands to Rosa's face, which remarkably untouched. The girl's brown eyes were pried open, the whites whiter than the moon, gazing at the hideous world above.

Sterling silently cradled Rosa in her arms and wept softly, letting her head fall against Rosa's wet hair and softly rocking her to eternal sleep. She gently brushed a strand of hair away from Rosa's face with a sad smile and said, "Goodbye, sweet girl."

Chase had helped carry Rosa's body inside the station. They'd brought it down to the basement and reverently wrapped her in one of the tarps. It was wrong, Sterling knew, but it was the best they could do without getting Leo the Coroner down here, and there was no way in hell that was going to happen in this storm.

They didn't tell Max what had happened. Chase had just explained that Rosa was tired and had decided to go home for the night. *If anyone deserved a break from this job, it was Rosa,* Sterling thought.

Georgia, on the other hand, was a mess. Sterling had excused the tired old woman, telling her to take a minute to fix herself up before she went back to watching Max. She wasn't going to be useful to anyone if she couldn't take care of herself.

Sterling wasn't faring much better herself. She'd cried more that night than she had her entire life, even more than when she'd watched Ovi take his last breath that morning, and at this rate she wondered if she was just about out of tears.

She and Georgia walked like the dead, shuffling back to the break room. Sterling had an arm hooked around the woman's broad shoulders, and both their hearts were heavy with loss. They stopped at the doorway, finding Max asleep. He was cuddled up on the torn leather chair, a vintage Winterview Watchers baseball cap pulled down over his eyes.

"I don't understand, Sterling," Georgia said quietly, sniffling. "Why would she do that? I mean, what would make her run out there into the storm by herself? It was like she went crazy in less than ten minutes."

Sterling frowned, shaking her head. "I don't know. I'm sorry," she said, knuckling tired eyes. "I wish I did."

But the truth was, she *did* know. Somehow, in a way she couldn't explain, she knew who was responsible, even if she couldn't prove it.

Georgia looked at her sadly, pulling Sterling into a warm hug. "She didn't deserve that. Good Lord, she didn't ever deserve anything so horrible." Georgia began to sob quietly, and Sterling pulled her tighter before tenderly releasing the old woman.

"Just stay here with Max until Chase and I can figure out what to do."

Georgia nodded, sniffling and wiping her eyes. "You don't think it's something to do with *her*, do you?" she said, shifting her eyes toward the dim corridor leading to lockup.

Georgia watched as Sterling carefully pondered the question in her head, her face widening as she came to the same horrifying revelation.

"Oh my god," she said, puzzled how she hadn't seen it before. "You think it's her, too, don't you?" It was rhetorical. "It *is* her, isn't it?"

Sterling exhaled, as if she couldn't believe it herself. "I don't know. But it sure as hell feels like it, doesn't it?"

Georgia's face was grave, like she'd just found out the world had ended. She blinked slowly. "What about Chase?" she asked, hushed. "What does he think?"

Sterling shook her head. "That it's this storm that's making people go crazy."

Georgia scoffed. "Isn't that just like him, though? Wouldn't believe in aliens if a spaceship fell out the sky and landed on his house. What more does that man need to see to believe it?"

Sterling shrugged. The fact was, there *was* nothing that would make Chase believe. He'd heard the tape, seen most everything she had, yet he refused to even consider the possibility that the witch was responsible for anything happening in Drybell.

A wicked glint shone in Georgia's eyes, something Sterling had never seen till that day. The old woman leaned forward, her breath cold and sweet. "You could make her disappear," she whispered. "You could just take her out in the woods and…" her eyes fell away before she could finish the sentence. But she didn't need to. Sterling knew what she was insinuating, and she'd be lying if she said she hadn't entertained the thought herself.

Sterling's face went hard. "I am a *peace officer*, Georgia. Not an executioner."

"But after tonight, you won't—" Georgia caught the mistake before it left her mouth. She gaped at Sterling, mortified.

Sterling said, "I help people, Georgia. Do you understand that? I am *not* a murderer."

Georgia frowned, ashamed of herself. "You're right. I'm sorry, Sterling. Forgive an old woman? Please?"

"Everything is gonna be all right, old girl. Just holdfast while we get this sorted out." She lightly patted the tops of Georgia's hands.

She nodded hesitantly. "Rosa—"

"I know," Sterling interrupted, looking at her friend with understanding. "I will figure out what's going on here. I promise you that. For Rosa."

Georgia smiled then, comforted as much as she could have been under the circumstances.

Sterling said, "Just stay here with Max and try and get some sleep. Daylight is only a few hours away. As long as we can keep it together until then, we'll be all right."

Georgia smiled resignedly, thumping a hand on Sterling's shoulder. "I can't promise anything, but by God I'll try." She gently slapped Sterling's cheek a few times, as if proud, then disappeared into the darkness of the break room.

The power surged again. The lights wavered above Sterling, sputtering.

A roar of static behind her.

She spun on her heels.

Dispatch.

She heard the static clear and a man's voice come through like he was talking through a blizzard.

Shit!

She sprinted into dispatch. The voice grew louder.

"Drybell come in, this is the Connecticut State Police, over," the man said.

Her face lit up like Christmas morning. The voice was music to her ears. She quickly grabbed the receiver and the cord yanked the radio off the desk into her arms.

"I repeat: this is the Connecticut State Police in Middletown. Marsh? Rosa? Is anyone there?" the voice said hastily.

"Phil?!" she shouted. "Is that you, Phil?"

Phillip Gilmore was her oak. She'd met him back in her days at the academy and never lost contact, even during all her years in Drybell.

"Marsh?" The static was coming back. "Marsh, is that you?"

The lights blinked and the radio briefly cut out.

She smiled with relief, laughing happily. "Oh, thank Christ! Yes, it's me. Phil, listen to me. Something terrible has happened here, people are dead and the storm—"

"What? Marsh—you're breaking up."

"We have an emergency here! People are dead, Phil! This is Drybell requesting *immediate assistance*. Please send all available units immediately!"

There was a moment of quiet as the static cut off again.

"Emergency?" the radio hissed. "What're you talking about? What's going on?"

The line dissolved into a roar of static. The lights in the building groaned one final time like its dying breath, then powered off completely.

"Phil? Phil?! *Shit!*"

The line was silent.

"Fuck!" she yelled. Her head fell on the terminal with a thump. She slammed the radio back on the surface with a clatter of plastic and metal and then exhaled, trudging back to the hall.

The corridor leading to the cells was nothing more than a black tunnel.

What's happening?

She looked up high on the wall beside her, where thankfully the floodlights were still glowing, the only lifeline keeping the midnight crew from dissolving into utter chaos.

Not them. Me.

She knew where that road would take her.

What waited at the end.

Who waited.

She cursed herself for being so close to getting help, a new void forming in the pit of her stomach, thinking about their last hope for survival going up in flames.

She stood at the mouth of the tunnel; her heart finally calmed to a normal rhythm. She listened to her blood pump in her ears, felt the beat in her hands and chest. She ran her tongue over aching lips.

"You could make her disappear." Georgia's thick, Southern drawl echoed in her head, a woman she'd never heard so much as mutter a swear.

"You could just take her out to the forest and…"

Georgia was right about one thing, she concluded.

Perhaps it was time to pay the witch a visit.

CHAPTER 26

THE TEMPERATURE DROPPED.

Lockup was beyond silent. She stepped into the room and waved the flashlight around, the beam slicing through the frigid air. The smell of wet concrete and urine permeated the oppressive space. Lightning crashed in the mountains through the slit windows, and thunder quaked the tomb-like walls.

"Sterling," a male voice said loudly.

The prisoner. His hands were fastened around the bars.

She cautiously walked forward, washing the light over him before turning it to the cold concrete floor.

"You're okay?" the man said skeptically, his doubting eyes scrutinizing her.

"Figured you'd be sleeping by now," Sterling said.

"Ah," the man said. His gaze trailed up and down her, astonished to see her in one piece. "Never was much of a sleeper. And with this storm?" he said, watching the flares of lightning through the small windows, "Forget about it."

Sterling regarded the man, then turned, gazing out the

windows into the eye of the storm. No trace was left of the mountains; even with the lightning, there wasn't much to see anymore. Darkness had nearly overtaken the world by that point, leaving only the few lonely souls in the station and more Christmas decorations than any one town should have.

"I heard gunshots," the stranger said.

Sterling sighed, nodding silently.

"Everything okay?"

Sterling shook her head. "No," she said regretfully. "No, it is not. Quite the opposite, in fact."

"You wanna talk about it?"

Sterling turned to the man. "Who are you? *Really?*"

The man turned away. Sterling could see that he was conflicted, like he wanted to tell her, wanted to confess all the bad things in his life, but he couldn't. For whatever reason, he could only stand there, breathing in the piss-stained air. She just couldn't figure him out.

The man brought his chin up and said, "I'm just an old man running out of time."

The man's hands were stone, his knuckles marred with splotchy pink scars and white nicks. His left ringer finger had a white band over the skin.

"You married?" Sterling asked. She saw a flash of Rosa in her head and nearly broke down again.

The man turned his hand, thoughtfully inspecting the strip of white flesh. "No. No, not anymore."

Sterling studied the man's face. His eyes were troubled but strangely at peace, as if he'd met many demons in his life and still somehow managed to hold on to his sanity. The longer she studied him, the more she thought she didn't mind his company. There was a way about him that not many people had these days. Something like decency.

"She leave you?" Sterling asked. She realized how callous she sounded and lifted a hand to her mouth, embarrassed by her insensitivity.

"It's all right." The man smiled wistfully. "In a way, I suppose she did."

A beat passed as they stood there looking at one another, each trying to figure the other out.

"She died," the man said. "Few years back."

Sorrow was etched in every word he spoke, and she imagined that whoever the woman was, she had meant the world to him.

The man cocked his head. "Aren't you going to say you're sorry? Isn't that what people do nowadays?"

Sterling shook her head. "No," she said with a dry laugh. "People say that like it's supposed to mean something, but I never understood why. Can't be sorry for something you never had control over in the first place. You ask me, it seems worse than saying nothing at all."

The man blinked, then nodded in agreement. "Yeah, I guess you're right."

"But I do hope you find peace," Sterling added.

The stranger smiled.

"You miss her?"

The man's smile fell away. He shifted uncomfortably behind the bars, head hanging. "Every day," he said. "She was like sunlight. Warm. Bright. Now all I can see is shadows. Just this…endless darkness. A road that never really ends, just keeps going…" He paused, then said, "But eventually, the clouds will clear up, and we'll see each other again."

Sterling mulled over the words, then stepped forward and wrapped her fingers around one of the bars, pulling herself closer.

The man exhaled. "What I wouldn't do for a cigarette right now."

"I don't smoke," she told him.

"I know."

Sterling looked at him.

"What was it, softball?"

Sterling raised her eyebrows.

"No," the man said, studying her hands. "Soccer?"

Sterling smiled. "Track, actually."

"Ah. That was going to be my third choice," he said with a smirk.

"I bet."

"Why'd you give it up?" he asked.

Sterling's eyes fell away. "I didn't have a choice. I was in an accident during college. My mother...she ran a red light Christmas day, and we got sideswiped by a moving van of all things. I had four surgeries but...my knee was...I can't run anymore. Not like I used to." Her eyelids beaded with tears and she turned away so the man wouldn't see them.

"Afterward, things changed between us. Our relationship before already wasn't great. Growing up there was always this...space between us. The sad part is, to this day I still don't know why. We both felt it, but neither of us would ever admit it," she said. "I didn't talk to her for *years*. I blamed her for it. For everything. Because it wasn't just my knee that got fractured that day. It was my whole life. I felt...broken," she said, swallowing. "I still do. Like there's a part of me I can't fix."

There was a long moment of silence before the man finally spoke. "Sterling?"

She wiped her eyes, looking back at him.

"I'm *not* sorry, Sterling," he said, smiling.

She choked up with laughter then, and her face broke into a smile. "Yeah..."

"Ain't that just like life, though? It will never hesitate to take the things we love most in this world."

"How'd you know?" she asked.

The man studied her face closely, taking in every blemish and line. "It was my job in another life—understanding people."

Sterling's lips parted. "You're a detective?"

The man looked at her, then reluctantly nodded his head.

"*Was*. But that was a long time ago."

She felt a tether of trust forming and knew that somehow, someday, this man would be someone vastly important in her life.

"One of our dispatchers was killed tonight," she revealed, deciding to reciprocate.

The prisoner's face hardened. "What happened?"

"Freak accident. It was..." her voice trailed off. Sterling cleared her throat, wiping her eyes. "She was attacked by a black bear. Out in the parking lot, if you can believe that."

"Shit." The man released the bars, pacing back in the cell. "That means..." he muttered to himself, mind racing, massaging his temples. "It's her. She's one of them."

"I don't understand," Sterling said. "What do you mean? One of who?"

"Sterling, this is very important," the prisoner said, deathly serious. "Has anything else happened tonight?"

"What do you mean? Like what?"

"I mean have you *seen* anything strange? Heard anything weird that you can't explain? Just—anything out of the ordinary."

Sterling nodded but didn't elaborate.

"The woman in there—have you ever met her before? Ever seen her here, in town?"

Sterling shook her head. "No. Not before tonight."

The prisoner's panic seemed to escalate further then, and it was as if he'd experienced everything she had that night.

"Have you been able to raise anyone on the emergency channels?"

Sterling shook her head. "I tried but...I don't think anyone's coming for us. At least not until morning."

The prisoner stepped forward, his face severe. "Sterling, listen to me very carefully. That woman in there? She's not who you think she is."

Sterling's posture stiffened. She pushed herself up straight. Had she made a mistake confiding in this stranger? "What do you mean? You know her? You know who is she?"

The prisoner quickly shook his head, gritting his teeth impatiently. "No," he snapped. "Look, I need you to listen to me. We're all in grave danger. You need to get your people together and get them out of here. Get them out *right now*!" The man was practically shouting now, warning her.

She raised the flashlight, quickly moving to the second cell and swinging the light up.

The weak funnel cut between the bars, lightning the concrete bunk and sink and connecting with the cinderblocks on the other side.

The cell was empty; the witch was gone.

Sterling's mouth fell open like she was trying to speak but couldn't get the words to come out. "Shit!" she shouted. She sidestepped, flinging the light back on the prisoner's face. "She's gone!"

"What?!" The man rushed to the corner of his cell and threw himself against the bars, trying to steal a glimpse of the empty cell.

"Wait, Sterling!" the man yelled. "You don't know what's out there!"

But she was already gone.

Her first thought wasn't of the others. It was her. How she'd be remembered by her friends. The Chief. How come morning, when the dust settled, *she'd* go down in history as the woman who let Drybell fall apart overnight, singlehandedly destroying the legacy of a town more than two centuries old. She knew it was a horrible thought, to be so selfish, but it was like a rusty nail jutting out of the corner of a decrepit wall that had torn open an old wound.

You really fucked up this time, Marsh, she thought to herself. *How could you have let this happen?* During her entire law enforcement career, she'd never had a prisoner escape. It was unheard of. As far as she was concerned, it had never happened in the history of the town, and now here she was, a gun in her hand with a lunatic loose in a building with a handful of civilians.

One less, now, though.

She winced, thinking of Rosa's gaping throat. The wet, torn artery and raw muscle. Her friend's blank, lifeless face, her dark eyes set on the storm hovering over them.

Had he helped her escape, the man in the cell?

No. It was possible, but she didn't think he was the type. He seemed just as worried about the witch getting out as she was.

More than worried.

Frightened.

Then how?

It didn't matter how she got out. What mattered was finding her before anyone else did.

She sealed the door behind her, the prisoner's muffled yells locked in with him.

He knew something. That much was obvious. But there wasn't time for that now. She needed to find the witch.

Up ahead, the fluorescent bulbs buzzed and flickered, blinking their sickly white light down the cinderblock walls. She thought about shouting, but she didn't want to alarm anyone she didn't need to. Especially Max. God, the kid looked terrified of the witch. She didn't blame him. The woman had an unnatural way about her, like when you watch a person just long enough to notice something is off, but can't really explain what.

She worked her way forward, emerging from the tunnel and skimming the corridor with her eyes. She blinked and saw herself back in that hallway in the hospital outside Ovi's room.

She blinked again and it was gone.

There was a cramp the size of a fist in her shoulder. She felt the muscle pulling taut, coiling in an acid bath.

"Sterling?"

She about jumped out of her skin. She whirled to the right, throwing the gun up.

Chase flinched at the pistol in his face, the cup of coffee in his hands splashing onto his jacket in a hiss of steam. "Christ, Sterling!"

Heart pounding, Sterling lowered the gun, exhaling.

"What the fuck are you doing waving your gun around like that?"

Sterling ignored him, quickly stepping into his office and easing the door closed behind her. "She escaped."

"What?" Chase said, brushing the coffee from his coat with his hands. "Jesus, that's hot!" he said.

"The witch—she got out of her cell."

"What're you talking about? She's out?"

"I went in there to check on them and she was gone. She's not in there."

"What do you mean *gone*? Then where the hell is she?" he asked bluntly. His face went red with panic. "Max…" He pushed past her, throwing the door open and rushing into the hall.

Sterling hustled out after him, breaking into a run.

Out in the hallway, they found Georgia and Max casually strolling toward them, practically sleepwalking, the woman holding the boy's hand.

Chase and Sterling halted upon seeing them. Chase sighed with relief. They looked at each other, feeling a bit ridiculous.

Georgia cracked a weak smile. "Sterling? Chase? What are y'all doing?"

Chase quickly made his way over, joining them at the junction in the hall that led to the elevator. He leaned down to get a good look at Max and smiled, wrapping an arm around the boy.

"Hi, Daddy," Max said.

Sterling exhaled, shaking her head as she approached. "What are you doing, Georgia? I thought I told you to stay in the lounge and keep an eye on him?"

"We was heading over to grab some snack food, weren't we, Maxy?"

Max bobbed his head, rubbing his eyes.

"Haven't been able to sleep much on account of all this lightning." Georgia looked terrible, at least ten years older. She flashed Sterling a grim look that what she really meant was what happened to Rosa. "We figured maybe we just induce it with a little sugar. We been craving all sorts of sweets, tonight, some reason."

Sterling frowned.

Max was latched to the side of Chase's leg while Chase kneaded the boy's messy hair with his fingers. He let his hand fall down to Max's shoulders and said, "Guess none of us are getting any sleep tonight, are we, Ace?"

Sterling said, "With the lights out, it's not safe walking around here right now. How about you two let us bring you back something?"

She gave Georgia a look and Georgia got the message loud and clear. She nodded, then dropped her hands on Max's shoulders. "You heard 'em, Maxy. Apparently, the Drybell Sheriff's Department is doing delivery tonight. That outta save us some trouble. Anyway, my knees are hurtin' something fierce tonight in this cold."

Ding!

The elevator.

They all turned to the end of the hall, where the elevator doors slid back and forth, malfunctioning. The bell kept on, chiming every time the doors opened and shut.

And inside, bathed in an unnerving red light, was the witch.

CHAPTER 27

THEORETICALLY, THE ELEVATOR shouldn't have been functioning. The backup generator had enough power to sustain the emergency lights and the radio equipment, but the elevator?

Not so much.

The group stood at the crossroads in the hall, mouths hanging open, faces frozen in shock. Max dug into the side of Chase's leg like a tick.

The air was sucked out of the corridor as the elevator doors closed with a final *ding!* and the witch was swallowed by blackness. They listened as the conveyance hummed to life, the worn steel cables creaking inside the shaft.

Georgia crossed herself, groping for Max.

Sterling stepped forward. "Georgia, take Max and get him safe. Don't open that door until either Chase or me is on the other side saying so."

Chase kneeled, peeling Max off his leg. "Daddy, don't go!"

He put his hands on the boy's shoulders. "It's going to be fine, Ace. We just want to talk to her. Stay here with Georgia until

I get back."

"But the witch—" Max cried.

But they were already gone, down at the other end of the hall.

Chase jabbed the elevator button, but nothing happened. He stepped back, perplexed. "What the hell?"

Sterling tugged on his sleeve, yanking him away from the sealed stainless doors. "Come on!" she snapped, shoving open the door to the stairwell.

They quickly descended through the darkness; their footfalls were heavy on the metal steps, echoing as if they were spiraling down a staircase to the center of the Earth.

The basement was silent. Sterling could barely believe this was the same room they'd been in no more than an hour ago. It seemed like a completely different place now, filled with unseen dangers and littered with gruesome true crime mementos. She thought of the witch hiding among the clutter, lying in wait in the shadows to spring on them. A ridiculous thought, she noted. As far as she could tell, the witch hadn't physically harmed anyone. On paper she would look as innocent as a nun at a murder trial.

But Sterling knew better.

She thought maybe even Chase did now, too.

Their flashlights crisscrossed the room, revealing lofty metal shelves crammed with hefty plastic evidence bags and boxes. The basement was damp, smelling of wet concrete and plastic. Black mold crept along the ceiling like moss, and hairline cracks in the walls bled rainwater from the surface. As irrational as it would seem, the thought occurred to her that the room would eventually be underwater.

Something wasn't adding up. Why would the witch come here? There wasn't any way out of the basement. No emergency exit. Just the stairs they'd come in from. Not even any windows.

Sterling surveyed the room, Chase flanking her side, his face knotted in a scowl. The gun was heavy in her hand and, holding the flashlight up in the other only made her realize just how exhausted she really was.

Sterling

The whisper fluttered through the air like bats. It was almost like the darkness was whispering to her, lulling her closer. Her fingers slid tighter over the pistol, swinging it out in front of her. A horrible notion came to her then, and her flashlight beam skittered along the cracked concrete floor to the tarp where Rosa's body lay.

She exhaled in relief.

It's still there.

Some part of her thought it might have been gone, that she'd turn around and Rosa would be standing there behind her, her dead, mutilated form fumbling for her, neck splayed open like a vivisected animal.

But no. The corpse was still in the same place, right where they'd left it. *Look at you*, she thought. *You think dead bodies just get up and walk away? How much longer are you going to keep chasing ghosts, Sterling?*

She heard Chase growl from the other side of the room and indignantly kick a pile of boxes. "Where the fuck is she?" he said, waving his light. The beam zipped about the room, raking over the swollen walls.

"There!" Sterling announced.

The witch stood at the end of two long shelves.

A dead end, Sterling realized.

"Hey!" Chase roared, voice climbing. He threw his light on the witch, rushing to Sterling's aid. He pushed past her, charging the witch like an angry dog.

"Don't you fucking move!" he yelled, stopping short of the figure. Chase was dumbstruck, as if words had escaped him. He'd become wary of approaching, and it dawned on her that the witch had retrieved her hat. It sat atop her head, completing the nightmarish caricature.

"That's why she's down here," Sterling breathed. "She

wanted her hat back."

Her skin slithered. She felt snakes scurrying through her hair, up and down her legs and tunneling inside her ears.

"Get your fucking hands on your head. Now!" Chase ordered. He stopped, keeping his gun trained on the witch and looking over his shoulder at her. "What are you doing?" he asked irritably. "Come on, Sterling, get your head in the game."

Sterling stepped forward, pulling her cuffs out of the leather pouch on her belt.

"I said now!" Chase barked.

This was all familiar. It was just like what had happened at City Hall. Only she was alone then.

"Chase," she started, holding a pacifying hand up, "just calm down…"

"No!" he snapped. He turned back toward the witch, growing more unhinged by the second. His posture tightened like a rusty spring. He paced another step closer, and Sterling could tell he was barely hanging on. "I have had just about as much as I can take of this freak," he said through gritted teeth. He took another step toward the witch, the barrel of the gun mere inches from her head.

"You come into *our* town. You *ruin* the last night we could have had together. And now you break out of your cell just to get your goddamned hat back? You just can't stop looking for trouble, can you? It's almost like…" Chase said, eagerly wetting his lips, "well, I'd say it's almost like you want to die." Chase's face relaxed into a sadistic grin Sterling had never witnessed before, and it made her heart race.

"Chase," Sterling said harshly. "You need to calm the fuck down. *Right. Now.*"

"You knew this bitch was the one causing all this, didn't you, Sterling?" he asked her, forcefully jamming the gun to the back of the witch's head. "You knew from the beginning. That bear that ripped Rosa to shreds? That was her. This storm. The bridge. All of it. I don't know how…but she's doing it." He paused, as if questioning himself, then repeated in a whisper, "Somehow, she's doing it."

"Okay, Chase," she said. "Say we're right. Say she is. Even if that's true, even if she is, well…that doesn't make this right. We are *not killers*." Then, with conviction, "It is not up to us to decide who lives or dies."

"Bullshit!" Chase barked. He unexpectedly lashed out, violently shoving the witch into the wall. "You and I both know she'd never see the inside of a courtroom. And if she did, it'd only be because she wanted to. To fuck with us. To fuck with our heads some more. Because that's what she does. She gets inside our heads."

Sterling lowered her gun, holding her hand out to him. "This is not the way, Chase," she said softly. She put a gentle hand on his shoulder. "This isn't you. You are not this man. You're Max's father. You are a *good father*. And that boy's daddy would not murder someone in cold blood like this. He wouldn't do it."

Sterling felt a wall inside Chase crumble. He stayed there shaking, breathing hard, his gun crammed into the back of the witch's head. He blinked lost eyes, like he'd been somewhere else altogether, then exhaled, hesitantly lowering his Glock.

"That's it," Sterling said softly, putting a steady hand on his gun and pushing it down.

And still the witch did not move.

CHAPTER 28

THEY LET THE witch keep her hat. Call it superstition, or fear of the unknown. Or maybe it was just a good old-fashioned lack of common sense.

They didn't care. The witch had gone through an awful lot of trouble just to get her hat back, and Chase figured letting her keep it was for the better. After all, if she didn't have a reason to want to leave the cell, maybe she wouldn't. Maybe she'd just stay there hibernating, like some kind of slumbering animal. They never did figure out how she'd escaped, and could only assume that one of them had forgotten to lock the cell door when they'd originally brought her in. It still wouldn't explain how she'd gotten through the entryway door, but they just wanted to put the incident behind them, wanted to pretend the witch couldn't just leave anytime she pleased.

The mystery man housed in the other cell hadn't uttered a word when they'd brought her back. He'd simply watched from the shadows as they'd shepherded her past him into the cell and closed the door behind her. The witch had stood there in the middle of the space, just as she had the time before.

That's the way they'd left her.

And she was in exactly the same place when Chase came back two hours later.

Sterling had taken the first shift. They'd decided that leaving the witch unattended was too big a risk, so they'd opted to take turns watching her instead. Sterling had told him she'd take the first shift, give him some time to ease his nerves, maybe get some father-son time with Max. God knows he needed it.

Chase found his son snuggled up next to Georgia on the leather couch in the lunch room, Max's chest blissfully rising and falling in shallow breaths. Georgia saw him coming and wearily formed a smile.

"Everything all right?" Georgia asked, blinking groggily. The back of her auburn mane was stuck up at an odd angle, and there was smeared mascara around her eyes like a raccoon.

Chase ran his fingers over his stubble and nodded. He quietly sunk into the chair beside them, lightly brushing a few strands of hair away from Max's closed eyes. "Thank you for watching him."

Georgia tipped her head.

"I don't know what he'd do without you, Georgia. Same goes for the rest of us."

Georgia sighed, readjusting on the couch. "It just keeps going, doesn't it?"

Chase cocked his head.

"The storm," she clarified.

Chase nodded. "Hmmm…"

"The rain keeps going like this, the town's gonna be underwater by the end of the week."

Chase didn't say anything, only kept watching Max sleep.

"How's Sterling holdin' up?" Georgia asked.

"I don't know." Chase didn't lift his eyes. "Sterling

is…*Sterling*," he said with a morose chuckle. "You know how she is. Just…sort of trapped in her own head. Keeps everything close to the chest, because God forbid she let anyone actually see what's going on inside there."

"Girl's just been hurt an awful lot, that's all," Georgia said shrewdly. "Hurt by people she don't have no business getting hurt by."

Chase was quiet.

Georgia took a deep breath. "Sometimes I wonder what life be like if I just did everything crossed my mind. Acted on every impulse, didn't have to think about who it was gonna hurt, or how it was gonna hurt them."

"She had a choice and she made it," Chase said unapologetically. "I wasn't the only one there that night. It took two people."

Georgia scoffed. "You damned fool. When you gonna understand that people liable do anything if they're hurting bad enough. Come on, Chase. Did you really think jumping into bed together would solve all that girl's problems for her? Did you really think you could 'rescue' her?" A beat passed between them. "No. Course you don't. And that's because she don't need you to save her. What she *needs* is to find her own way. To find the path she's meant to walk down. Ain't nobody that can show her where that is. Not me. Not you. Not anybody but her."

Chase smiled, shaking his head and standing up from the chair. "Isn't many people that will give it to you straight, Georgia. But I'm afraid in this case, you don't know what you're talking about."

"You look me in the eye and tell me that again," she replied. "Only this time take a good hard look at what's happening around here."

He exhaled with frustration, checking his watch.

"Y'all go on down to the chimney now. Burns," Georgia murmured, snickering softly. "Burns. Black chimney… Smoke."

"What?" Chase asked blankly. "You say something, Georgia?"

Georgia looked at him oddly and smiled. "Oh. No. Just dead tired is all."

Chase chortled, easing back in the chair and kicking his feet up.

She was right. Every word. But what was done was done, and right now all he wanted to do was sit with his son in peace, and enjoy the sound of the rain, and maybe, just maybe, let his eyes close for ten minutes of undisturbed peace.

So for the next two hours, that was exactly what he did.

He'd woken later to the sound of Georgia's rattling snorts. Max was splayed out next to her, one leg dangling over the side of the couch, his head dug into the woman's side, the leather bag still slung around his shoulder.

Chase wiped the drool off his face and scrubbed the sleep from his eyes, checking his watch.

Right on schedule.

He rose from the chair and made his way back to the cells.

Sterling was wide-awake when he arrived. She stood up, astutely looking him over.

"You feeling better?" she asked.

"Yeah, I think so. Slept damned near two hours."

That seemed to make Sterling ease up a bit.

"How's things here?" he asked.

The prisoner was flat on the concrete bed in his cell. Chase couldn't tell if he was asleep or awake, but he was quiet enough it could have been either. Chase turned to the other cell in disbelief. "She hasn't moved this whole time?"

"Not so much as breathed," Sterling said. A beat, then: "Look, if you're not up for this…"

"Just give me the damned keys before I change my mind."

"Be careful," she warned, slapping them down in his palm. "And if you need me for *anything*—"

"I'll be fine," Chase interjected.

"Chase..." Sterling said.

"I'm *fine*, Sterling." There was a tense moment between them. "I had a moment, but I'm fine."

Sterling regarded him. She didn't trust him to be left alone. He could see it clear as day.

"I promise," he said, softer this time. "Okay?"

Sterling's frown lightened. "You want anything? Coffee?"

Chase shrugged. "No. Thank you."

"You sure?"

Chase nodded. "Thanks anyway."

Sterling turned around, closing the door behind her.

Chase took a deep breath, putting his hands on his hips. He moseyed toward the prisoner, thumbs tucked behind his belt, peering in through the bars to find the man sitting up on his bed looking out at him.

"What're you looking at?" Chase said.

The man laughed, twisting his head until there was a dusty crack.

"Something funny, stranger?"

"This department."

"Come again?" Chase asked, stepping forward.

"It's a joke," he replied. "I've seen better run DMVs."

"That a fact?"

"That's a fact," the man said dryly.

"You've seen the inside of a lot of jails, I reckon."

The man chuckled again, grinning. "More than you know."

Chase scoffed. "Well, unfortunately for you, you picked the wrong town this time."

The two men stared each other down a moment, the tension fueling the fire in the room.

"That right?" he asked, his voice gravelly. He stood up and it was then Chase noticed just how tall he was. Easily over six feet, the man could have been a million different things. A criminal. A boxer. An old war hero. A politician.

A policeman.

The man casually approached the bars, fearless. "Small men usually use big words," he said. "You a *small man*, Chase?"

Chase glowered, feeling the blood rush to his face. Beads of sweat leaked down his temples and neck, slipping under his shirt.

"You just picked the wrong night to piss me—"

The man's arms flew out between the bars. Before he could reach him, Chase squeezed the Taser's trigger.

The man jerked back violently with a hiss of electricity, collapsing hard to the floor, his body convulsing.

Chase sighed nonchalantly, unlocking the door and stepping into the cell. He loomed over the man, shaking his head. "Tsk tsk."

The man groaned, gritting his teeth.

"I told you," he began, drawing the club from his belt, "you picked the wrong person on the wrong night."

Just as the man began to stir, Chase whipped the club through the air, cracking him on the side of the head and knocking him out cold.

Chase got down on his heels. "You should have kept your mouth shut."

He lugged the man across the floor, working up a worse sweat and heaving the man's body onto the concrete slab, folding his arms so it would look like he was sleeping.

Chase leaned down and put his ear to the man's face.

He felt his stale breath, weak but there. He chided himself for taking the risk, but then again, he was done putting up with everyone's shit.

He closed the cell door, twisting the key and securing it before casually walking along the bars, raking the club against them with a series of metal clangs, stopping in front of the second cell.

The witch was still as usual, and it made him uneasy knowing that she could stir so much fear in him without so much as lifting a finger.

God, you're a sorry excuse for a deputy, he thought to himself.

"Fucking scared of a Halloween statue…" he murmured.

Chase twisted his head and saw the man was just as he'd left him.

That'll teach him to mouth off.

A warm air brushed his face, heating his skin like he was standing next to an open flame.

He turned back and gasped, "*Shit!*"

The witch's frozen eyes burned holes through him, mere inches away from the bars, practically within arm's reach. He stumbled back in surprise, knocking the metal folding chair over with a shrill clanging sound. He was pressed to the wall like a fly, arms braced at his sides, breathing hard as he beheld the horrible thing across from him.

She moved!

"What—the—fuck!" he shouted. He tore himself off the wall and flattened a hand on his thundering chest. "You fuck—" he muttered, laughing to himself. "You stupid…"

What was the worst that could happen? She was locked up. She could have grabbed him if she wanted to, but she didn't.

Which meant that she was just toying with him.

His laughter molted into a growl.

She'd made him look like a fool.

Not once, but twice over.

He thought about how nice things were before the witch had come to town. How routine. And how now, they were anything but.

The witch remained there on the other side of the bars, staring across the room in his direction, the hat tall on her head, a reminder of the power she held over them.

"Fuck it," he muttered, picking up the chair and setting it back upright. Without lifting his eyes from the witch, he swung down, hunched forward.

And the witch remained, staring across at him. His eye twitched and he slapped a hand to his face, kneading it out of his skin.

Maybe the witch wasn't looking at him at all. Maybe what she saw was deeper, the place where his darkest impulses lay dormant, waiting for just the right thing to come along and wake them up.

CHAPTER 29

THE MAN IN the cell over was sleeping peacefully. Chase had made sure he was going to wake up with one hell of a headache come morning.

An hour had come and gone, and the witch still hadn't moved an inch. Fortunately for the Drybell Sheriff's Department, Deputy Chase Adkins hadn't either. He'd sat there and stared right back at her, a scowl on his face like the witch was the physical manifestation of everything he'd ever hated in his life. His left eye twitched and he felt it deep inside his head. Like something inside him was waking up. He just didn't know what.

The witch stared, and he stared right back.

The room was on fire. He thought this strange on account of the storm, thought he should be able to see his own breath by now without a working heater, but no.

Just a fever, he told himself. *That's all it is. Just a fever...*

An uncomfortable shiver trembled through him. The bite from the cold was getting in, he just couldn't feel it because he was burning up from the inside out. The nagging thought came to him that he was getting sick right before Christmas, and that was all he needed. He'd promised Max they could go down to Jennifer's parents' place for Christmas, and he'd never seen the boy look so thrilled. He liked Jennifer's parents well enough, but man were they hoarders. Every room in the house was crammed with trinkets and knickknacks. He just didn't understand it. Jennifer had learned to live with it growing up in that house, yet she wasn't a fan of the clutter either. But her parents loved Max. Every time they'd visited they'd bake him a fresh Pumpkin Pie and enough extra gravy to turn his mashed potatoes into soup. Then come morning, they'd exchange gifts and make a trip to Silvers Hollow for breakfast, where they'd stroll the town plaza after and build a snowman that'd make Jack Frost proud.

The daydream iced over in his head, freezing solid before his very eyes. There was a pressure in his chest like he had an elephant sitting on him, and his throat was raw like he'd been screaming his lungs out.

He glanced outside, watching the lightning flash beyond the mountains. He wondered how many more bears roamed the valley, how many were out there this very moment in the storm, stalking through the darkness for blood. The same kind that had ripped poor Rosa's throat out.

He turned and glared at the witch.

Hands shaking, he zipped his jacket, popping the collar up.

As he sat there uncomfortably on the cold metal chair, pondering everything that had become of his life in the last month, he eventually arrived at the biggest question of all:

Who was the witch?

He stood up and heard his body crack. Small beads of sweat rolled down his face. He reached up and brushed them away. His shirt was sticking to his ribs, and his boxers were pulled up awkwardly on one leg under his pants.

He stopped in front of the witch, looking her up and down.

Her face was attractive, there was no denying that, but it had an eerie quality about it, like the people you saw in old oil paintings from centuries past. Her unblemished skin had a sheen to it like a snake, and the hollows around her eyes were dark, like she hadn't slept in a hundred years. With the exception of her face, neck, and hands, her skin was concealed under a dark coat and dress embroidered with intricate patterns. Clothes from an older time was his guess.

And finally, the hat. The final detail to complete the bizarre ensemble. A tall, pointed thing fashioned of dozens of leathery patches in all different shades, most of them so dirty they were practically black. The scraps were crudely stitched together, and his mind went to dark places thinking about what they might be.

He realized his face was twisted in disgust. He rubbed the fatigue from his eyes, forcing himself to relax.

He slowly lifted his hand in front of the witch and waved it back and forth. She didn't flinch, trapped there in a stasis of sorts, his wave going unnoticed.

An idea came to him.

He walked back to the chair and picked up his flashlight.

The beam snapped on, the funnel bright as gold. He grinned, proud of his cleverness, then looked at the witch.

He swung the beam up.

The light poured onto the witch's face like a blast of fire.

An electrical hiss.

A sharp crack.

The light went dark.

Did he see…

No, it couldn't have been.

He could have sworn in the split-second before the light shut off that the silver in her eyes had gone black.

He stood there shaking, the useless light pointed at her face, listening to the lull of the rain.

His heart was pounding.

The witch hadn't flinched. In the shadows, her eyes were

practically glowing now, two moons in the darkness. As soon as the light had died, he'd immediately known he'd made a mistake.

"What are you?" he breathed.

He stood frozen, a mouse trapped in a shoebox with a snake; a thing so terrifying it could swallow him whole and leave no trace.

Maybe even the entire town, too.

A muffled voice.

Thank you! he thought.

He turned toward the entrance door, where on the other side, he listened to a garbled voice calling for him.

He looked one last time at the witch and saw the glow in her eyes had gone, leaving her a dreadful silhouette in the moonlight, and he counted his blessings she was on the other side of those bars right now.

The voice grew louder.

He heaved the heavy door open with a groan.

A woman lingered under one of the pale floodlights in the corridor.

"Is anyone there?" she cried. She had her back to him and she sounded frightened. "Please." Her voice was infinitely louder than before, bouncing off the brick walls.

Was it... Could it be...

"Jennifer?"

The woman turned and all of the weight of that night lifted off him like the world had woken up.

"Chase?" she said.

Her eyes lit up and she ran to him.

"Jennifer!" he shouted.

She threw herself into his waiting arms.

"Chase!" Jennifer sobbed. "Thank god, Chase, thank god."

Chase held her tight, clutching at her as if she were a life raft and realizing for the first time that he never wanted to let her go again.

"I was so worried," Jennifer said softly in his ear. "The phones weren't working, and I haven't been able to get a hold of you these last few hours. I was scared to death something happened."

Chase fumbled for words, speechless, and the rush of emotion was almost too much after everything that had happened. The smell of her hair, the warmth of her skin. His senses fired back to life, and the reality hit him that she was here with him now. That he wasn't alone to face this nightmare anymore. That their family was back together like it should have been in the first place.

They stood there under the emergency lights in the corridor, and it was like standing in a dream. Only he couldn't decide if he wanted to stay, or wake up.

Chase gently pried Jennifer from him and said, "What are you doing here? Sterling said you were at the house?"

Jennifer sniffled, pulling her arms across her chest.

Chase took off his jacket, draping it over her shoulders. Her teeth chittered and her skin was wet with rain. She grabbed the sides of the coat, pulling it tighter over her.

"After we talked earlier the power went out and I got scared. I couldn't get a hold of you and I—"

A panicked look washed over her face. "Chase, where's Max?"

She began to turn, but Chase put a hand on her shoulder. "He's fine—he's with Georgia. I checked on him a little while ago. She's been looking out for him while we deal with this mess."

Jennifer eased a hand on her chest. "Oh, thank god. Are you sure he's all right? I should go check on him…"

"No, don't," Chase said. "He's fine. They're sleeping. He needs it." And while he wasn't lying, the truth was he wanted her here with him. *Needed* her here. He couldn't face this night alone anymore. His strength was dried up like a river of sand and rocks, and he needed his family if he was going to survive until morning.

Sterling had been there, sure, but she really wasn't. Not in the way he needed her to be. She'd been all over the place that night, her mind off somewhere else entirely. He'd tried and tried to get through to her, but she'd rebuffed him at every turn. It was pointless, he'd decided. And who was he kidding, there was no turning back time. They'd made one bad decision and ruined a good thing. He thought it was cruel the way the world worked. How one bad choice could change the trajectory of your life, derailing a million good things in the blink of an eye.

Sterling had never forgiven him for what happened, even if she'd said otherwise. Even if she said it wasn't his fault. He wondered sometimes if she blamed him, but he didn't think as much. Georgia sure as hell thought he was responsible, but Sterling had taken responsibility for everything that'd happened since he'd met her, and he didn't see her changing that now.

Tigers don't change their stripes, Jennifer's mother used to say. *Once a cheater, always a cheater.*

What a disaster.

The truth shall set you free.

Bullshit, he thought.

All the truth had done was ruin what little sex life they had left. Well, that and get Jennifer to threaten him with divorce papers, alimony, and custody talks. All within the span of a few days.

He cringed thinking about it. He couldn't imagine a life where he didn't come home from a long night and find Max sitting at the dining room table eating a bowl of Cheerios and working on a jigsaw puzzle.

All because of one bad night.

He thought back to that night in her office. Sterling had been in bad shape, hardly herself. She'd never been particularly talkative, but at that point she was just downright silent. Sure, there had been something there between them all those years. Small flirtations here and there, holding each other's eyes a little too long. But they never acted on it. *He* never acted on it.

Because he was a married man. Not necessarily a *happily* married man, but a married man all the same. He wasn't miserable by any means. He loved Jennifer. There wasn't any part of him that disputed that. But after eleven years of marriage (and another two when they were engaged) the spark had dimmed considerably. They'd made love three, four times a year, if that. He'd try sometimes and she'd try others, but the timing just always seemed to be off. Between raising Max and their jobs, they were exhausted.

That night Sterling had been the worst he'd ever seen her. He'd come in to check on her and she'd looked up at him with those breathtaking dark eyes.

Jennifer had been after him about the gutters again. Hounding him about clearing the leaves before the rain, snow, and Connecticut wind came and made a mess of the property. The trees were already shedding like dogs, and the leaves were everywhere by then, like orange and yellow splotches of paint covering the forest.

Couldn't she just understand that he was tired? That he'd get to it when that pain in his shoulder calmed down and he could actually turn his neck just once without feeling like his head was going to snap off?

So he'd left then, Jennifer firing off a string of expletives as he slammed the door behind him, her voice exploding like a star. He'd arrived at the station not long after, hauling all that simmering resentment to work that night. He'd been in and out most the evening, responding to one call after another while Sterling had stayed behind to work on her correspondence.

When he'd arrived back at the station and walked into her office, Sterling had looked up at him and he'd seen the sadness and desperation in her eyes and had reminded himself that he was flesh and blood, that he needed love too. That he deserved something better than what was waiting for him at home.

They'd taken each other then without a word, hungry and reckless, oblivious of the fallout it would bring to both their lives.

But as it turned out, the grass isn't always greener on the other side.

Chase regretted it the moment they'd finished.

He'd laid there with her the rest of the night, holding her the way he knew she'd yearned to be held. He'd stayed there, eyes open, staring off into space while she breathed in and out. The arrogant slice of him thought he could actually fix whatever had broken, maybe help her move past it while helping himself retain his sanity at the same time.

She was his boss.

His friend.

And in a moment of horror, he realized he'd successfully ruined three relationships in one fell swoop.

At first, he tried to go on, keeping this secret that was burning a hole through him. He carried it around like a cancer while he tried to act like nothing had happened, just going on with his life like the world hadn't shifted beneath him.

He'd betrayed her, the woman he'd loved all those years, the way he'd vowed he never would. Eventually, the secret became unbearable.

So he'd told her and they'd fought into the night until the sun came up. They'd both fallen asleep that morning holding each other, agreeing to salvage what was left of their marriage. But the betrayal would linger, like a ghost living among them, reminding them what had died.

Yet somehow, miraculously, Jennifer had forgiven him.

And now she was here.

She'd come back after all.

He didn't think he'd ever been so happy to see her than at that moment. A swell of emotions began to rise up in him, and a dam broke inside. "I'm so sorry," he said, choked up. "I'm so, so sorry."

Jennifer's face softened. She stepped forward, putting a hand on his face. Chase held it there, closing his eyes and feeling the cold of her skin against his. "I wish I could take it back, but I can't," he cried, tears falling down his cheeks. "I fucked it all up, and now I don't know how to fix things. I don't know how to get us back. I don't want to lose you."

A glint of lightning flashed and he saw a silhouette of bars on the walls beyond her. His eyes caught them and began to lift, but Jennifer gently turned his face to her.

"You're right," Jennifer quelled, and he could see her eyes pooling with tears. "There isn't anything we can do to go back. You made a mistake. But you? Max? You're my whole world, and I will *never* let you go."

Chase's sobs quieted then.

Jennifer gazed at him and he at her, two people lost in the storm that had uprooted their once complacent lives. Unexpectedly, she stepped forward, pressing her mouth to his like she was saving his life.

He felt the heat of her breath, the chill of her hands on his face. His eyes went wide with surprise, his heart kicking in his chest. He began to kiss her more urgently, pulling her body to him. His hands worked their way under her wet shirt and found cool skin as her hands moved down his body, desperate in a way he'd never felt before.

Minutes later, they weren't but two shapes in the darkness, breathing fast and heavy, hoping to bring back to the world everything that they'd lost.

Chase was too preoccupied to notice the fly merrily buzzing through the air, zigzagging and whirring over their vigorous bodies while outside the stomach that was the sky grumbled, hungry and awake.

CHAPTER 30

THE BUZZING. MAX heard it loud as lawnmower blades in the darkness. His mouth was bone-dry, and there was a tickle on his cheek; tiny legs soft on his damp skin, scrambling up his face. His eyes twitched beneath closed lids, caught halfway between a dream and sleep.

He smelled Georgia's perfume, the one that smelled like roses, and he remembered how he'd fallen asleep on her shoulder earlier. He didn't mind. She was like a big pillow, and he thought he fit nicely there slumped up against her.

There was a harsh snap and the hat was in front of him. He saw himself hurtling through the black hole inside until he was so far gone nobody could find him and there was nothing left *to* find.

A pop of glass, like a bulb detonating. His eyes shot open to find a fly using his eyelashes like a ladder. His back was soaked, and the collar of his shirt was wet with a ring of sweat.

Georgia was nowhere near him.

He heard keys jangling and glimpsed Sterling as she patrolled past in the hall.

He was breathing faster now, could feel his chest going up and down, and he squeezed his eyes shut and prayed the fly would go away.

He wanted to shout for Sterling, tell her to come quick, but he was stuck, paralyzed while the fly skittered over his face. He listened as her footsteps echoed down the hall, then heard the big door at the end open and close with a metal groan.

The buzzing was so shrill it was unbearable. The fly casually scuttled across his naked blue eye like it was a frozen pond, and for an alarming second, he thought the foul thing might try and force its way inside.

Sheer panic jolted him into action. He sucked in a giant gulp of air and bolted upright on the couch, slapping at his face like he was on fire. The fly dodged his slow hands, zipping into the air in a loop before disappearing into the hall.

Panting, he spilled off the couch onto the floor and used the table to push himself up. One half of his shirt had come untucked and his collar was flipped up in the front. He straightened his bowtie and tucked his shirt back in, then glanced around the room to find Georgia standing in front of the Christmas tree.

"Georgia?" he murmured.

There was a crunch of broken glass, then more crunching.

He heard something slip from the tree, colliding with the train in a tiny derailment. The cars launched through the air, wildly flying off the track. He tracked it with his eyes as they slipped past his feet and across the room, crashing into the wall.

"Georgia? Are you okay?" he asked, a quiver in his voice.

He saw her doing something to the tree but couldn't see what.

The sound of branches and ornaments moving.

Was she redecorating the tree?

He took a step closer, his hands tight on his satchel. He had a bad feeling about this. That was what Rosa always said, and now he was starting to understand why she said it.

More glass crunched, like it was being smashed up in

someone's hands. Georgia was breathing heavy and her hands were busy doing something on the other side where he couldn't see.

"Georgia?"

She stopped and lifted her head as if she were listening for something.

"What're you doing?" Max asked with a gulp.

He could hear her wheezing breaths, could practically hear his own heart beating in his chest like a drum.

Something wasn't right. No, something was not right at all. She'd been acting sort of funny before. He didn't think too much of it when she'd say things he didn't understand, but now…well, now he most definitely did.

He listened to her moan like she was trying to speak, and he took a step back, bumping into the table.

Georgia's voice climbed like she was holding a scream in her throat, and it chilled him to the bone like he'd just jumped in a pond of ice water.

"What's wrong, Georgia?"

He needed to get someone. Anyone.

He looked out at the hall, but remembered hearing the door slam closed after Sterling had passed by. She'd never hear him here. And his daddy was already in there!

Georgia shuddered, and it sounded like she was blowing a gallon of snot out of her nose.

He took a few more steps back, anticipating what was coming next.

Georgia cocked her head toward the ceiling and screeched something awful, like a bird gone crazy. He clapped his hands over his ears as the hulking woman whirled around.

Max gasped, slamming into the bulletin board behind him. There was a flutter of papers like doves flying past his head.

Georgia's mouth was a bloody mess of broken Christmas bulbs and flaps of jagged flesh. Her gums were shredded, and her teeth were covered with so much blood he couldn't even see them.

He tried to scream, but a squeak came out of his throat instead.

"You've been a naughty boy, Max. A naughty, naughty boy," she growled, cackling manically. Georgia let loose a wet laugh, and it caught in her mangled, bloody mouth, bubbling up like she was using a voice changer.

There was a glint in the moonlight, and Max noticed something shiny in her hand. Georgia raised it into the air and screeched, charging toward him, her voice crazed and low. "So naughty! You're a naughty boy! And naughty boys need to be punished!"

Max screamed.

CHAPTER 31

CHASE WAS GONE.

The metal folding chair was empty. The world was submerged beneath a steely gray darkness. Sterling watched the air shimmer the way it did when the asphalt was supercharged during the grueling summer heat.

Make no mistake, it was *hot*.

Her skin was sticky, and for once she almost wished she was out in the rain letting her skin get drenched with cold.

"Chase?" she called out.

Heavy rain blasted the thick windows like a carwash. She imagined the station hurtling through space, destined for a black hole, and pondered what would happen when they got there. She heard once that if you jumped into a black hole it would stretch you in opposite directions, transforming you into a nightmare resembling elongated strands, like spaghetti noodles. That's how she felt now, this thing being pulled in a million different directions, stretched to the breaking point.

She looked up at the window, where the shadows of ragged branches writhed like tentacles from monsters hidden away in the darkest corners of the universe. She thought of the black hole again and questioned if she'd already reached it.

Would she remember anything after?

Would she go crazy, losing what little peace of mind she had left?

Would the matter she was made from be rearranged this very moment, transformed into something else entirely?

Or would she still just be herself? Alone and afraid.

Guarded, Sterling stepped forward, eyes darting about the jail.

Where the fuck is he?

In the cell closest, she saw the prisoner stir, looking up at her with a troubled expression. He groaned, letting his head fall back on the slab.

"What's wrong?" she asked.

The man nodded. "Where is he?"

"I was hoping you could tell me."

There was a flapping sound.

Sterling drew the Glock from her holster.

She could barely hear it at first, thought maybe it was a sound riding the wind in from the storm, but the longer she stood there while the lightning screamed at the world, the clearer it became.

She frowned at the man in the cell, noticing a smear of dried blood on the side of his head. "What happened?"

"He did this."

"Who? Chase?"

The man nodded.

"He did that?"

"I figured it was fairly obvious." Without getting up, the man gently fingered the laceration, wincing in pain. "He's not thinking straight."

Sterling stepped closer, looking him over.

"What are you talking about?" she said.

"He started talking to me, and it was like he couldn't hear anything I was saying. He just kept talking and getting madder and madder." The man noted the empty chair and rose from the concrete slab like he was coming off the worst hangover of his life.

Movement in the witch's cell.

Heavy breathing. Grunting.

The cell door was wide open.

The man in the cell put up a hand, cautioning her. He mouthed the word, "Wait."

Sterling shook her head. She was the Sheriff, and she'd be damned if she was going to let anyone tell her procedure in her own station.

She rushed forward, gun out in front of her, throwing herself in the entryway to the cell.

Her breath hitched. The blood left her face as her eyes widened in revulsion.

Inside the cell, Chase was breathing hard, pants around his ankles, his white buttocks flexing in the shadows, the witch pinned beneath him like a corpse.

Sterling stood in disbelief, hands shaking, watching him writhe on top of the witch, her soul ground to dust.

"CHASE!" she roared.

Chase froze as if he'd awakened from a dream.

He was a mess of labored breaths, his hair matted to his forehead with sweat. He turned sluggishly and peered over his shoulder at her, finding the gun trained on him.

"Sterling?" There was an innocence in his voice that made her heart ache. He gazed at her, fixed in that awkward position as the light returned to his eyes.

The gun was a hundred-pound weight in her hands. She wanted to scream at him. Unleash all of her fury and anger and hate like poison, but all she could do was look down at him with pity in her eyes.

Chase studied her for a few seconds, like he was waking up, remembering an old friend.

His face went hard, the wrinkles tightening. His confusion morphed into horror as he came to. His eyes went giant as he flipped around, a moan escaping his throat as he found himself on top of the witch.

The witch stared back at him like a dead body, her big, otherworldly eyes reflecting his own appalled face at him. A sound came out of him, a mix of disgust and horror. He lurched back from her, clumsily falling to the cold concrete. Violent and shaking, he grabbed the bars and heaved himself to his feet, jerking his pants up.

Sterling wanted to call out, to ask what happened, but she was too upset to speak.

"Fuck—what the—" Chase sniveled, wiping the sweat from his face, staring impossibly at the witch. "What—" His clumsy hands fastened his belt. He half-shrieked, half-screamed as the full realization of what he'd done hit him. He backed away, slamming into the bars with a crash.

"Sterling! What's going on over there?" the prisoner called.

Chase was pressed into the bars as if he was trying to pass through them. He had his hands held up in front of him, trying to shield himself from the realization that he'd committed the horrific act.

"It wasn't her," he murmured quickly. "It wasn't her. Wasn't her. Wasn't her."

Sterling looked at the witch, who was slumped against the wall.

"Sterling? What is it? Are you okay?" the man repeated.

"Just shut up a minute!" Sterling snapped.

"Wasn't her. Wasn't her. Wasn't her," Chase muttered, a blubbering mess. He was white as white could be, and he was practically catatonic. Chase retracted his hands toward his face like a frightened child. He began to whimper, sinking down to the floor.

Sterling steadily got down on one knee.

"Chase," she said sternly, lightly slapping his face.

"It wasn't her. Wasn't her. It wasn't her. I saw her."

"Chase!"

There was a *snap!* and something in her voice finally broke through to him. She gently put her hand on his face and pried it away from the witch.

She said, "What're you talking about? What happened?"

"It wasn't the—" His voice broke like he didn't want to say the word. "It wasn't her, Sterling."

"What are you talking about? Who was it?"

Chase's face relaxed as the thought came to him. "It was Jennifer. She was here. She was here with me."

"Jennifer?" she asked, her voice going up an octave.

Chase swallowed, eagerly nodding. "She was here," he repeated, jabbing a finger at the ground. He was coming back. His voice was settling, coming down to its usual low timbre.

"She's not here, Chase," Sterling said softly. "She was never here."

Chase laughed sharply, shaking his head. "No. No no no no no," he argued. "She was here. She was right. Fucking. *HERE!*"

His scream startled her, and she sprang up, tripping a few steps back.

"Goddammit, Chase! What the hell is the matter with you?"

Chase scrambled to his feet and stormed out of the cell. "She was here, Sterling! I touched her. I held her in my arms."

Sterling chased after him. "You better explain to me what the fuck is going on in your head because what this looks like—"

"What?!" Chase asked, whirling around. "*What this looks like?*"

"Talk to me, Chase," she said. "I am trying really hard to understand what's going on here…"

"That's the whole point! It's exactly what it fucking looks

like!"

Sterling held her hands up in front of her, attempting to calm him down.

"It's her!" he said, poking an incriminating finger at the witch. "She's been doing something to all of us! Trying to make us go crazy or…or…something!"

Sterling looked at him pleadingly. She had wanted so badly for him to see what the witch had been doing all night that she almost regretted it now.

Chase paced around the room like a nervous dog. He combed the sweat into his hair with his fingers, then turned to her like he'd had an epiphany. "Jennifer was here, Sterling. She was right here. *She* did something to her. I know it."

Behind Chase, Sterling saw the prisoner standing idly at the bars, looking forlornly at her.

She had to tell Chase the truth.

As if the prisoner could read her thoughts, the man subtly shook his head. *No*, he was saying. *Don't do it*. Eyes locked on her, he mouthed the word, "Don't."

"It wasn't her, Chase," Sterling said, and she saw the prisoner's eyes turn sad, as if she'd let him down, shunned his advice yet again.

"I told you, Sterling, I *saw* her. She was here—"

"She's dead." The sentence cast a spell of cold through the room like a winter breeze. As the words left her mouth, she saw the prisoner smack the bars with an open palm and curse under his breath. "Shit!"

The oxygen was ripped from Chase's lungs. He wobbled in front of her, drunkenly swaying, tears rolling down his cheeks.

"At City Hall," Sterling offered.

"What?" he said. Betrayal was etched into his face. His mouth hung open and there was a pinch between his eyebrows. "What are you saying, Sterling?" There was doubt in his tone. Panic was building now. His breathing was climbing, chest rising and sinking rapidly.

Sterling sucked in a deep breath, then turned and saw that the witch was still slumped in the cell against the wall like a broken doll.

"She's dead, Chase."

"No." Chase shook his head in disbelief. "That's not true."

"It is." The finality in her tone was evident.

"No." He was backing away, his face teetering on the throes of splendid horror. "That's impossible..." He was shaking his head back and forth. "I talked to her on the phone, hours ago. She... She called and I heard her."

"No," Sterling said, more insistently this time, stepping toward him. "The phones haven't been working all night. You know that. She's dead, Chase. I saw her myself."

Chase slid his gun out of the holster and leveled it at her.

She quickly raised her Glock, "What the fuck, Chase!"

"You're lying."

"Is this what we're doing now? Huh? Is this what all these years working together has got us, pointing guns at each other?"

"I don't believe you," Chase told her. "I don't believe you."

"Come on, Chase—I'm not lying and you know I'm not!" she said. "Now take that fucking gun off of me and let's talk this through like friends."

Chase let out a choked laugh. "Friends? *Friends?*"

"Yes. Friends."

"I saw her," Chase said to himself. "You're a FUCKING LIAR!" he screamed. His emotions soared and crashed, lashing out at her manically. "You're lying! You're just trying to get back at me!"

"Get back at you?" Sterling said, stunned.

"Don't bullshit me, Sterling!" Chase barked, thrusting the gun in her face. "You blame me for what happened. You think it was my fault! Ever since that night together you've acted like you were the only one with something to lose around here." He glared at her, and she never thought she'd see him look at her with such loathing and it broke her heart. "Well I've got news for you! You are *not* the only one who lost something that night," he spat. "My marriage is *fucked* because of you!"

Sterling took the blow like a kick to the stomach.

"I tried to help you, Sterling," he cried, tears streaming down his face. There was regret in his words, and she knew in that moment that their friendship was over and could never be saved. "I tried to help you."

"Chase, I'm…"

"You never said sorry before," he said, "and you're not sorry now. I can see it in your eyes. And I'm the stupid asshole that never wanted to see it."

They stared each other down, guns drawn.

"You know, it all makes sense now, what you said back at the diner. That man you shot," he said, lifting his eyebrows, "I thought maybe you said what you said because he deserved it. But now I see that has nothing to do with it at all.

"It's why they didn't clear you to come back, Sterling. Because they knew there was something fucked up inside you."

"Chase, please—"

"Those psychological tests the court ordered? The ones you *failed?* They were right, weren't they? You're so fucked up you want to take everyone down with you. You're just like *her*," he said, nudging the gun at the witch. "You want to watch the world tear itself apart."

Chase flipped the gun back on her. "Where's my wife, Sterling?"

Sterling stared at him, the gun trembling in her hands, her face red with tears. "I already told you."

"*Where is she?!*" he snarled.

"At City Hall!" Sterling shouted.

A beat passed between them as he waited for her to elaborate.

"Rosa got a call from City Hall and I went there and… I tried,

Chase. I tried so fucking hard," she admitted. "When I got there, Jennifer was standing on the balcony. About to jump off."

"No."

"I tried to talk to her," Sterling continued. "I *tried* to help her, but…she jumped. She's dead."

"No…" Chase shook his head.

"It's true."

"No!" Chase yelled. "You're a fucking liar!" He paced back and forth, shouting, "She wouldn't do that! She would never do that!"

"I saw her jump," Sterling said. "She's dead, Chase."

"Liar!" Chase screamed.

He rushed toward her.

Her finger tightened on the trigger.

His smile came to her then. Not the demented grimace he wore now. His real smile. The one she'd fallen in love with all those years ago. She remembered his kind blue eyes. His generosity. His crooked smile.

She couldn't do it.

She couldn't pull the trigger.

She closed her eyes as Chase slapped the gun out of her hand. He seized her by the throat, practically lifting her off the ground, and slammed her against the bars.

She could hear the prisoner's distant shouts echoing in the room; metal clanged like he was trying to break out of the cell.

"What did you do to her, Sterling?!" Chase bawled.

She raked her chewed nails at his face, carving jagged scratches through his skin. His burning hands squeezed her throat, suffocating the life out of her. He dropped a hand away and grabbed his pistol, painfully jamming the gun into the side of her neck.

His breath was rotten, hot and rancid with rage. "So help me God, Sterling, I will *end you* if you do not start telling me the FUCKING TRUTH!"

She could only stare up at him helplessly as his eyes blazed.

There was a flutter of air to her left. A dark blur whirled out of the corner of her eye.

Chase grunted in surprise. He released her, jerking his head to the right.

The witch stood a few feet from them, facing the wall.

"Goddammit!" Chase roared.

Coughing, Sterling clutched at her throat, falling to a heap on the ground.

Chase's attention burned on the witch.

"You fucking crazy bitch," he spat. He stomped forward and violently shoved the witch from behind. Her face slapped the cinderblock wall with a thump and her head bounced off.

He seized her by the back of the neck and slammed her forward again, pinning her against the wall. He twitched, wincing as if in pain. "It's her," he said through gritted teeth. "It's her, Sterling."

"Chase..." Sterling pleaded, fighting to get her breath back. "Wait..." She had to find a way to get through to him.

"Shut up!" he yelled. "All of this—it's her. And I'm going to put an end to it before it gets to all of us. Right. Now." He dug the gun into the back of the witch's hair until it met her skull.

"Max," Sterling croaked. "Max..."

Chase froze.

"Chase..." Sterling panted. "You kill her...and you are...never... going to see...Max...again. No matter what they find here...they'll lock you up. He...will have...no one."

Sterling pushed herself to her feet, holding onto the bars to steady herself. Her legs were Jell-O, and her throat felt like it had a snake coiling around it.

"You can't...do this...Chase," she rasped.

The wrath that burned in Chase's eyes dimmed. The gun slowly withdrew from the witch's head. Chase held it out in front of him, the heavy thing shaking in his hand, fighting whatever had overtaken him.

"There's still time. You still have time." Sterling gently talked him away from the edge of the abyss.

He shrank away from the witch, letting the gun fall slack at his side. He looked at Sterling and his bottom lip trembled.

She massaged her throat and nodded.

It's okay. Everything is going to be okay.

Chase broke down crying. Sterling moved forward and took him in her arms the way Ovi held her the day she found out she'd never run again. Never soar the way she once did.

His body was racked with sobs, quivering like a dying, suffering animal. Chase groaned and, as she held him against her, she felt the deep cuts in his heart, the wounds that nobody would ever see below the surface, the pain of a lifetime of mistakes and regrets.

The same ones she wore so well herself.

We're the same, she thought, and then she looked to the witch who, despite having her face battered into the wall, didn't have so much as a nosebleed.

"I'm so sorry, Sterling…" Chase said.

"Shhhhhh…"

"I wish things could have been different. I wish—"

There was a wet *splat!* and Chase's body subtly jolted.

"Chase?" she said. She gently pulled back and found his eyes open wide, the whites showing far too much.

She felt something warm on her hand.

No.

There was too much of it now. It was trickling over her skin, sticky and hot. She lifted her hand and gasped.

There was a wet sucking sound, and she watched a geyser of dark blood spray out from his neck.

Chase's rigid hand went to the wound, his other clutching at Sterling.

"Ster—" he wheezed, "—ling…"

She backed away in horror as he collapsed, blood spurting halfway across the room from the gaping hole in his throat.

Standing behind him, Georgia grinned dementedly, a blood-stained letter opener in her hand.

And she heard Chase's voice in her head one last time. Something he'd said less than a week ago, when he'd caught her listening to one of the voicemails she'd saved from her mother.

You can listen to those voicemails as many times as you want, but it's never going to bring her back. Anna and Ovi—they're gone. It's time to move on.

Georgia started toward her.

CHAPTER 32

GEORGIA GRINNED, THE gleaming letter opener clasped in her plump fist. She threw her head back and chortled, half-coughing, half-choking, shaking herself to pieces like a dying machine.

Sterling dove to the ground where Chase flailed around like a fish, weakly holding a hand to the gaping hole in his throat.

There was blood everywhere. It was pooled around his head on the concrete floor. The vessels in his left eye had burst, leaving a bloom of red around his iris. He coughed, choking on his own blood.

"*No no no no,*" Sterling said, panicked. "*Georgia?*"

The massive woman loomed over them, her face expressionless.

"What'd you do, Georgia?" Sterling said. "Christ!" She pressed a hand to the side of Chase's neck, her fingers smearing hot blood. He coughed again and spit up blood. "What the fuck did you do?!" she shrieked. She looked up at the woman and saw her staring down, face blank.

She felt Chase's body snap rigid; his arms and head contracted tight. He convulsed, and she fought to keep him steady. His jerky movements settled into quiet shivers.

"Hang on, Chase, hang on!"

He was losing too much blood.

His movements grew weaker.

His arms and legs stopped shaking, settling to stillness. His face was pale and ashen, the blue sparkle gone from his eyes. He stared up at her like he didn't understand what had happened, and Sterling realized he was gone.

"*No, Chase, no!*" she screamed. She began to weep, letting herself fall on his chest. Her hands slid over his face. She felt him the way she'd remembered that night and cried harder.

She heard the man shouting in the cell, screaming at her to get up, to move, but couldn't bring herself to look up.

To care.

All that was left now was that infernal buzzing in the air and the sadistic storm carrying on in the Painted Mountains.

Georgia teetered like a house of cards in the wind. A trickle of drool leaked from the side of her mouth. Her eyes were glazed over. She breathed slow and long. Her fingers twitched, tightening and loosening around the letter opener.

Sterling sniffled, listening for Chase's heart, but heard nothing.

She listened as Georgia breathed steadily above her.

She couldn't bring herself to face the woman. The woman she'd confided in all these years. Told secrets to she'd never told anyone else. The only true friend she had in Drybell.

An eerie moan escaped Georgia's lips.

Sterling heard Georgia's foot squelch in the pool of blood a few feet over.

The gun was out of the holster before Georgia could take another step, cocked up at the woman.

Kill her, Sterling told herself.

Georgia was fighting it. She groaned like she was crying inside, and Sterling couldn't bring herself to look up at her friend. She held the gun out in front of her, her finger hovering on the trigger.

She squeezed her eyes shut and tears rolled down her face.

Unless you want to die right now, pull the trigger!

The man had stopped shouting now. All Sterling heard was the demented buzz in the air.

She let out a choked sob as Georgia took another wet step.

Kill her unless you want to die!

The gun trembled in her hand. She squeezed it harder to get control of the gun. Of herself.

Georgia crooned the horrible noise, lumbering closer.

She's coming!

The woman took one last step and this time Sterling saw her white shoe sink into the puzzle of red on the floor.

You have to. It's self-defense. She remembered another time she'd told herself that very thing. The night she'd looked Jimmy Glanzer in the eyes as he'd choked on his own blood, clutching for her. Her mother's face came to her then. The bruises. The convenient injuries. The police had done nothing, even after Anna had fallen down that staircase and cracked her head open on the floor. Ovi had been taken from her by way of cancer and now Anna was gone too thanks to her stepfather Jimmy Glanzer and his temper. Only, unlike with the cancer, this time there *was* someone responsible. Someone who needed to be punished. Someone who deserved what was coming.

Sterling began to squeeze the trigger.

Do it now!

The buzzing was in her head now, crackling and incessant. It was the voices from the tape recorder. The yattering of something ancient.

Sterling, a voice whispered.

Then silence.

She couldn't do it.

She cried out in agony and frustration as if she'd been stabbed already, letting the gun fall away.

She forced herself to look up.

Georgia held the letter opener rigid in her hand, her arm cocked back behind her, her mouth twisted into an insane smile. Her bloodshot eyes were so wide they looked like they might pop out of her head.

She remembered the way the lightning lashed beyond the windows, remembered the way the blood was sticky on her hands, the sound of her heart slowing in her ears as if time was coming to a stop.

She let her eyes fall closed peacefully, not wanting to see what was coming, and she almost smiled then, thinking about how nice it might be to be gone from the world, a place where hurt and loss seemed to be the only things she could remember.

There was a sound, like something striking metal.

The next twenty seconds happened fast.

Georgia grunted sharply, like the breath had rushed out of her.

Sterling heard a jingle of metal echo off the concrete floor and a whoosh of cold air. She opened her eyes and saw a blink of confusion on Georgia's face. She locked eyes with the stunned woman, as if held by some unseen force.

Georgia grunted as she was yanked back, brutally slamming into the bars with a grunt like her soul was fleeing her body.

Sterling winced, nearly feeling the blow herself.

It was the prisoner.

Powerful forearms flexed around Georgia's thick neck. She strained like a rabid animal, her bloodstained teeth bared. She dug her fingers into the man's skin to pry his arms away, but it was no use.

Chords jutted out in the man's forearms as Georgia gasped for air. Sterling watched her flail against the bars, struggling to get free.

The man grunted, straining harder yet, and Sterling was surprised Georgia wasn't decapitated by his sheer strength.

Georgia rasped, and Sterling could see she was slipping.

She saw her old friend come back just long enough to say goodbye, and then her body went slack, held up only by the prisoner.

The man released her, and Georgia's body collapsed to the floor.

On the other side of the bars, the man panted, looking down at his own hands in shock.

It was over.

Rosa. Chase. And now Georgia. They were all gone. All her friends. She was the only one left, now, aside from the prisoner.

And Max.

Max! her mind shrieked.

She quickly composed herself, standing up. She looked over to find the witch standing in her cell, just like before. She rushed forward, cautiously grabbing the door to the cell and swinging it closed with a metal screech.

She half expected the witch to move, but she didn't.

Georgia was right, I should have done it when I had the chance.

"Hey." The prisoner's gruff voice.

Sterling paced over to the man. She skidded to a stop, Georgia's crumpled remains at her feet. A dagger twisted in her heart, and her eyes welled with tears.

"Sterling," the man repeated, more harshly this time.

She looked up to see him on the other side of the bars, an edge to him she hadn't noticed before. Like he'd been places she'd only ever seen in nightmares, survived things nobody else had. And it scared her.

But he'd saved her. Done what she couldn't. Part of her hated him for it, for choking the life out of one of the only good people she'd known in the world. But there was no other choice. And right now, he was the only one left, and she thought she just might need someone dangerous if she wanted to make it until morning.

The prisoner's dark eyes blazed, and he said, "Get me the fuck out of this cell."

CHAPTER 33

A SHEET OF thin glass crunched into a web as Sterling's fist collided with the WORKPLACE SAFETY GUIDELINES.

When it remained there, she ripped the frame from the wall and hurled it across the room. She threw a leg out and caught the monitor square in the center, kicking it off the edge of the desk with a weighty crash of glass.

"Hey!" the prisoner shouted. He moved forward to calm her and she shoved him away. "You need to *calm down*!" he snapped, nodding his head toward Max, who sat huddled in a chair in the corner of the room, his head slumped down, his worn eyes locked on the floor.

"Listen to me, goddammit!" the man yelled. He seized her by the arms, and she fought him every inch, kicking and shoving.

Seeing her extraordinary pain, the man forced his arms around her like he was attempting to calm an angry, frightened child. She fought him still, but she finally relented in sobs, her body juddering.

"It's all right," the man whispered. He spoke with the

confidence of a father, a man who knew when to push and when not to. "That's it. You're all right. Just breathe. That's right. Breathe…"

But she wasn't all right.

She was anything but.

She stood there with her head against his shoulder, heart pounding, Max looking across at her as if she'd gone crazy. She took a deep breath, letting the wasps in her chest settle.

After she'd secured the witch as best she could, she'd released the prisoner from his cell. By this time, the rules had gone right out the window, any policies and procedures serving no purpose now other than to annoy her. And as far as she was concerned, this man was the only help she had left in this shit show.

Together, he'd helped her scour the station for Max, finding the young boy hiding in the janitor's closet under a pile of mops and cleaning rags. Max was shaken up pretty badly, explaining that Georgia had started acting funny not long after the incident with Rosa. Georgia had frightened him, he'd said. She'd looked at him scary-like with a mouth of blood and picked up that shiny thing and come after him.

So he'd ran.

He'd tried to find Sterling and Chase but he couldn't, so he'd hidden himself away the best he could, praying his daddy would come along eventually.

After they'd found him, Max had called for Chase, wanted desperately to see his daddy. He'd pleaded with Sterling, begged her to know where his father was, and Sterling could only look at him with a frown.

She couldn't do it. Couldn't be the one to destroy his life.

After a while, Max had given up asking. She could see he was just happy to be safe, and the creeping thought that she'd eventually have to tell him the truth lingered in the back of her mind.

Sterling stared at the boy, blinking with tired eyes, and he stared back. God, she was a mess. She turned away from them and unzipped her blood-stained jacket, balling it up and throwing it aside.

She drew in a long, exasperated breath, as if trying to absorb all the calm left in the room to ease her strained nerves.

"Max?"

Max perked up in the chair as much as he could.

Sterling said, "I'm going to go out in the hall and talk to my friend here. Just wait here for a minute till I get back, okay?"

Max nodded, pulling his knees to his chest and resting his head on them.

Sterling led the man into the hall, pulling the door to the office closed.

"The DHS aren't coming, are they?"

The man shook his head. "No. I'm sorry."

"Then who? Who's coming?"

The man stared at her.

"Four people have lost their lives tonight," she said furiously. "Four people I've known for what feels like my entire life. *Good* people."

The stranger looked away.

"I don't care who you are or what you did, but I need an explanation as to why these people had to lose their lives tonight," she finished.

The man slowly shook his head, and she sensed that he was debating something much bigger than himself.

Sterling put a hand on his shoulder and the man smiled sadly.

"You ever looked into the eye of the storm, Sterling? I mean really looked and seen what's there, wrapped up in all that... violence? Seen what's behind the rage, and darkness?"

Sterling was silent.

"Because I have," the man said. "And once you've seen what's inside, you can never, ever unsee it. Do you understand?"

Sterling's face was grave, etched with new lines she didn't

remember having before tonight. She nodded.

The stranger sighed, almost relieved, like he was glad he would finally have someone to share in his secret. He peered down the corridor, where he knew the witch waited patiently in the cell.

"They've been rounding them up," he admitted.

"Rounding *who* up?"

The man considered her, then said, "The monsters. They've been searching for them. Trying to collect them. The ones they could, anyway. Some of them they can't. They've tried. They've been trying to keep them locked away. From the cities." A pause. "From people."

"Who?" Sterling asked.

"People who want to study them. They think that if they can understand where they come from, how they work, they'll be able to use it somehow for themselves."

A terrifying thought came to her. "Wait," she said. "You're saying there are…there are more of them out there?"

The man tipped his head. "A lot of them are like animals. Just mindless, hungry things running around in the dark. Forests. Basements. The ocean. Most the places you'd imagine."

"My god," Sterling whispered.

"But there are others that are smarter. Ones that think," he said, tapping his temple with his finger. "And *those* are the ones that are the most dangerous."

The man was quiet for a moment, lost in thought, and Sterling tried to imagine what skeletons he might be drudging up in the graveyard he called his memory. What sort of awful things he knew about the world that others didn't.

The man cleared his throat. "About a week ago, I got word from one of my contacts that a 'package' was being transported due south. I don't know where."

Thunder rumbled in the Painted Mountains, and they both listened to the wind.

Sterling cracked the door and peeked into her office. Max was still curled up in the chair, attention set far away as he stared out the window at the storm.

She gently tugged the door closed again.

"Why'd you crash into it?" Sterling asked. "The truck. Why here? Why Drybell?"

The stranger shook his head, smiling out of the corner of his mouth. His hand raked over his stubble, and she thought of Chase. Thought of how he was lying dead in lockup in a pool of his own blood.

"So?" Sterling asked sharply. "Why'd you do it? Why crash the truck?"

"That wasn't supposed to happen," the man laughed. "It was an accident."

"An accident?"

"I didn't mean to crash it—I was trying to steal it."

"Why?"

"Because I am one dumb sonofabitch. And I wanted to make things right," he replied. She saw the sincerity in his eyes, the man's words drenched with a profound regret. One which Sterling couldn't truly fathom. The stranger smiled wistfully. "I wanted to send her home."

"What is she?" Sterling asked, shaky.

The stranger put his back to the wall and let his head tip back, exhaling. His breath carried a hint of cigarettes.

"You've seen her," the man said with a chuckle, motioning down the hall. "What's it look like? She's a witch, Sterling. An honest-to-God, real live witch."

"No shit. I mean where did she come from? The Salem Witch Trials? Some fucked up black magic ritual?"

"No," the stranger said, shaking his head. "Nothing like that."

"Then where?"

Sterling's persistence amused him, his mouth curling into a smile. "She's not from the Salem Witch Trials. Not from any event you'll find buried in a book. No, our lady is from somewhere else entirely. I've been tracking her for months now. Ever since I got wind one of them was here. Didn't know it was her back when, but still…"

"One of *who*?" Sterling asked, more urgent this time.

The man looked at her gravely. "The Thirteen Witches."

"The Thirteen Witches?" she repeated. "Is that supposed to mean something to me?"

A shadow fell over his face then, and Sterling sensed she was about to be dropped into a rabbit hole of which she'd never return.

"Imagine a place, Sterling. It's sort of like here," he said, glancing out the window at the end of the hall. "It has mountains and rivers. Valleys and trees. Only they're different than the ones out there that you've known your whole life. They're vibrant. Strange. Like a painted world you'd see in a dream. Bright and glowing with these *impossible* colors. Colors no one's ever seen in their life. Least no one here. It's kind of like Heaven, really, this beautiful place where magic and fairy tales are real…

"And at the top of the world, where the sky met the clouds, there was a mountain." There was a sorrow in his voice that made her chest tight. "And at the top of that mountain was a great castle," he explained. "A school. Unlike anything anyone's ever seen. Nobody really knows much about what goes on inside, only the ones that are chosen, and one day, something goes horribly wrong with their magic and they open a door to somewhere they shouldn't and something horrible spills out."

The stranger moved closer, and said, "So what do they do? They flee. Escape with their lives. Or so they think. And when the smoke clears, of all the people that lived in that place, only thirteen remain. Thirteen women who decide to stay behind and face it, to try and stop what's come."

Sterling suddenly remembered the tape recorder.

The voices!

The terrible whispers came rushing back into her head like

bubbling acid, filling her mind with horrible growls shaped in ancient words, chaotic and vehement.

Her left eye began to twitch and she immediately put a hand to her face and massaged it.

"You can hear them, can't you?" he asked. "In your head."

Sterling nodded. "What was it that came?"

The stranger shrugged. He reached into his pocket and pulled out a pack of cigarettes, packing them on the top of his hand before plucking one out and lighting up.

Sterling looked at him and he chuckled. "Swiped them off the desk in there." The cherry glowed as he sucked in a long drag. "There is so much more out there than you think, Sterling. People look around and think this is all there is but…"

"What happened?" she asked again.

"But they're wrong. There's more. Other places. I've seen it."

"What. Happened?" she asked petulantly. Her patience was running on empty.

"Nobody really knows what it was. Some called it Hell. Some called it the Void. Just some dark plane of existence, home to all the things that would make a man mad just by catching a mere glimpse of it." The man blew the smoke out of his nostrils in two plumes.

"Personally, I like to think it was Hell. Yeah, that's what it was," he decided, almost pleased with himself. "Those women…they opened a door to Hell. They saw hell, and it saw them. And somehow, by some fluke of time and space…they survived."

Sterling stared at him severely.

The man continued, "Anyway, it changes you, seeing something like that. The way men change when they go to war and come back after seeing their friends slaughtered before their very eyes. Doing unimaginable things. Terrible things. Seeing true horror. *True fucking evil*, Sterling. It changes you." A beat, then, "Rumor says they were able to stop it, but it was too late. Whatever came through…it transformed them."

"Into what?"

The man pointed his cigarette down the long hall, where the witch was housed. "Into her."

Cold fear flushed through her veins like ice water. She swallowed. She imagined the witch standing in the cell in the pitch-dark, patiently waiting.

But for what?

Sterling said, "What was it? What came through the door?" she asked, a tremble in her voice.

"I don't know," he said simply. "But legend goes, after they'd killed *whatever* it was, they kept it there in the castle, as a reminder."

"A reminder of what?"

The man smirked. "A reminder that some things are worse than Hell."

Sterling chewed her lip, pacing in front of him. "Wait. Thirteen witches," Sterling muttered. "*Thirteen.* So…where are the others?"

"Don't know," the man shrugged. "I suspect they're out there in the universe somewhere…turning out the lights, one at a time."

"How do you know all this?"

The man chuckled. "You dabble in this shit long enough, eventually you hear a little bit about a lot. Some of it I've read in books people don't know exist. Some of it I've been unfortunate enough to see myself. And some things…well, some things I wish I didn't know at all. But occasionally, it comes in handy."

Sterling shook her head, her mind racing with the impossible new information. "Why didn't you warn us?"

The man scoffed. "And say *what*, exactly, Sterling? Say what? That that woman in there is an actual witch?" He snickered. "Don't kid yourself, you wouldn't have believed me and you know it."

"You could have tried," Sterling protested.

"Yeah, well," the man said, "what's done is done. You know now."

"But why hasn't she done something? Why doesn't she move? Why does she just *stand there* and stare at the fucking wall?" Sterling said, slapping the cinderblocks. "She hasn't tried to attack us. Hasn't tried to harm us."

"From what I've seen, that's exactly what she's been doing all night," he said matter-of-factly. "Just because you haven't seen it, doesn't mean she isn't doing exactly what she does."

"You think she's just toying with us…?" Sterling asked.

"Yes. And if she's done this much damage from the inside of the cell, I can only imagine what she can do when she finally decides she wants to come out."

"I don't understand," Sterling said. "Why us? What does she want?" Sterling asked, even though deep down she already knew the answer.

She wanted to be wrong. *Had* to be wrong.

The man looked at her, his jaw compressing. "If I had to guess, I'm gonna say she wants the little guy sitting on the other side of that door."

CHAPTER 34

"MAX?"

The man nodded.

So she was right. After everything that had happened that night, it all came down to Max. For one reason or another, he'd caught the witch's eye.

"But why?" Sterling asked. "What does she want with him?"

"I wish I knew," the man replied. "There's a million stories out there about witches and kids. Something in their youth, maybe. Maybe to keep themselves young. But your guess is as good as mine."

"But witches are supposed to be *make-believe*. They're fairy tales. Stories people made up for books…aren't they?"

"Most legends are based on some form of the truth. Exaggerated sure, but still. Maybe our ideas of witches came from them. Maybe someone here met one, once upon a time, and decided to write a story about it."

The idea was ludicrous; the thought the witches could have been here before now. That someone could have met that *thing* in the cell more than a hundred years ago. Maybe centuries. And if he was correct in his assumption, if all of the stories people knew were based on the Thirteen Witches, then what else might be out there?

What other nightmares could be out in the world that very moment?

"I don't believe that," Sterling said finally. "I can't."

"Unfortunately for you, it doesn't matter *what* you believe. *Whatever* she is, she is in there right now," the man said, "which means we have a serious problem to deal with, Sheriff."

"We have to kill her." She didn't recognize her own voice.

Georgia was right. So was Chase. She should have taken care of the witch back when she had the chance.

The man looked at her and his eyes twinkled. "Kill her?" the man laughed. He spun on his heels, pacing the room. "We just...*kill her*?"

"Yes." She wasn't backing down.

"And how exactly to you propose we do that, Sheriff Marsh?"

Sterling glanced toward lockup, where the witch waited in the darkness. "I can take her outside, into the forest."

"What makes you think it'll be that easy?"

Sterling rolled her shoulders. "She's flesh and blood."

The man grumbled. "In my experience, these things are never this easy..."

"Wait," Sterling said, an idea forming. "I need to show you something."

She led him back inside the office.

Max stirred in the seat, his face downtrodden.

Sterling hitched over behind the desk and produced the container from the river, setting the weighty thing on the desk. She noted a crack running through the glass viewing pane that wasn't there before.

The man's eyes narrowed. He cautiously stepped forward, studying the strange object.

"What is it?" His voice sounded like he'd swallowed nails.

"I found it in the river under the bridge—where the truck crashed."

The stranger picked up the case, peering inside.

"There's something in it," Sterling said, "but I can't tell what."

Max watched them quietly from the chair.

"This writing…" he said, "it looks familiar."

"There was more of it on the transport."

"Latin," the man clarified.

"What's it mean?"

The man shook his head. "I don't know. Maybe some kind of warning."

"The inside of the transport—it was lined with gold."

This caught the stranger's attention. He looked up at her. "Gold?"

Sterling nodded. "The whole inside was gold."

"You're sure?"

"Yes."

The man scratched his stubble. "So the old girl doesn't like gold…" he said. "Well, unless you've got a stash of gold bars down in your basement, that doesn't help us a whole lot." He traced his fingertips around the edge of the capsule the same way she'd done countless times before. He held the etched pane up close and squinted in. "I can't make it out," he said. "It's long, whatever it is." He fumbled with the plethora of hinges on the side.

"Don't bother: it's locked," Sterling said.

The man shook his head, dropping it back on the desk with a heavy thud. "Doesn't matter. Unless you have some way to melt down the inside of this thing and turn it into some bullets, it's not going to help us."

"Can I see?" Max asked.

Sterling and the man looked at the small boy, his legs dangling off the chair, his face puffy and red.

She couldn't say why she did it. Maybe it was pity. Or maybe she just felt responsible for ruining the child's life, for letting his mother and father die horribly along with any chance of a decent childhood.

She smiled wryly, and for the first time since she'd known the boy, she felt her heart swell the tiniest bit. She looked at the man and he looked at her and tipped his head in approval, then turned away as if they were wasting their time.

She picked up the case and handed it to Max. The boy's beaten eyes lit up, bringing him to life. His slumped posture pulled taut, his chin lifting. He swallowed, taking in steady breaths as he fondled the strange thing.

Sterling wasn't sure why she was so surprised by what happened next. Maybe she'd forgotten how much Max adored puzzles. He'd carried some variety of them with him wherever he went. That Rubik's Cube was so worn down, Chase had had to paint the colors back on the individual squares. And it hit her then how much she'd actively tried to push any thought of the boy from her mind when he wasn't right there in the room with her. How much Chase had been the only person to dominate her thoughts, and how all Max had been up until that point was a nagging reminder that the life she really wanted wasn't hers and never would be.

Her eyes welled with tears at the realization, and she made a promise to herself that she'd do better. *Be* better—*if* they survived the night. And against all odds, she found herself smiling, watching Max's tiny fingers glide over the case, carefully taking in every intricacy and minute detail that even the most attentive might have missed.

There was a mechanical *click!* and the boy's eyelids lifted.

Sterling and the stranger stepped closer, the three watching a series of mechanisms cycle with a soft hum and a series of clacks.

She gasped as the entire upper portion of the case let out a spray of air like a space hatch opening.

The motorized hum grew louder, and the reinforced door to

the case artificially swung open, revealing a sparkling golden interior.

Sterling and the man kneeled down beside the boy and peered inside.

CHAPTER 35

MAX HAD DONE it.

Sterling and the man were crouched down next to him. They both looked like they were holding their breath, like they'd seen something amazing that they couldn't explain.

Sterling was smiling at him in a way he'd never seen before.

He didn't even know she had teeth! And now that he saw her smiling, he decided that he liked that smile. It made her look so much happier and younger than she ever had before.

He didn't understand why the man was out of his cell, but Sterling seemed to be okay with it, so he was too.

When he'd solved the box, it had hissed and shot him with a spray of cold air. The scare had made his heart flutter like a butterfly, and when he'd looked up, Sterling was right there on one side of him, and the man was on the other, both looking at him like he'd done something amazing.

Max looked at them with fascination, then let his eyes fall to the thing in the box.

He'd gone to a museum once with Mommy and Daddy.

They'd drove all day in the car to this great big building that started with an S (he couldn't remember the whole name). They'd spent all day walking around inside, looking at each and every glass box and case. The ceiling was so tall it made him dizzy to look up, so he'd tried to keep his eyes on the ground. He'd walked with Mommy and Daddy, hand in hand, hearing the sound their shoes made on the tile. He had watched them smile and laugh, listening as they'd whispered things to each other in a way so he wouldn't be able to hear. The truth was, he'd loved every second of it, seeing all the shiny and rusted things together with his two favorite people in the whole world. He couldn't read just yet, so they had to take turns reading him the little squares mounted in front of each display. His favorite sight was this giant gold coffin with the strange face of a man with his crossed arms on the front. Daddy said it belonged to the people who made the pyramids, and Max remembered wondering why they didn't make those out of gold, too. He must have stood there for twenty minutes, just staring at that shiny coffin. It looked old and new at the same time, and Max recalled being confused at how such a thing was possible. *Artifacts*, Mommy had called them. He'd contemplated what was inside, wondered if maybe there was a mummy in there like he'd seen late at night on the TV when his parents were fast asleep.

That was a good day, he mused. His lips curled into a smile.

He never did find out what was inside that golden coffin, but now here he was, with a discovery of his own. Miraculously, he'd solved his own mystery, and was about to glimpse what was on the inside.

He sucked in a deep breath and felt the air flow into his chest.

The first thing he noticed was how long it was.

Maybe a little longer than the wooden things he used to make straight lines with when he'd draw at the kitchen table with Mommy. She'd use them too for something she called "homework," although he didn't understand what she meant since she worked at City Hall during the week and didn't have to go to school like he did.

Rulers! That's what she'd called them.

The object was long and pointy at the end, and it reminded him of a bone, except that it was black instead of white. Whatever it was, it looked *old*. It reminded him of the things he'd seen in the museum that day resting on top of those dark red pillows. He imagined it there, tried to think of what Mommy or Daddy would read about it to him.

Hadn't he seen something like this before? His nose crinkled.

There was something...*familiar* about it.

There was a handle toward the bottom. That part was shiny as a dull nickel, with a bunch of little squares going around it. In each square were these funny little markings, almost like they could slide around between each other the way his Rubik's Cube did.

Was it some sort of puzzle?

At first, he thought they were letters, but after a minute, squinting his tired eyes as hard as he could, he realized they weren't letters at all, but something completely new to him. He couldn't recall seeing anything like it at the museum or school, either.

He looked up at Sterling and could tell she was just as confused as he was. The man, too.

Why did it look so familiar?

Had he seen something like this before?

And why keep something so pretty locked up inside a box where no one could see it?

"What in the hell is that..." Sterling murmured.

Without thinking, Max reached out and plucked the thing from the supports built inside the container.

A chain of fireworks exploded in his head, cascading in deafening crashes. He felt ice rush into his body as his heartbeat crawled to a standstill.

"The cold," he whispered.

He tried to move.

No no no no no.

Whispers.

They were far away, but he could hear them.

There was a roar of thunder and the world went black.

What's happening? His words were muffled and came to him slow, like the cars of a train longer than the state of Connecticut. He heard a protracted wail in the darkness, like some sort of whale breaking apart the water at the bottom the ocean.

The whispers grew louder.

It was adults.

Women, like Mommy. They were scary, growling like animals.

He began to feel frightened but he couldn't move. He could only sit helplessly, trapped in his own head as the voices talked and snapped at each other like adults gone crazy, like the kind he'd seen in the hospital in that one movie. He couldn't understand them. Couldn't understand anything they were saying. They used words he didn't know, and even if he *did* know them, they were all talking at the same time so fast it was more like noise than anything.

A flash of light seared the front of his face like the sun had blown up. He was looking into a room now.

Only it wasn't like any room he'd ever seen. The ceiling wasn't as high as the museum, but it was close. The walls were blocks of stone, with lamps mounted high on them.

The light flared like a match with a ghostly shriek, imploding into a black hole in midair.

A dozen or so women in strange clothes scrambled around the black hole and he recognized one of them:

The witch!

Only she looked different. She wasn't wearing the hat and all her witch clothes. She was wearing long robes like he'd seen sometimes at fancy schools, and her hair wasn't black anymore but yellow like his daddy's. She looked beautiful and powerful like an angel, and she stood with the other women and watched that scary black hole open in midair.

Tears pooled in his eyes. It felt like he was sitting in front of an airplane engine; the skin on his face rippled like a sheet in the wind.

Sounds he couldn't describe poured from the darkness and there was a loud crack like lightning in his head.

He screamed, but only a spray of dust came out.

He wanted to run and get as far away as he could from here.

He didn't want to see.

But the women didn't run. They stood their ground as the hole in front of them opened wider like a bottomless, hungry mouth.

A sound worse than anything he'd ever heard bellowed and the world shook; it tore through his ears and just as something hideous and slimy began to crawl out of the darkness toward the women, he was whisked away.

He soared through the castle as it transformed, watching as beautiful stone corridors and immense colorful banners were touched by a flood of darkness and transformed into something ugly. He felt the cold; it was freezing, spilling forward through the giant building like a sea of oil.

As he reached what he assumed to be the entrance, there was another blast of light and a clap so loud his ears popped.

He felt a rush of warm air as he was drawn out of the castle and into the sky.

He was flying now.

The world was a brilliant green, sprinkled with winged things that cascaded through the sky across twin moons. He thought at first glance that they were birds, but they appeared bigger and he felt relief that they were in the distance, so far away from him.

He smelled the witch.

Cinnamon. Chocolate. And hidden beneath it all, he smelled the rot. The same odor he remembered when he'd found that dead dog out in the forest on his fifth birthday.

The world exploded like a star, and the land beneath him lit up like Christmas.

His mind faltered, jarred from the extreme change, and the sensory overload was almost too much. His dream hiccupped like lost power, darkening, but then roared back to life, bright and glowing and glorious.

The castle sat atop a world of candy.

Among the impossible things he saw there were:

Vast mountains formed of jagged chocolate cliffs and ridges.

Roads dotted in Peppermints and three-story, multicolored candy canes trailing alongside them.

Marbled rocks like Jelly Bellys.

Licorice vines dangling in the air like telephone wire.

Houses and buildings fashioned from gingerbread and wafers and frosted like cupcakes, the rooftops pressed with colorful foot wide gumdrops.

Just like Mommy and Daddy helped me make!

His breath snagged as he beheld dozens of islands suspended against the swirling pink sky, hulking masses in the shape of strawberries. He made out tiny houses with chocolate chips and mint doors. Lawns of gumballs and gummy bears as tall as he was, and some candies he didn't even recognize! Crimson taffy stretched through the sky, forming elongated bridges that led to places unknown.

And at the center of the valley, a vast river formed of pure chocolate.

Max breathed the river in, and it was more real than anything he'd ever smelled in his life. He admired it as it lazily oozed past, spilling over hard candy rocks. Giant cherries bobbed on the rich brown surface, and he wondered what it would taste like to bite into them. He marveled at the incredible world of his dreams, pondering how nice it might be to stay there forever. To drink from the chocolate river, and befriend the gummy bears in the gardens.

But then he remembered the castle.

Remembered the rot, and the black hole.

He quickly detected the scent beneath all the sweets and wonderful colors.

Hidden.

There was a colossal *BOOM* and the sky exploded in a million shards of red glass.

And then he remembered.

His eyes shot open to find Sterling's hand clamped down on his shoulder, her face in a grimace, she and the man leaned in close.

Her voice was far away but unmistakable.

He watched her mouth open and close as she shook his shoulder.

"Max!"

He was back now. He was breathing so hard it was like he'd just run to catch the bus for school.

"Max, are you all right?!" she shouted.

"I know…what it…is," he panted. "I know what it is…"

"Max? What are you talking about?" Sterling said. "Goddammit Max, tell me you're all right!"

"I know what it is," he rasped, staring down at the thing in his hands. "I know what it is now."

Sterling and the man looked at each other.

And Max said, "It's her magic wand."

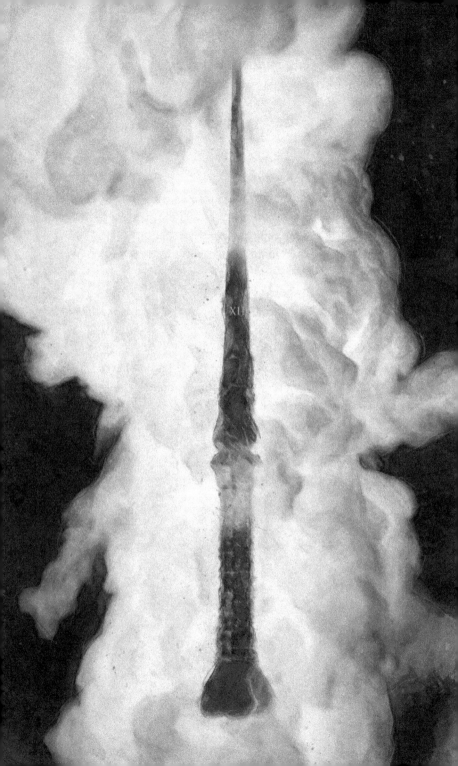

CHAPTER 36

"MAGIC WAND?" Sterling parroted. "As in *Harry Potter* and *The Wizard of Oz* magic wand?"

Max nodded. "It's true, Sterling, I saw it!"

She'd about had a heart attack when he'd reached out and touched it. His eyes had rolled back in their sockets and his hands had set on the wand like stone. They'd tried to pry it out of his fingers but didn't want to risk hurting him in the process, so they'd let it play out. Luckily, after a moment, he'd come to.

He told them what he'd seen, recounting a fantastic tale about a castle that existed in a world of candy.

A castle with *thirteen witches*, to be precise.

She didn't want to believe it, but she had little in the way of contesting the evidence.

Max had essentially seen exactly what the stranger had told her no more than twenty minutes ago.

The man's face was tight with tension. "Well, I guess we know what they did with it now."

"Did with what?" Sterling asked.

"The thing that came through the gate."

Sterling cocked her head. "What'd you mean?"

"The wand," he explained. "Max said it was bone."

Sterling smiled and thought she must look pretty crazy about now. Because it *was* crazy. All of it.

"You don't think—"

He went on, ignoring her skepticism, "The witches must have used its bones to create the wand. And I'm going to venture a guess that this isn't the only one."

"This is crazy," Sterling said, throwing her hands up.

The man pointed at the open case, where the wand lay resting inside a tarnished gold interior. "You see that?"

"What?" Sterling leaned down and peered into the case.

"That writing there, carved into it?"

"I don't see anything."

"No," he said. "There." He hovered a finger over its marred surface. The roman numerals XII were whittled into the bone.

"Twelve?" she said out loud. "So...what? This is wand number twelve?"

"It's true, Sterling, I saw it!" Max said again.

"Just give me a minute here, Max."

She turned back to the man, who fingered the side of the case. The automatic cover swung closed, securing the wand once more.

Sterling laughed. "You can't seriously believe this?" she said. "I mean...this is just...crazy—isn't it?" There was a hesitation in her voice. Doubt.

"Is it harder to believe that the woman in there is exactly what you think she is? Or to believe that she's not? Because deep down I think you already know. I think you've known from the second she showed up here tonight."

He was right, and it might as well be raining cats and dogs tonight, too, because somehow, along with every other crazy thing that had happened, she'd also decided to take the advice of a perfect stranger without thinking twice about it.

The situation was impossible. She tried to rationalize everything that had happened, scrutinized it and dissected it over and over in her head, but at the end all she saw waiting for her at the end of the road was the witch.

She knew what she had to do.

"We can't win this fight, can we?" Sterling asked him.

The man looked at her grimly and shook his head. "No. I'm sorry."

Sterling swallowed, skeptical, her eyes falling to the scared little boy in the chair. "We leave?"

The man breathed deeply, and thunder clapped white light. He nodded in agreement. "We leave. Now. You two just get in your car and drive. There'll be people coming for her."

"They'll be able to stop her?"

The man shrugged. "They'll have a hell of a lot better chance than we do."

Sterling ran her tongue along her bottom teeth. "What about you?"

"Me?" the man asked modestly. "Hell, I don't know…" his voice trailed off. "I guess they'll just have to keep looking, won't they?"

Rain fell like nails from the night sky. The parking lot was a muddy pool, littered with half-sunken cars and debris from the storm.

She could see their frozen breath huffing out in front of them. Ever since the power had wound down, the station had gradually been getting colder, but for whatever reason when the witch was nearby there was always an abundance of heat. The same heat that had cocooned over the station and kept them warm most of the night.

Her mind flashed with a glimpse of Chase and the witch, his naked body squirming on top of her.

Whispers.

She heard them skip around from one corner of her head to the other, ricocheting around like pellets. They were disorienting, whipping around her in circles, throwing off her sense of balance.

She stumbled, and her knee dropped into ice water.

The man was there in an instant, helping her up.

"You all right?" he asked.

"Fine," she told him, steadying herself on the trunk of a patrol car.

They trudged on, past floating branches and leaves before arriving at a patrol car and an unmarked SUV.

The wind howled and the rain poured.

They weren't but three survivors in the eye of the storm.

Sterling took one final look at the man she'd known most the night only as "the prisoner," and as she admired him for who he was—the cut through his brow, the rough, callused skin—she couldn't help but wonder how many other nights he'd had that were just like this one. Maybe even worse. She wished she'd gotten a chance to know him better. They may have even been friends in another life.

She reached into her jacket and fished out a set of keys. She pressed the fob and there was a honk. A set of brake lights flashed on a nearby SUV.

"That's you," she said. She tossed him the keys, and he caught them without looking.

"Where will you go?"

The man gazed up at the sky like he'd never seen anything so magnificent. He closed his eyes and smiled as the rain touched his face. "My wife...she used to love the rain. Every time she'd get a sense of it she'd go outside, sit on this wooden swing in our front yard. Just stay there for hours listening to the world, breathing it in." When he opened his eyes, there was a longing there that Sterling hadn't seen before. "I never understood why until after she was already gone." He paused, as if he could read her thoughts, then said, "The sad truth of it is sometimes there is no hero of the story. No way to win. Because when a tornado is comin' all you can really do is get the hell out of the way. My advice? Take him and get as far away from here as you can. Enjoy your life. Not always, but sometimes the smartest thing to do is just walk away."

"Yeah…" Sterling smiled, extending a hand. "Thank you."

The man looked down at her hand like he was pleasantly surprised. "My friends call me Bill," he offered, taking her hand. There was a warmth to his touch. Not like the witch, just the right amount to keep the cold away.

"Take care of yourself, Sheriff Marsh," he said, smiling.

He climbed into the SUV, and the engine purred to life. The vehicle sliced a path through the water like a ship at sea, lost to the night.

She was saddened more than she thought she'd be seeing him go, but by now she was so numbed by loss she found herself more in a perpetual state of shock than anything else.

She looked down and noticed she had Max's hand in her own.

The boy shivered, his face scrunched up, his round cheeks red with cold.

"Are we…leaving…now?" he asked, teeth chattering.

"Yeah, Max," she said, "we're leaving now."

The patrol car glided through the parking lot, a rippling pond of black glass and splintered branches.

Sterling had the heater cranked up as high as it would go. Max sat in the seat beside her with his hands held out over the vent.

She looked in the rearview mirror, watching the station grow smaller and smaller.

She exhaled, shaking her head.

What the hell are you doing?

She thought the weight in her chest would have lifted the

further from the witch she got, slowly easing away and leaving her feeling light again.

But instead, it only got worse.

This was wrong.

How could she just walk away?

What if "they" didn't come?

What if the Chief walked in tomorrow, blissfully unaware of everything that had happened in the last twelve hours and found the witch waiting inside the cell along with most of his staff dead?

She could call him.

In this storm?

Come on, Sterling, that's never gonna happen and you know it.

She'd barely gotten a few sentences through to Phil over in Middletown, and that was practically a one-in-a-million shot in this storm. Whether the State Police were actually on their way or not was impossible to know at this point. And even if they were, how would they get around the wreckage at the bridge? The fire access roads? No, that would have taken hours, maybe longer.

The windshield wipers cut across the wet glass. She listened to rain pelt across the surface like tiny pebbles as the engine rumbled.

Just as the car reached the edge of the parking lot, she made up her mind. She stomped on the brake, throwing an arm across Max as the car slid across the wet asphalt to a stop.

Max turned to her, confused. "What's going on? Why are we stopping?"

She looked in the rearview mirror again and saw the faint outline of the station in the moonlight under a halo of mist.

"I can't..." she whispered.

"Can't what, Miss Sterling?"

The engine idled there at the fork, the tailpipe blowing out warm exhaust into the breath of night.

She looked down at Max and knew she had a decision to make.

"Max?"

Max watched her.

"Why do you call me 'Miss' Sterling? Why not just Sterling?"

Max shifted in his seat, adjusting the seatbelt on his belly. "I don't know," the boy said. "Just felt right, I guess."

Sterling smiled. "Just Sterling. Okay, Max?"

Max nodded his head.

Get out of here. Just go. Leave the witch like he said. Let them figure out what to do with her.

"I can't..." she repeated.

She couldn't go through with it. Couldn't run. The witch was her responsibility now, and she owed it to her friends to see it through to the end.

Max stirred in the seat beside her, growing more uneasy by the second. "Can't we go now, Sterling?"

The inside of the car was borderline hot now. They'd sat inside for the last ten minutes while the engine warmed up. She'd let it flood with enough heat to last a good hour or so. At least enough for her to run inside and finish what needed to be done.

She shifted the car into gear and wheeled it back toward the station. "I want you to listen to me, Max," she instructed. "I need to go back inside the station for a minute."

"For what?" Max asked. She could see the worry in his eyes and hear the apprehension in his high-pitched voice.

"I forgot something," she told him. She was telling the truth. She *had* forgotten something. She eased on the brake, crawling to a stop. "I'm going to be right back, but I want you to promise me that you will stay right here until I get back. Can you do that, Max?"

Max looked around like he'd been cornered.

"Max? I need you to *promise* me, okay? Please?"

"I promise."

She smiled and tussled his hair, throwing the door open and starting back into the storm.

CHAPTER 37

FLIES WERE IN her head.

The buzzing had gotten worse. The sound droned on, incessant and ruthless. She tried to remember a time when it wasn't there and couldn't.

It was time.

Sterling had prepared everything in the span of less than five minutes, quickly setting up a failsafe if things went sideways. More specifically? Gasoline. And plenty of it. Sprawling yellow veins trailed in and out of offices, halls, and down into the basement. There would be nowhere to run. The witch would be trapped.

Sterling stood at the foot of the corridor leading to lockup, the pistol snug in her hand, a determined expression set on her face. She listened to the gentle lull of thunder in the Painted Mountains and heard the rain on the metal rooftop and her own heartbeat in her ears.

She wondered, would they find her body too come morning?

Find her lying in a pool of her own blood like Chase and Georgia?

She shuddered at the thought, squeezing her eyes shut hard and forcing it out of her mind.

Not you Sterling. Never you.

She started the march to lockup, passing through a world of shadows like a ghost herself.

The long track of lights on the ceiling sprang into a flicker, hissing and fluttering with sprays of ghastly light. She heard a needle scratch across vinyl, and after a few seconds of crackling, "Silent Night" began to play. The vines of Christmas lights chasing the walls brightened and dimmed to her own pulse, like the station and everything in it had become an extension of her energy.

She marveled at the station in wonder, as though she was walking the inside of an alien spacecraft, then continued on with renewed resolve.

She arrived at the door, using her weight to wheel it open.

A flutter of intense heat breathed out of the room, tossing her hair, and for a split-second she thought maybe the room was engulfed in flames.

Unperturbed, she shouldered the door open the rest of the way.

She scoffed, shaking her head. "Sonofabitch," she said, finding nothing but a gloomy room suspended in a prison of shadows. "Just another goddamn trick."

The first thing she saw was Chase's body. His face was ashen, the blood completely drained from his body and pooled around him like a crimson pond.

Tortuous wind moaned beyond the window, erratic flashes of lightning revealing glimpses of the macabre scene before her.

Georgia was still slumped upright against the bars where she'd been strangled, her eyes frozen open in horror, her mouth twisted in a grimace.

She swallowed, feeling her nerve slipping.

Do it, before you change your mind.

Without lifting her eyes, she carefully sidestepped the mess, finding the door to the witch's cell wide open, inviting her in.

The witch stood like a demented sculpture in the center of the cell, like she'd been there just as long as the rest of Drybell and had become a part of it in a way. The woman wore the same empty expression as before, and her eyes shone with a brilliant silver reflection.

Sterling approached with the gun held down at her side.

The witch didn't move.

She wasn't surprised. She hadn't before, so why would she now?

Sterling stepped in front of her so that the two were face-to-face. She felt the heat radiating from the woman, the sickly undertone of death hidden among the cloying smell of sweets.

The music played on, eerily filling the deserted corridors and offices with scratchy, haunting music.

Silent night, holy night

Sterling said, "I don't know who you are…*what* you are—but I know what you're doing."

all is calm, all is bright

Sterling's sweaty palm tightened around the grip. "This is *my* town," she said with a scowl. "Those people that you killed? Those were *my* people. My friends. My family."

Her eyes pooled with tears. She raised the pistol, easing the barrel onto the witch's forehead. "I don't know why. I don't know how. But you know what I do know? It was you," she whispered. She dug the barrel into the witch's skin, forcing her head back. "*You* did this. *You* killed them. And I'd say I'm just about out of things to live for."

She harshly grabbed the back of the witch's neck and jerked her forward, jamming the gun under her chin.

"You won't be the first person I've killed," she said, shoving the gun into the witch's throat. She paused, grimacing at the monster she'd become, like she'd finally relinquished all control and surrendered to the inevitable. Anna's voicemails painfully replayed in her head, letting the words rip the scabs off of fresh wounds.

I love you, Ling.

Ovi came next.

Be true to yourself, love.

She remembered the way his face had looked while he'd lain there dying, his chest hiccupping with shallow breaths. She'd watched the light go out in his eyes. Watched his last heartbeat on the monitor.

"You won't be the first," she repeated. She remembered how her mother's face had looked in the morgue. Her skin was waxen, and it almost looked like she had finally found peace in her life. She remembered Jimmy, remembered what it was like to put a bullet in him.

"He was like you," she explained. "He liked to hurt people."

Without warning, Sterling pitched her weight to the side, pistol-whipping the witch across the face with a hard *thwack!* The blow would have floored anyone else, but the woman merely kept staring into oblivion.

"He got what he deserved, in the end. You see, nobody seemed to care about what he liked doing in his free time. My mother...she thought he was this charming, perfect person..." Her voice trailed off. There was a beat, then, "But he wasn't. He was a monster. Just like you. And I made sure that sonofabitch would never hurt anyone ever again."

Sterling roared as the gun whizzed through the air like a sledgehammer, catching the witch on the side of the face with a meaty *crack!* Her face snapped to the side like a doll, then slowly twisted back. No blood or markings marred the woman's face the way they rightfully should have. In fact, her skin appeared as if it'd never been touched at all, beautiful and ghastly at the same time.

Silent night, holy night

"He begged me to help him. Begged me to save his life as he was dying in front of me." She took a sharp breath, then said, "I watched him die that night. Watched him take his last breath. And I'd do it over again if I had to, because I will not let you or anyone else try to take my life away from me, and I *will* protect what's mine," she warned.

All is calm, all is bright

"You're here for the boy," she said. "You've come to take him, haven't you?"

Sterling calmly breathed in and out, patiently waiting for the witch to answer.

"Only you've got a problem," she told her, "because you can't have him. Not tonight. Not ever."

She raised the gun to the witch's head a second time, only this time she left it there.

"He said you came from a land of fairy tales…" She paused as if lost in thought, imagining such a place, and the corner of her mouth curled into a smile before falling away. "But I've been on this earth long enough to know there's no such thing. There are no happy endings. Not for me," she said, tears rolling down her cheeks, "and not for you."

Sterling wept quietly, tightening her fingers around the grip.

"I'm going to give you one chance."

She sniffled, tears slipping from her eyes like glass beads.

"One last chance to do something besides *STAND THERE LIKE A FUCKING STATUE!*"

She was crying harder now, taking in short, shallow breaths.

"Goddamn you," she breathed.

Her index finger tightened on the trigger.

She wondered if when the bullet erupted through the witch's head and out the other side if the woman would still be standing after. She anticipated the recoil, heart hammering faster and faster until it was so loud it was like small explosions in her head.

BOOM. BOOM. BOOM.

Sleep in heavenly peace

The buzzing cut like wire.

The sounds in the air settled.

She could hear again.

Hear the thunder and the wind like fresh running water, magnificent and powerful and real.

Her heart stopped; the blood rushed to her face and she was shaking so bad she thought she might pass out. She held on and fought through the spell of dizziness, the gun stretched out in front of her, her gaze lost in the horrible silver coins that were the witch's eyes.

And then, just as she went to pull the trigger, finally put an end to it all, the witch blinked.

Sterling gasped, stumbling back.

It was a surreal sight, and a disturbing one at that, like watching an inanimate object unexpectedly come to life.

The horrible thing blinked her eyes again, and Sterling's heart about leapt out of her chest onto the floor in a bloody mess.

Her feet caught the puddle of blood and slid out from under her.

She went down hard on her hip with a wet smack and a grunt.

The gun went spinning away.

She immediately came to, scrambling to get her hands on the tile to push herself up.

Her palms slid through blood. She twisted upright and threw herself in the direction of the gun.

The witch hadn't moved yet. She waited there in the cell, her skin eerily pale against the darkness, as if luminescent.

Sterling watched in horror as bursts of lightning showed her glimpses of the inside of the cell.

The monster slowly stirred to life, each flash revealing short, jerky movements of an ancient being.

There was a snap. Then another, like the limbs of a tree being broken off.

Sterling stayed there petrified on the floor, her hand extended toward the pistol in the corner of the room.

There was a series of cracking sounds, and then something heavy and wet flopping onto the concrete.

A guttural moan, more animal than human reverberated from the shadows.

Sterling seized the pistol and flipped around on her back, leveling it at the cell. A cold bolt shot through her as she beheld a hulking mass sprouting inside the cell like a vision straight from hell itself.

The thing let out a piercing rattle and a prolonged chitter, like a great insect and serpent fused together.

Her jaw went slack as impossible lengths and numerous appendages writhed inside the small area, a grotesque masterpiece of shadows.

She tried to scream and couldn't. She was too terrified.

She pushed herself from the floor and darted for the door.

The creature wailed, an awful sound that violently rattled through her bones.

She flew through the door, flipping around and screaming as she threw her weight, wheeling it closed in time to see the thing in the cell scuttle toward her on impossibly long legs.

She fell back as a force like a rogue rhino collided into the other side of the door. There was a heavy crash and dust sprayed from the frame.

THUMP

It's not going to hold!

THUMP

Shit!

She had to get to the lobby—fast.

She reached into her jacket pocket as she slowly backed away, the pounding against the steel growing more powerful by the second.

THUMP

Shit! Where's the keys?

She flushed with panic.

THUMP

She didn't have much time. She beelined for reception, tearing across the tile.

Behind her, the door let out a protracted groan as it finally gave way. Metal slammed so loud it was like a submarine had been crushed.

Her feet tangled as she ran and she nearly tripped, correcting herself just in time. She caught the doorframe, using her momentum to veer into reception.

She hurdled over the front desk like she was back in high school, crashing into the rolling chair and taking the phone with her.

She withdrew under the desk, pressing her ear to the narrow space in the corner.

Just the rain. Always just the rain.

Cinnamon.

The spice wafted into the room on a wave of sweltering heat.

She listened as the quiet patter of feet moved along the tile.

There was a skittering sound followed by a squeak.

Something furry rolled over her hand.

Hey eyes snapped down in time to see a fat rat bite into the fleshy skin between her thumb and index finger.

She shrieked unexpectedly, and her head slammed into the top of the desk as she shot up.

Five more rats scurried up her legs squealing, their beady black eyes and jagged teeth climbing her legs like a fruit tree. She squirmed, slapping the hairy, plump things off of her. Panicking, she hurled herself out from under the desk, heaving the rolling chair away and crashing into the fax machine.

She swatted at her clothes like she was on fire, the rats nowhere to be seen. Her eyes darted about the floor, looking for any trace.

The rats were gone.

A shadow stretched in her peripheral, creeping to life.

Her eyes rolled up to find the witch on the other side of the counter, watching her.

There was no mass, only the same woman from before.

Had she imagined it?

No, she shook her head. *An illusion.*

She brought the gun up, leveling it at the witch's head.

She didn't hesitate this time. There was a deep blast and the room flashed white.

Ribbons of smoke curled from the end of the pistol, and she saw the witch standing on the other side of the counter.

"It's not possible…" she muttered.

She began to move around the counter, pumping rounds into the witch.

One.

The witch still stood. "No," Sterling said, shaking her head. She squeezed the trigger again. And again.

Two. Three.

"It can't be."

Another flash.

She quickened her pace, loosing more bullets in bright flares of light. The sound was deafening, like grenades going off in her head.

The witch took everything she gave without hesitation, anchored to her spot in reception.

A roar began to grow in Sterling's throat. She was only a few feet away now. Her eyes burned holes in the witch, and her mouth was twisted into a grimace, teeth biting down, bared like a lunatic.

The trigger went soft, like she was squeezing rubber.

Her face softened, feeling the gun turn to dough. It began to pulsate, kneading in her hands. There was a rattle and a protracted hiss and the thing in her hands twisted back on itself.

She didn't know what it was. It looked like a snake, but wasn't. It was dark, covered in spines and patches of wispy hair. Thin, spidery legs twice its size squirmed and wiggled between her fingers.

She gasped, releasing it.

There was a clatter as the gun knocked to the floor.

She stared down at it dubiously, then looked at her hands.

The witch was within arm's reach now.

Her eyes darted about for a weapon.

There!

A letter opener.

She snatched it from the counter and brought her hand down from high over her head.

She watched the witch's face, waited for the moment the blade would sink into her brilliant silver eye.

Without warning, she was off her feet.

The world flipped upside down.

Her body soared into the maintenance door with a crash, the wood exploding open. Her body careened into the mop cart and shelves, and the wind was knocked out of her as she connected with the drywall. A cascade of cleaning bottles and rags rained down on her from broken shelves like an avalanche.

She coughed dust and rolled over, digging her way free.

She scanned the floor.

The pistol was within reach.

She dove for it, directing it at the witch.

The witch blinked.

Unexpectedly, Sterling turned the gun to the floor at the last second and let loose one final bullet.

The concrete sparked—the floor roared to life with a wall of flames; they swept down the hall in either direction, trailing through the station.

The wind left her sails and all hope was extinguished as she beheld the witch waiting just as before, completely unfazed by the fire raging around her.

Sterling coughed, tasting the gasoline in the air.

Black smoke began to fill the station. The heat was intense, eating away at the paint on the walls, bubbling glass and spreading to the ceiling.

Sweat dripped from her neck and face. She stumbled to her feet, eyeing a broken broom, one end a jagged stake. Half-conscious, she took it solidly in her hands and vaulted out of the closet, charging at the woman. She was covered in dirt and grime and blood, and the broken wood was like a javelin in her skilled hands.

The broom punched into the witch's shoulder.

Sterling screamed between her teeth and hurled her weight, driving the witch back like a freight train. They slammed into the counter with a crash of hard plastic and metal.

The witch's hand clamped around her throat like a vice, squeezing as Sterling helplessly looked into her dead eyes. The fingers tightened, and the weight in her neck increased tenfold as she was hoisted into the air, her feet dragging along the tile.

Casually, the witch seized the broom with her other hand and jerked it out in one swift movement, letting it fall to the floor with a wooden clatter.

Sterling wheezed, fighting for oxygen and straining to pry the fingers away.

"What…do you…want?" she rasped.

The monster blinked again, and a wave of dread coursed through her body. She felt her life slipping away as she beheld the flames licking the walls and razing everything she'd known. She struggled, kicked, and screamed as the witch choked the life out of her.

Images of her life soared past her like dark clouds.

Rosa.

Georgia.

Chase.

Max.

Ovi.

And Anna.

She heard her mother's voice push through the darkness.

I love you, Ling. Take care of it for me. And take care of you.

Just as the fight began to leave her, her eyes shot open.

Shaking, on the verge of death, she dug a hand into her pocket.

There!

She clamped down on it and ripped it free from her pants.

The witch's hand tightened, and she felt her consciousness slipping.

"Merry…Christmas…you bitch!" she screamed.

She shoved her mother's tarnished gold ring into the witch's mouth, and the monster's eyes flared with molten silver light.

The hand locked around her throat released her, and Sterling crumbled to the floor, flames tearing down the room around them, the entire ceiling buried beneath a canopy of dark smoke.

The witch whirled around, clutching at her throat, smoke pouring off of her. She drunkenly crashed into a burning wall and caught fire. She screamed, and it was unlike anything Sterling had ever heard: alien and human at the same time. The monster spun around, engulfed in flames, then stumbled into the wall of fire.

Sterling was done, had nothing left to give.

It was time.

She rolled onto her back, struggling to breathe in a room choked with black smoke, and peacefully watched bits of the ceiling crumble away, content to know she'd finally done something good for once in her life.

Exhausted and beaten, bathed in divine light, she smiled, and let her eyes fall closed.

CHAPTER 38

"STERLING!"

The voice was distant, echoing in the blackness.

"Miss Sterling!"

The steady sound of crackling. Intense, blistering heat. And the smell of burning plastic and wood.

Fire.

She blinked dreamily at Max, watching him shout, but he sounded so far away. She could feel heat, like she was being cooked alive.

"Please, Sterling!"

Her eyes sluggishly opened to find Max above her, his face alive with panic. The light was too bright, like looking at the sun.

"Come on, Sterling!" the boy screamed.

Max?

He tugged on her hand urgently, nervously eyeing the front doors.

"Hurry!" he pleaded.

Max!

The full force of the fire roared to life, and she found herself thrust into the middle of it.

She grabbed his hand and rolled onto her side.

Max started beating at her leg and she noticed it was on fire. She felt her skin begin to blister, searing with pain.

She sprang to life, slapping it out with her hands.

"Hurry!" he shouted.

She pushed herself to one knee, using him to steady herself. She threw herself over him as flames ten feet high exploded from the hall.

She looked down at him as fire climbed the walls, and realized she had one more friend than she thought. She was grateful that she didn't have to face it alone and realized she'd been wrong about him. About everything.

He wasn't a reminder of the things she'd never have, the life she'd lost.

He was hope.

Forgiveness.

But more than that, he was a second chance.

She smiled and he smiled back, like he didn't know why they were smiling in the midst of a burning building.

There was a loud splitting sound and somewhere part of the station collapsed in on itself.

Max cocked his head, an odd look on his face. The boy listened closely, and that was when she heard it too.

Sirens.

She grabbed the boy's hand, and together they ran for the front doors.

CHAPTER 39

STERLING COULD SEE them in the distance. It was the most glorious sight she'd ever set eyes on.

The State Police. They must have taken the fire access roads after all. *One hell of a detour*, she thought. *No wonder they're just now showing up.*

She and Max stood side by side, their chests rising and falling with pure adrenaline, eyes wild and desperate. They were a sorry sight if there ever was one, completely beat down by exhaustion and covered from head to toe with layers of grime, ash, and blood. Piping hot smoke billowed from the station windows in swollen plumes, feeding into the sky. Little flakes of ash dreamily drifted around them like black snow.

They stood in front of the station among the destruction and listened as a chorus of sirens rose in their ears.

Sterling's heart swelled three times its size, and for the first time that night an honest smile broke across her face.

The procession of blue and red lights wound through the

forest down the mountain, working their way toward Main. She could hear their engines, feel the rumble in the earth as an army of reinforcements fought through the storm.

They were here. The State Police had finally come.

Against all odds, she and Max had made it to daybreak.

They were survivors. For better or worse, they'd gone through hell and come out the other side alive.

It was finally over.

Max looked up at her and smiled in the genuine way only a child could, gently taking her hand. His skin was warm and his hand was small, and she thought about how fragile he was in the world, among so many awful things. How precious and good.

Their hearts nearly jumped into their throats as the glass entrance doors detonated and an otherworldly scream broke out in the station.

Sterling's heart dropped; she threw herself over him as Max spun around in a clumsy panic, nearly losing his balance.

The witch was still alive.

She did a quick pat down of her pockets and realized she didn't have the keys; she must have lost them inside the station.

Sterling reached down and scooped Max up in her arms, racing down the cracked concrete steps. She ran and ran, hauling Max in her arms like a frightened, crazed mother. She thanked God that she'd been a runner all her life, otherwise they'd probably be dead already.

Her legs burned and there was fire in her chest, but she pushed through the pain, grit her teeth, and barreled down the road.

She wanted to cry. Wanted to scream for them to please help them, beg them to hurry! But she couldn't, she simply didn't have the energy. It was pointless. They were just too far.

The inferno raged behind them, the embers crackling, razing her old life like a fallen empire. The smoke was substantial now. It fused with the bleak gray clouds, filtering the sunrise to a blood-red horizon. There was a heavy groan behind her from what she assumed was the roof of the station giving way. She stumbled, nearly dropping Max as the earth shuddered and the station collapsed under its own weight.

They had made it to the middle of the road now at the entrance to town, where a long banner arched over the street that said, WELCOME TO DRYBELL!

She stopped in front of the diner to catch her breath, chest burning, and Max said, "Sterling, look!" He twisted in her arms, pointing down the road where the convoy of police vehicles zoomed toward them in a cloud of dust.

Her hope renewed, she trudged forward. She was on the verge of collapsing now, Max held tightly in her arms, pressed to her chest, her frosty breath pluming out in sharp white jets. She hurried forward, shambling past empty storefronts and gloomy windows. Past the barber shop and the fish and tackle store. Past the electronics store and dog groomer.

"Help us…" she wheezed, but the words barely came out. She couldn't get enough air to her lungs. "Please."

The sirens grew louder, the cycling emergency lights lighting up Main like a carnival.

She could hear the engines now, practically feel their heat.

Max shouted, "Sterling, they're almost here! The good guys!"

She slowed, her body on the brink of total failure as the entourage roared around the bend in the road.

There's so many of them, she thought. Police cars and SUVs and all the help she could have hoped for. She'd never seen so many of them at once in her life.

Her muscles screamed and cramped, and the pain in her knee was unbearable, but she endured, summoning her last remaining reserves of strength.

The first vehicles slammed on their brakes, screeching to a halt in the road mere feet from them. The black and white patrol cars parked staggered in the street, a beautiful mirage that had turned out to be real.

Sterling felt her last bits of energy begin to slip away. Her arms were lead, the feeling in her legs gone altogether aside from the throb in her knee. She stumbled to a stop and fell to her knees in the middle of the road before the blockade, releasing Max.

They had made it.

They were safe.

The doors began to open simultaneously; police officers of all shapes and sizes poured from at least a dozen emergency vehicles.

"Come on, Sterling!" Max shouted elatedly. He tugged on her hand, but she was too weak to move. She just stayed there in the street on her knees, tears of joy steaming down her face.

A man with a neatly trimmed goatee and a plaque that read P. GILMORE marched up to them, a hand held firmly on his holstered sidearm. A few others followed closely behind him, their faces alert.

"Been a lifetime, Marsh," he said, reaching down and offering a hand.

Sterling looked at his hand hanging in the air as if she didn't have the strength left in her to grab it, then looked up at him and nodded, taking it. He was strong but gentle, easily helping her to her feet. The man looked down at Max and smiled, amused.

"Captain Phillip Gilmore," the man said. "Looks like you two had a hell of a night, Sheriff."

The storm began to kick up again, and debris and the smell of smoke wafted over the road from the burning station. The wind was coarse and ragged, and the sky had a sinister glow to it.

Phil said, "What the hell is going on here, Sterling? We haven't been able to get through since—" He stopped midsentence, and his hard eyes shifted past them, staring down the road from which they'd come. Some of the other officers took notice, nosily wandering forward.

Alarmed, Sterling slowly turned her head.

The witch stood in the middle of the road no more than fifty feet away. An electrifying, threatening presence, if she'd ever seen one.

Max yelped and held his hands up in front of him, shielding himself from her.

Sterling's eyes widened and her heart punched the inside of her chest.

"It's her! The witch!" Max shouted, latching onto her leg. She threw an arm around him and slowly began backing away. "She killed them!" He was crying now, reverted back to the frightened child Sterling had forgotten he was.

"Captain, you have to get these people away from here," Sterling warned, her tone heavy with urgency.

"We can handle this, Sheriff Marsh."

"No," Sterling said. She pleaded with him, getting in his face and pawing at this arm. "You don't understand; you need to get your people out of here right now!"

Gilmore remained steadfast, shepherding her and Max away. "Strellson, get them inside a car," he ordered.

"Captain, please listen to me!" she begged. "I'm telling you, you don't understand!"

Gilmore looked at her with pity in his eyes and said, "It's going to be okay, Marsh, just let us handle this."

His face softened as he saw the fear in her, and for a fraction of a second, she almost thought he'd relent to good sense.

But it was too late.

Calm and collected, Gilmore sucked in a tired breath and took a step forward, ushering them behind the line of officers.

Those fools, she thought. *Those goddamned fools are going to die.*

She had to get Max away.

Sterling and Max shrank back, weaving their way between the patrolmen. The officer called Strellson threw open a door to his SUV, guiding them into the backseat. They climbed into the warm air and Sterling pulled the door closed with a *thump!*

Back at the frontlines, Gilmore waited, curiously watching the witch at the end of the road. The flock of law enforcement looked on unbelievingly, their mouths agape, faces rapt in awe. Murmurs rose and fell in waves. Some of them chuckled, like they thought someone was playing a joke on them, but others weren't laughing.

Sterling listened as thunder rolled in the sky and snow began to fall, and before long it truly was a winter wonderland.

It was like they were the last ones left on Earth. Max scooted forward in the seat and worked his fingers into the steel mesh divider. The two held their breath, fatigued beyond all hope.

After an unbearably long silence, Sterling watched as the witch finally twitched to life like a broken toy.

Two things happened simultaneously: The witch's ghastly white hand disappeared into her coat, and Gilmore unfastened his holster, wrapping his fingers around the grip.

The witch drew her hand slowly down across her body, unveiling an object hidden beneath the layers.

"Don't move!" Gilmore shouted, swiftly drawing his firearm. The other officers joined suit, training their weapons on the woman and scattering behind open patrol car doors and their vehicles.

The wand was impossibly long; its sleek surface glistened, at least fifteen inches of pure black, and Sterling knew somehow that in the right hands it was easily capable of some of the worst things imaginable.

The State Police held there opposite the witch, guns out in front of them, ready to do what needed to be done.

The witch stood ominously in the middle of Main Street, her tall hat both strange and surreal, the long black wand at her side. Her coat flapped in the wind like crow's wings and she was like the figure of death itself, a nightmarish fairy tale come to life set against the protectors of the modern world.

The witch's empty, mirrored eyes blinked dreamily, just once, and then her mouth contorted into a demonic smile.

There was a crack high above their heads, and it was like the world had broken open as the sky began dumping snow like they were in the North Pole. Snowflakes the size of Frisbees carelessly drifted down from the steely gray sky, and with a final groan, the greatest blizzard in the history of Drybell commenced.

CHAPTER 40

THE SKY WAS a white void. The snow dumped heavier, and most of the road and rooftops were blanketed, leaving dirty brown patches along the gutters. The chill in the air was biting, and the wind carried the sickly sweet scent of the witch down Main Street.

Sterling and Max waited in the back of the SUV, their attention glued to the witch. Sterling thought her heart might have slowed after the State Police had arrived, but it hadn't—it was beating faster than a hummingbird's and just as erratic. The cloying scent crept inside the vehicle, filling her head with memories of that night. Her stomach gurgled, and she felt vomit flood up her throat. Max turned and looked at her anxiously, and before he could ask if she was okay, she threw open the rear door and collapsed to her knees. She retched loud and painful, vomiting up steaming bile on the snow.

Hunched over on her hands and knees, she craned her head toward the road where the witch watched her like a hawk watching a mouse. There was a horrible smile on her face, and Sterling imagined her gums were black with slime, a mouthful of glistening teeth.

The intensity in the air was palpable. Captain Phil Gilmore and the rest of the Connecticut State Police waited, guns drawn, watching the bizarre thing in the street, growing restless.

Sterling slowly stood up from the wet road and wiped her mouth with her sleeve. The witch's dead eyes found Sterling's own and her demented smile spread wider.

Oh dear god, Sterling thought.

The witch began forward.

"Hold it!" Gilmore ordered.

Sterling listened as the officers readied themselves, getting into position. She heard the sounds their guns made and the whistle of the wind, feeling the giant snowflakes brush her face and ears. The majority of their voices had died down, anticipating the inevitable.

The witch seemed to float, eerily gliding down the road like a phantasm, wisps of steam curling into the air around her.

She was coming for them.

For her.

For Max.

Max!

"I said stop!" Gilmore yelled. "Hold it right there!"

The witch abruptly came to a stop.

A false sense of relief lulled Sterling forward a step or two.

No. Something's wrong, she thought.

The witch was much closer now, no more than thirty feet away.

Sterling held her breath. Her hands pressed into fists and the nails bit down into her palms.

"What's she doing, Sterling?" Max cried back inside the SUV. "Why'd she stop?"

"I don't know…" Sterling murmured, her brow pinched together. She slammed the door to the SUV and began through the snow. Max pressed himself to the window as if to protest, but was too distracted by the scene to be bothered.

The witch coolly raised her arms like a conductor, palms to the sky, the black wand glistening.

A single gunshot cracked in Sterling's ears and the sound echoed far and long, carried by the wind. Max ducked down inside the SUV and Sterling's heart sank.

The Drybell town flag whipped in the wind on top of Grayson's Market.

No. No, no, no, no.

"Don't!" she warned.

But it was too late.

Gilmore stared down the barrel of his smoking gun, eyes pried open with terror. The State Police looked on in disbelief, casting nervous glances at each other, as if they couldn't understand what had just happened.

The witch's grin stretched into a shark-like smile.

She raised her hands and metal groaned as two patrol cars lifted off the ground into the air, little trickles of water streaming off them. The officers stumbled away from under the vehicles, suspended in wonder. As the metal heaps hung there, floating twenty feet in the air, Gilmore turned and looked at the witch in complete and utter awe, fully aware he'd made a terrible mistake.

The witch met his eyes, unamused, and her demented smile fell away into a glare.

Sterling saw the look on Gilmore's face, saw the fear there, but there was nothing she could do.

The witch whirled her hands through the air and there was a heavy rush of wind. Sterling flinched, ducking down as the cars sailed past overhead, somersaulting through the falling snow and launching into the storefronts in a blast of destruction, detonating the plate-glass windows and collapsing tired walls of brick and mortar.

Sterling slowly rose as more bricks crumbled, spraying out moats of sparkling dust. She stepped away, surveying the destruction, then craned her head toward Gilmore, who was hunched over, taking cover behind a patrol car.

The man could no longer hide the panic on his face. Sterling noticed the other State Troopers staring at him, waiting for him to lead them, tell them what to do. The man caught himself shrinking away in the face of adversary and shook it off, standing tall and turning back to face the witch.

"Get away from her!" Sterling warned. She began to sprint toward the crowd, crunching through the snow. "Run!"

"*FIRE!*" Gilmore roared. He lifted his gun, squeezing the trigger. A flash of white lit up his hardened face as the gun kicked back. The other officers joined in, throwing themselves behind the remaining cars for cover and unloading a barrage of bullets.

The sound was thunderous, the hail of gunfire so loud she thought she were immersed in the middle of a war.

The witch was stone, unwavering as the bullets zinged through the air, fluttering her hair as they passed. Others hit an invisible wall, flattening in midair and disappearing into the foot of snow blanketing the street.

The men unloaded everything they had, emptying their magazines with their teeth bared. Some switched to shotguns, throwing wave after wave of lead at the witch in a brilliant volley of firepower. And for a fleeting, illusory moment, Sterling actually thought it would work.

But when all was said and done, when the shooting stopped and smoke poured from the barrels of their semiautomatic weapons, the witch still remained the same as before, the same as she had all night long.

As silence settled over Drybell, the witch abruptly erupted into an insane, maniacal cackle. The sound was overwhelming, a cross between an old woman and something much more ancient, like there were demons inside her. Her laugh poured from everywhere and nowhere, bouncing off the piles of rubble in waves.

Sterling clamped her hands to her ears as the dreadful sound amplified tenfold, sewing unease in the men.

The witch quickly sprung to life, gliding toward them.

The men panicked, eyes locked on the stranger, fumbling their magazines as they attempted to reload their weapons in a mad rush.

She floated into their numbers as if she were leading a parade. Her ebony wand cracked, and a bloodcurdling scream loosed from Sterling's right. She jerked toward the sound and saw a stumbling mass of sinew and blood vessels howling with pain. A second wave of nausea hit her as she realized the man's skin had been turned inside out. The walking horror drunkenly wobbled past her, wailing in agony, and slammed headfirst into a car door, smearing the glossy white paint with a trail of fresh blood.

The witch was at the front of the blockade now. She floated into the group of frenzied law enforcement and twirled the black spike again in the air, conducting an orchestra of madness.

There was a loud sucking sound and a flash of ghastly green light as a black hole tore open above the street in midair. A rush of screaming wind surged from the void, as if a portal to outer space itself had been opened.

Sterling gasped as a gigantic reptilian head sprang forth from the impossible hole. An unsuspecting man waiting below looked up and the color drained from his face. He went to lift his shotgun, but he wasn't fast enough. The monster's immense jaws snapped closed like a crocodile and the man shrieked. Blood sprayed from his chest as the gigantic teeth sunk in, crushing bone and organs. The creature lifted him off the ground with ease. He thrashed and kicked until it jerked him through the air, disappearing back into the hole just before it closed.

The men were in a flurry now, scrambling to escape the witch's murderous spree. Some ran for the hills, disappearing into the surrounding forest, but most of the remaining ones stood their ground, struggling to reload their weapons.

Two troopers charged the witch.

She quickly slashed the wand through the air and the men were cut clean in half, as if with a giant invisible blade.

A third came running at her, hollering at the top of his lungs.

The witch jerked the wand and there was a wet tear as the man's skin ripped clean off his body and splattered on the side of a car with a soggy splash. His fleshless figure collapsed right there in the snow, staining it red.

The witch callously waved her hand and the pile of dismembered corpses were tossed aside like ragdolls.

Another trooper dove off the hood of his car, throwing his arms around the witch's neck to wrestle her into a headlock. Unperturbed, she calmly lifted the wand, reached up, and tapped him on the forehead. The man gasped and released her. He shrank back, clawing at his face in panic. A fellow officer rushed over to assist him. Sterling watched as the man's teeth fell out all at once, swallowed by the snow. There was a sucking sound and the man whimpered as a bouquet of black tendrils blossomed from his mouth, ensnaring the man beside him and latching onto his face. The man's screams were muffled as he tried to pull the writhing things away, eventually collapsing to the road.

Another man stepped directly in the witch's path.

The witch slowed to a stop, watching him curiously.

He waited there, gun drawn, then fired.

The witch's head kicked back from the impact, slowly rolling forward.

Sterling watched in horror as the hole closed itself, the skin mending back together. The witch tilted her head oddly at the man, as if tickled by his courage, then flicked the wand in his direction. The man's eyes bulged and his breath rushed out of his throat like he was attempting to scream. Sterling ran forward to help him, but just as she reached him his body sagged like he'd lost everything that made him solid, and his skin fell into a pile on the road like a suit of rubber. Where his eyes had been were two empty holes, like he'd disappeared right out of his own body.

Another man darted out of the crowd.

The witch cracked the wand, and he exploded in a mist of blood like a popped water balloon, spraying Sterling's face and clothes.

She stood there in shock, face wet with blood, gaping at her hands. They were coated with grime and flecks of snow. She spun around to find herself face-to-face with the witch. She roared with a sound she didn't even know she had in her, lunging forward.

The witch hastily waved her hand as if swatting a fly, and Sterling was batted off her feet and tossed through the air. Her body slammed into the corner of the nearest patrol car, shattering the lights and tumbling over the rooftop to the street with a sharp grunt.

She laid there on the freezing snow as the men screamed, doing everything they could to stop the witch.

Get up! she told herself. *Get to Max! Get out of here, now! It's too late to save the others, just run!*

She roused, head spinning, trying to get her bearings back. She pushed herself from the ground, bracing herself on the car.

On the other side, a group of troopers were engaged in a shootout with the witch, having taken cover behind another cruiser.

"Run," she croaked. She cleared her throat. "Don't fight, just go!" She shuffled around the car, attempting to get closer, but she was too weak. She stumbled, falling to the ground.

The witch approached the car and raised the wand. A crack of energy shrieked and a dazzling flash lit up the street as white-hot electricity poured from the tip, shattering the windows and impaling the car. Nearby snow instantly evaporated as veins of lightning webbed to the three men and their clothes caught fire, the sheer force of the electricity violently launching them into the street, their corpses chased by trails of smoke.

Sterling fought to her feet and smelled burning flesh as pure power flowed from the wand. The heat was unbearable. It was so hot she could feel it on her face like the breath of a dragon. She watched helplessly as the electricity sizzled and crackled, destroying anything it touched. The car slowly began to slide, the white-hot metal glowing. There was a groan and the power overloaded the car, flipping it into the air and sending it tumbling backwards, crushing the three burning men before disappearing over the side of the road.

Two others who'd been hiding sprang from behind the car nearest the witch. They threw their weight, swinging with their batons, but the witch was too fast. She effortlessly snapped her wand and their bodies rocketed from the ground like magnets, smashing into each other with a heavy thud. Sterling heard an ear-piercing scream as their bodies shuddered and smoked, fusing into a horrific sculpture of flesh and fabric. Once it had completed, the disgusting thing fell to the street with a wet plop. She saw little wisps of steam rising from the mass of blood and muscle, and noticed she had tears rolling down her cheeks.

The witch looked over her shoulder and smiled.

CHAPTER 41

STERLING WAS ON her feet, weaving between contorted bodies and corpses. Her face and hands were stained red and her clothes were so filthy they almost looked black. Fires burned and screams echoed in the air.

After she'd thrown up, Max had seen her run off toward the witch, but he didn't know why, and he couldn't think what to do except watch her go. He'd screamed his lungs out, calling for her to come back, but she'd left him. Just like Mommy and Daddy.

As soon as he'd seen the lightning start arching over the street, he knew it was bad. He'd heard the gunshots and seen bright flashes of light, listening in horror as the policemen screamed out in the road when the witch came to them. He was too terrified to move. So he'd hid there instead, behind the seat where Sterling had told him to stay. Some of the policemen had gotten back in their cars and driven away while others had run into the woods like the devil was chasing them. He'd waited there in suspense, praying that someone would come before the witch did.

And then his prayers had been answered. He'd seen lightning

shoot across the street and he'd nearly fainted. A few moments later, Sterling had appeared, racing toward him.

"Hurry!" Max screamed, pounding the window with his palms. He didn't think she could hear him through the window, but he couldn't help it.

He watched as Sterling found the body of the policeman called Strellson who had brought them to the car. She quickly reached down, ripping the keys free of the man's belt.

The witch was coming. He could see her making her way down the road, dispatching the State Police in gruesome fashion. She stopped for a moment, and Max realized she was looking at him. He tried to swallow, but it felt like he had a bone in this throat. He didn't think he'd ever breathe right again. The witch waved her wand, and he saw a policeman explode with green light, and when he looked back, he saw a big plump rat on the ground instead. And that wasn't all. He'd seen horrible things. Things he never even thought were possible. A giant monster head like some sort of dinosaur coming out of a black hole in the air. A man walking around without any skin. Another man that popped like a balloon. And some things so awful he couldn't even put them into words.

The witch glowered in his direction and arched the wand over her head. A gigantic ball materialized out of nowhere, like a tiny steel bearing had just grown a thousand times its size in a split second. It looked just like the one from Which Witch? only as big as a car. It must have weighed over a million pounds, he thought. The uncanny sphere sailed through the air toward Sterling with a whistle like a bomb being dropped.

"*Lookout, Sterling! Move!*" He slammed his fist so hard on the window the glass webbed, and Sterling jerked up at him. Panicked, he jabbed his finger toward the giant metal ball.

Sterling's eyes went wide as saucers.

She dove out of the way just in time for it to splat what was left of Strellson, the sheer weight demolishing a blockade of police cruisers. Less than ten feet away, a policeman scrambled for his keys. The man heard the sound gaining on him. He looked up, screaming as the thing crushed him like a boulder, paring a path through the snow.

Max watched as the giant thing reached a bend in the road and rolled into the forest with a splintering crash. He watched Sterling scramble to her feet. She threw the door open and jumped into the driver's seat, slamming it closed behind her.

"Sterling!" he shouted happily.

"Put your seatbelt on!" Sterling was panting, soaked in cold sweat. She twisted the keys in the ignition and the engine rumbled to life.

Max listened as outside the vehicle men screamed and gun shots cracked like horrible music.

Sterling switched on the headlights and gasped.

The witch stood in front of the SUV, trapped in the funnels of light. A trail of dead bodies and destroyed vehicles littered the road behind her. What was left of Captain Phillip Gilmore was stretched over two nearby cars, his limbs drawn-out like grotesque flesh-colored taffy. It was pure and unadulterated carnage.

"Go, Sterling, please!" he pleaded, sobbing.

"Hang on!" she said, throwing the car in reverse. She stamped her foot down on the pedal and the tires squealed, spitting powder from the wet road. She turned back in confusion, mashing down the pedal.

"Go, you sonofabitch!" she screamed. The vehicle shuddered like it was hung up on something. "*Come on!*" She pounded the steering wheel with her hand before turning her attention to the windshield.

The witch stood in front of the vehicle, the wand raised out in front of her.

Max whimpered in the backseat. He wanted his Mommy and Daddy. He didn't care how much they fought all the time, he'd do anything to have them back right now, to be home safe, away from the witch and the skinless men and the giant monster heads.

Sterling awkwardly reached back and took Max in the crook of her arm without lifting her eyes from the witch.

"Just close your eyes, Max. Don't look," she said calmly. "Everything'll be okay, sweetie. Just close your eyes."

She watched helplessly as the witch started forward.

The SUV rocked on its wheels; the earth shook and a blur of yellow lightning flashed from the left.

The bulk soared past the SUV with a mechanical roar, slamming into the witch like a freight train. The school bus rocked from side to side as it plowed through squad cars, etching a path to Grayson's Market. Sterling saw the prisoner named Bill jump out of the open side door, rolling onto the ground into a wall of snow-covered hedges. The rogue, golden titan weaved forward, leaping the sidewalk and blowing out its front tires in a loud *pop!* before crashing headfirst into the wall in a spectacular display of destruction, all the while donning the witch as a hood ornament.

Afterward, the man lay motionless on the ground, and Max could see Sterling was fighting the impulse not to go to him. She let out a choked sob, tears streaming down her face, and threw the gear in reverse.

She stomped down on the pedal once more, only this time, they went.

CHAPTER 42

THE SUV CARVED through the snow, winding alongside the mountain with a steep cliff on one side, a sheer mountain face on the other. At the bottom, the Connecticut River had turned to ice. She wheeled the SUV madly, like she'd stared death straight in the face and lived to tell the tale. Max had quieted down, sitting in the backseat drowsily slumped against the door. Sterling knew the feeling all too well. Her body was depleted to the point where she could barely lift her arms, let alone walk, but the spike of adrenaline was going to keep her going long enough to get the hell out of Dodge.

Her face broke into a smile. She let up on the gas, letting the vehicle straighten itself out, and for a very brief second all was right again in the world.

She saw Ovi and Anna smiling at her, proud of her, and they nodded at her as if her time had come. "Goodbye, Little Star," they said.

It was like hitting a wall.

The world went black and she was weightless, head reeling.

There was a loud crunch like a soda can, and she felt a pressure building in her head. Her body slammed forward, her head bashing into the window in a web of glass.

"Max?" she called out. Her voice trailed; it sounded so far away. "Max?" She whimpered as a terrible pain burned through her leg like acid. She screamed, but her voice barely made a sound. There were piping hot embers burning in her chest, and she could feel that some of her ribs were broken.

She forced open her eyes.

The SUV faced a horizon of snow-covered forest. The windshield was splintered glass, half peeled away from the frame. "Max?" she cried out, fighting the pain. She struggled to turn around, but realized she was still locked in with the seatbelt. She groaned, unbuckling the belt and letting it drop aside.

She pushed through the pain and shouldered open the door, spilling onto the wet concrete. The snow was speckled with pearls of broken glass. She hacked weakly, and syrupy blood spilled on the snow like an abstract painting. Her breaths were labored, and the world was going cold again. "Max?" she called out feebly.

A soft moan.

"Max? Can...you...hear me?" Her body was racked again with a coughing fit and the broken ribs painfully shifted inside her chest, biting into tender muscle. She screamed in agony, gritting a mouthful of bloody teeth. "I'm here, Max..." She struggled up the side of the wrecked vehicle until her hand found the door handle. She summoned her last bit of strength and jerked it open.

Max collapsed out of the SUV into her arms. She cried out, catching him and pulling him close to her. A thin trickle of blood leaked from his nose, and his face was bruised across one side.

"Max?" She shook him in her arms, lightly slapping his face. "Come on, Max!" Tears welled in her red eyes and she sobbed. "Please be alive, *please!*"

He moaned, half unconscious, and Sterling cried out with joy. She sniffled, smiling and wiping her eyes. She pulled him closer and held him tight, feeling his heart beat and his warmth and life.

A flutter behind her.

She beheld a dark blur out of the corner of her eye and twisted around painfully to find the witch watching them inquisitively, her dark clothing flapping in the wind.

Sterling's arms tightened around Max. She slid on her butt through the glass, sheltering herself alongside the SUV. Her heart sank, and she felt that the end was near for them.

The witch gazed at them with her empty, hollow eyes, as if considering them. She took a step closer and Sterling recoiled, burying herself in the wreckage and barring her teeth like a frightened animal. She searched for a gun, a weapon, anything, but found nothing.

The witch stepped to her feet, and Sterling knew all hope was lost. The monster got on one knee, gazing at them, and Sterling wept because she knew she had lost. Knew that she couldn't save Max, or herself.

She shuddered with Max in her arms, the cold setting in. She glared at the witch with a deep hate burning within her. She sniffled. Tears rolled down her face, and she said, "You can't have him."

The witch looked at her oddly, then at the boy in her arms, as if confused. And for the first time that entire wretched night, the witch spoke with a hollow, otherworldly voice and said,

"I'm not here for him."

Sterling shook her head and more tears came then, sliding down her face as the final revelation hit her.

She wasn't here for Max.

She had never wanted him.

It was her the witch was after. All of the bloodshed, everything that had happened…it was for her.

Sterling shook her head, crying, holding Max securely in her arms. She let her cheek sink down to his head and held him there.

The witch gazed at her benevolently.

Unexpectedly, the woman tenderly reached out and brushed Sterling's tears away. "So much pain, and fear. A lifetime of loss, broken by the wicked. But no more." The witch looked at her sympathetically, perhaps even kindly, and said, "It's time to let go. Only once you do, will you know what you're truly capable of."

Sterling sobbed, holding Max tight and squeezing her eyes shut as tears flooded out.

The witch rose silently, a true horror in the storm to end all storms, and offered her hand to Sterling.

Sterling looked at the horrible white thing, stripped of its humanity, and shook her head. "I can't..." she cried, shaking her head. "*I can't!*"

"But you're one of us," the witch replied. "*Soror Tredecim.*"

Sterling shook her head. "*No,*" she sobbed. *"I'm not like you!"*

"Your time in this world has come to an end," the witch announced joylessly. "Destiny awaits."

The witch began to raise the wand at Max, and the sight of it made Sterling cower in fear.

"Wait!" she cried out, waving it away. "Just—wait."

She knew now what she had to do.

It was the only way to protect him. The only way to save him.

She looked up at the witch and blinked miserably. She unfastened the gleaming star on her chest and placed it in Max's palm, gently closing his bloody fingers around it. She kissed him on the forehead and smiled, then released him from her arms, carefully laying him on the road. "Goodbye, Max," she whispered.

The witch offered her hand again, only this time Sterling took it. She felt the witch's burning hot skin, felt the power that flowed through her veins while the witch helped her to her feet.

Off in the distance a pillar of black smoke gushed from Drybell, a town that would be lost to history the same way Roanoke Colony had been in 1590.

The witch pointed the wand one last time at the frozen sky

over town.

Sterling watched as the tiny etchings in the bone began to glow, pulsing to life. She winced, holding her ribs as the steely clouds began to stir, slowly braiding together into a black funnel. The wand vibrated in the witch's hand, growing more animated as the sky worked itself together, pooling into a massive, destructive force. There was a clap of thunder and the wand bucked just as a massive tornado twisted out of the sky with a deafening crash, powering into the heart of Drybell with a colossal *boom!* The earth rocked beneath her and the forest rustled alive around them, the birds escaping into the sky in a sea of black stars.

Sterling saw the burning cars and mangled bodies savagely sail into the sky, houses and benches whipping through its belly into the heavens. Even water from the Connecticut river threaded into the whirlwind, and she was speechless as nature was reclaimed, wiping away all traces of the events from the night prior.

Wiping away her past.

Her mistakes.

Her regrets.

Her life.

Her.

She smelled rain and cinnamon and looked to the witch, who calmly beheld the destruction with mirrored, wise eyes, as she had so many times before.

The devastation was magnificent, and even though Sterling knew she wouldn't remember this moment once the witch had taken her, it was one of the most glorious sights she'd ever laid eyes on.

And she was glad to have known it.

9/01/20-07/08/21

AUTHOR'S NOTE

Villains. Is there anyone else we love to hate as much as a good villain? In fact, I can think of a long list of fictional stories where the antagonists are almost more interesting than the protagonists themselves. I don't think that's a mistake. I think sometimes it's easy to point the finger at a villain and say, "Oh, that's why they're the bad guy," without looking any deeper. And then there's villains where you just get it. You understand why they did what they did, and maybe you can even empathize with them. And that's one of the ideas I wanted to explore with this book, the idea that villains aren't always so easily defined, that they can't just be filed into the "good" or "bad" categories. They're human too, after all (mostly, anyway).

Sterling Marsh is that character to me. She's someone who's experienced one trauma after another and is constantly being faced with making decisions that define her true self just a little more. Was she the Thirteenth Witch all along, or was she merely a victim? Did Jennifer fall from that balcony, or was she pushed? Was Sterling justified in murdering her stepfather after his actions went unnoticed time and time again by the authorities, especially considering what he'd done to Sterling's mother? I think in our minds it's easy to say it was wrong, but if it were you in that situation, would it still be so easy?

Either way, I want to thank you. I sincerely hope you enjoyed this Christmas tale and that you'll join me for more stories in the future.

I want to thank Ross Nischler for the brilliant illustrations and cover design. You've been in my corner from the start and I can't imagine any of these books without your art. Justin T. Coons for creating a jaw-dropping painting for the alternate cover. Ben Long, Julia Lewis, and Wofford Lee Jones for proofreading this manuscript and for being some of the coolest friends I've made on my writing journey. Phil Fracassi for the fantastic blurb. Tali Leonard, Celso Hurtado, Briana Morgan, and Brittany Hydorn for beta reading it for me. Your input was invaluable and I appreciate it immensely.

Kaylin, for keeping me sane enough to keep churning out books. I don't know what I'd do without you. To my friends and family, you know who you are.

And last but not least, I want to thank all the friends I've made through my books. Whether you're just a fan that's reached out via email, or we've spoken on Instagram, I'm glad this experience has allowed me to make so many new friends. While I wish I could list everyone, that would be another book in itself. Just know that I appreciate every single one of you. If you want to see more of the 13 Witches, don't hesitate to let me know. After all, who knows what could ride in on the next storm?

Sincerely,
Patrick Delaney
Pdred1985@gmail.com